The Glass Road

PRESCOTT FAMILY ROMANCE

BOOK TWO

ALYSSA SCHWARZ

ALYSSA SCHWARZ

THE GLASS ROAD

Editing by A Little Red Ink and Suzy Oakley Solutions

ISBN-13: 978-1-7379788-4-8
ISBN-10: 1737978849

Scripture quotations and references are taken from THE HOLY BIBLE, NEW INTERNATIONAL VERSION®, NIV® Copyright © 1973, 1978, 1984, 2011 by Biblica, Inc.™ Used by permission. All rights reserved worldwide.

Library of Congress Control Number: 2022919045

Cover design by Alyssa Schwarz

www.authoralyssaschwarz.com/

PRAISE FOR ALYSSA SCHWARZ

"The letters penned in *Dear Beth* bring back a beautiful sense of nostalgia ... With well-developed characters and a handsome hero to fall in love with, readers will be rooting for Tye Prescott and Beth to get their happily-ever-after. I can't wait to read more of the Prescott Family romance series. *Dear Beth* is highly recommended for fans of inspirational contemporary romance, especially for readers who enjoy novels by authors such as **Denise Hunter, Becky Wade, Melissa Tagg, and Susan May Warren**."
~ Goodreads reviewer

"If you enjoy an honest, thoughtful, character-driven story, *The Glass Cottage* will not disappoint. Debut author Alyssa Schwarz does an amazing job of balancing character development and plot while circling around romance, suspense, and small-town history. Simply spun, *The Glass Cottage* is a page turner with heart and a storyline like no other book I've read."
~ Becky Van Vleet, Award Winning Author

"Alyssa Schwarz has struck gold with a well-paced, intriguing tale that is sure to keep readers turning the pages. The Glass Cottage is a cozy, small town romance, with relatable characters and just the right combination of romance, mystery, and historical fiction."
~ Heidi Glick, Author of Dog Tags

"Alyssa Schwarz's debut novel, The Glass Cottage, reads like a Hallmark Channel movie. It's sure to make you laugh and possibly go out for a gourmet pizza. You may head straight to your favorite coffee shop for a latte and pastry too. Full of romance, suspense, and plot twists, it's definitely a must-read!"
~ Amanda Speights, Author

BOOKS BY ALYSSA SCHWARZ

A PRESCOTT FAMILY ROMANCE SERIES

Dear Beth (novella)

The Glass Cottage

The Glass Road

Fields of Glass (Fall 2023)

*To my grandpa who lived for
adventure and found solace
in God's creation*

"Let us run with endurance the race
God has set before us."

—Hebrews 12:1

PROLOGUE

THE FIRST RACE of the season, and Tess Prescott was already hyped on the thrill of competition and the chance to prove herself once again.

Languid waves lapped against the red and white hull of the troller boat, the seawater unaware of the anxious energy pulsating across Mission Bay Beach. She checked her watch for the tenth time.

Eleven minutes to go.

Excitement radiated through her limbs. She cranked the volume on her earbuds and blasted Katrina and the Waves' greatest hit into her ears. She hummed along and finished the last of her stretches.

The bay's briny scent rolled off the water and mingled with the cloud of coconut sunscreen rolling over the crowded beach. For an early February morning, the San Diego skies had peeled back their usual fog, and warm sun beat down on the triathletes.

The water was fifty-seven degrees, according to the morning report, and everyone was ready with their full wetsuits and swim caps in place.

"Okay, Tess," she whispered to herself over the hum of the music, "you've got this."

A rough hand tapped her on the shoulder, and she glanced up to see her coach, Ryan. His blond beach-boy waves skipped in the breeze, and he wore a smile meant only for her. He motioned to her ears, pantomiming for her to turn her music off.

She turned down the volume and gave him her full attention.

"Done giving yourself a pep talk?" He gave her arm an affectionate squeeze. "Looks like you've got the perfect day for a warm-up race. I know it's the beginning of the season and all, but I stand by what I said. With the right times, and a little luck, you could qualify for the U.S. Team at the National Championships in August."

Tess had been working her entire adult life to make the Olympic Team, and this was her year. Something great was about to happen. This had to be it. By God's grace, she'd made it this far. He wouldn't let her down now.

She readjusted the strap of her goggles and tucked a strand of chestnut hair back inside her teal swim cap. She was all in. "I'm walking on sunshine."

"Good. Now remember," he spoke over the crowd of voices around them. "This is the first race, so it's okay to take things easy. Especially after that sprain you got back in

December." His Ironman sweater stretched across a muscular torso when he folded his arms.

After working together for seven years, he knew her well enough to expect an argument, but that never stopped him from trying.

"Yeah, you know me. Like I'd ever take a race slow. Besides, it was only a minor sprain. The doctors gave me the all-clear weeks ago." She'd iced her ankle earlier that morning for good measure and detected only some slight stiffness when she stretched it.

Ryan shook his head, and a shock of sun-bleached hair fell over his designer sunglasses. "That's what I like about you, Prescott. Never one to take the easy way out. Keep it up, and we'll all be watching you take the podium in Paris in a few years."

He pushed his sunglasses onto his head, and his wink made her head spin. The warmth seeped into her shoulders and stayed long after he'd left to join the other coaches and spectators beneath the blue and white banners.

Prerace banter complete, Tess channeled her focus on the course ahead. She scanned the water while Elton John's "Don't Go Breaking My Heart" rocked in the background. A 750-meter swim through Mission Bay, followed by three laps around Fiesta Island on a bike, and a five kilometer run through the park to the finish line. Piece of cake. Tess had competed in this race the past five years and could trace the route in her sleep.

She took a last sip of water and set it beside her bike and running shoes before they called her heat to the starting line. All set, she padded up to the brisk water to wait her turn with the other competitors.

Tess's breaths grew long and slow. In and out. Sea air filled her lungs, and she zeroed in on the rippling water ahead. She checked her High Sierra GPS watch, her sponsor's logo cheering her on while she reviewed the racecourse one last time. As the timer drew closer to zero, the crowd hushed, and then out of the stillness, the starting gun cracked, propelling the racers into the cold water.

Tess cut to the front of the group with ease and rounded the first buoy. Her freestyle strokes sliced through the water, and her feet flutter-kicked in a steady rhythm. Each breath tingled her tongue with a salty spray, and she relished the familiar taste.

She pulled ahead, along with a handful of other athletes, taking full advantage of the draft-zones of the other swimmers. They turned right at the next buoy, and the gap grew wider within the heat. Arms and legs beat the surrounding water, and she occasionally felt a hand cut dangerously close to her head.

They came to the last turn and circled back toward the beach, where throngs of spectators cheered them on. Tess imagined Ryan's smile, and she kicked her legs harder. The water grew warm as they reached the shore. Tess dug her feet into the soft sand and sprinted across the grassy field toward the transition area.

In ten seconds flat, she'd stripped down to her sleeveless tri-suit and dropped her swim cap and goggles onto the discarded wetsuit. Without socks, she slipped into her cycling shoes, secured her helmet, and raced toward her lime-green ten-speed. One leg over the frame, she kicked away from the asphalt and clipped into the pedals with lightning speed.

Dunes and shrubs passed in a blur of green and brown. Others slowed behind her, waving at family members and friends along the sidelines. All Tess needed to know was that Ryan was there. They could celebrate after the race, just the two of them, as usual. Despite her family's support, it was a rare occasion that any of them came out to watch her compete, and while she would have appreciated the show of support a few years ago, she'd found solace in Ryan's friendly encouragement a long time ago.

Tess pushed her bike to a breakneck speed around Fiesta Island. A sharp wind threw needle-like sand against her skin, and the sun dried the remaining seawater from her low ponytail.

The space between her and the other cyclists grew, and the crunch of their tires over the road faded like a muffled baseball card against the spokes of her childhood trainer bike.

You can do this. She clicked up a gear and flew ahead. *This is your year.* She repeated the mental pep-talk and finished the last lap.

Back in the transition area, Tess leapt from her bike and switched into her running shoes with an extra shot of adrenaline in her veins. She didn't waste a single second with the speed laces before jumping back into the final leg of the race. It had taken years to perfect her swim and cycling times, but as soon as her feet hit the pavement, she was free.

Three-point-one miles was not a run, it was a sprint. Like in a hundred-yard-dash, Tess bolted down the palm-tree-lined path with one goal in mind:

To win.

The next runner had to be over two-hundred yards behind. Her legs burned with each stride, and a muscle twinged in her ankle. Almost there. She pumped her arms to keep up the momentum and blitzed around the last turn.

Through the trunks and palm fronds, the finish line came into focus. An enormous banner stretched across the road, and the crowd stood, waiting for the first woman to cross beneath the blue and silver flag. Ryan's loud cheers permeated her concentration, and she looked up in time to see him pump a fist in the air at her sure victory.

Their victory.

Tess was so focused on his tanned smile beneath the arc of balloons that she didn't notice the commotion to her right until it was too late. A monster of a German shepherd came barreling up from the beach and broke straight into Tess's line of vision.

Before she could stop, the animal cut her off. Tess flailed her arms to keep her balance. The tread of her shoe caught on the textured concrete, and she twisted in midair. Something snapped in her left ankle, and a searing pain shot through her leg as she crashed onto the unforgiving sidewalk. Her wrist smacked against the hard surface, shattering her watch with the sudden impact.

Tess clutched her chest and forced the air back into her lungs. Time slowed. The outside world grew dim. A steadying hand wrapped over her shoulder, and she blinked into the bright sunlight as a man in uniform knelt beside her. His voice barely registered in her consciousness, but he kept his steady gaze locked on hers.

The pain engulfed her senses, flooded her ears with a radiating throb that drowned out the approaching footsteps and voices. She opened her eyes and saw the paramedic talking to her, his face pulled into a grim line that seemed to make the pain grow worse.

Ryan. I need Ryan. She opened her mouth to say so, but all that came out was a stuttered moan.

A second person knelt on her opposite side and began a series of ministrations with her foot. Another bolt of pain shot up her leg that made her stomach churn.

Tess didn't catch the question the second EMT asked her. Or if she did, the words didn't register in her numb mind.

The only thing she could hear was the sound of her dreams shattering across the road like glass.

CHAPTER

One

THREE MONTHS LATER

AUSTIN WRIGHT STARED at the old Polaroid in his hand and then back at the dilapidated cottages in front of him. This couldn't be the same place. Could it?

Left vacant for over a year, his grandfather's property sat like a crumbling monument beneath the Colorado Rocky Mountains. The A-frame cottages looked as if they'd barely survived the past winter, and that didn't even include the main log house at the back of the overgrown lot. He'd had to use the set of tire chains on his Ford Explorer to make it up the snow-packed road. He could only imagine the infamous mud lurking beneath that frozen quilt.

A chilly breeze tossed a few dry pine cones from the trees. They bounced off the tired rooftops in a feeble welcome.

"You've got to be kidding me. We're not staying *here* for the summer, are we?" Austin's fourteen-year-old nephew, Josh, shoved open the passenger-side door and stomped over with a scowl, his headphones dangling around his neck.

Josh stood with arms crossed, his navy Converse Allstars submerged in four inches of slush. A mop of brown hair fell over his down-turned face, matching the dark mud at his feet. "Did you know there was no cell reception up here? How are we supposed to survive all summer without phones or . . ." His eyes widened in horror. "Don't tell me there's no internet either."

Austin bit back a grin.

"What about my friends? I'll miss everything. I'll be the loser who went dark all summer. And what if my mom tries to reach me but can't? We should at least have Wi-Fi."

He had to give the boy props for his tenacity, so much like his mom. What the camp lacked in modern amenities, it made up for with sky the color of an alpine stream and air so clean, it made one come alive. Of course, he didn't plan to keep the camp entirely off grid. Before the staff had arrived, he'd purchased a satellite phone in town, but even though it had all the capabilities of a normal phone, it was strictly for emergencies.

"If you need to use the computer, there's one in town at the library. But welcome to mountain life, kid. Besides," he looked back up at the weathered siding and the rustic moss-covered shingles, "we've got plenty to keep us busy for a few weeks until campers arrive."

More work by far than he had been expecting, but with some help, they'd bring the place back to life.

Josh glowered at the first cabin, having the sullen teenager act down to a tee. "I don't know why Mom ever agreed to this."

Austin held back a sigh. He'd promised his sister, Meghan, he'd watch Josh for the summer while she worked in Cambodia. Five months of doing what she loved would be good for her. She'd given up a lot to raise her son on her own, and it was high time she did something for herself. Besides, it had been too long since he'd spent any real time with his nephew. He could teach Josh some good life skills and, God willing, show the boy there was more to life than cell phones and video games.

"She knows what it's like up here. And when she gets back, you'll both have some adventures to share."

"I bet *she* has internet, though," Josh mumbled under his breath.

Austin felt a little sorry for the boy, but it was good for a kid to spend some time in nature, away from the digital world. To be reminded of the important things in life. It might not have been the summer in California he'd expected, but by Austin's estimation, there wasn't anything better for a kid than fresh mountain air and a project to keep his hands occupied.

"Tell you what." He took a mental picture of the property and strode back to the car. "I need to pick up a few things from town. How about you come along, and you can text your friends the news on the way?"

Josh's shoulders dropped as if the idea excited him as much as mud pie. "Fine."

"Great, then hop back in."

The two of them made the long drive back into Estes Park. As soon as they merged onto the main strip, Josh's phone lit up with half a dozen messages. His fingers flew across the touchscreen, no doubt to share his tale of woe with half his contact list.

Austin pulled into the hardware store's parking lot at the end of the street as his phone rang.

Josh gave him a look as if to say, *see, I'm not the only one who needs their phone.*

Austin ignored it and answered the call on the third ring. "Hello?"

"Austin. It's Caden."

"Hey, man, what's up?" Three years younger than Austin, his friend Caden had refused to settle down after college, but Austin hoped this summer camp would help give him some roots. Or at least a steady job for a few months.

With Caden, Josh, himself, and a handful of high school volunteers, Camp Kinnikinnick might actually stand a chance of succeeding.

There was a long stretch of silence, and Austin checked his cell connection. Three bars. "Caden, you still there?"

He heard a shuffling noise on the other end before his friend finally spoke again. "So, listen, man." His tone had lost its usual luster. "I know I promised to work with you this summer at the camp, but something's come up, and I won't be able to be there. My cousin Micah needs some last-minute help with the ranch this year. I'm actually heading out right now."

Austin closed his eyes and leaned his head back against the headrest. There went his grand plan of starting on schedule. He cleared the tension from his throat. "Sorry to hear that, man. Well, I've got Josh here, so we'll figure it out."

He always did.

There was another long pause before Caden responded. "I really am sorry I won't be there."

"No worries. Family comes first." Austin might not be able to ask his grandfather for advice anymore, but he knew he would say the same thing. The man had taught him the importance of family since Austin was young, and he'd been trying to live by that truth ever since.

A car door shut on the other end of the line. "I know this is short notice, and I don't want to leave you high and dry, but I think I have a solution."

Uh-oh. Austin recalled some of Caden's past solutions. Knowing him, he'd probably convinced some poor schlep to volunteer for the empty position, sight unseen. His friend sounded so excited, though, he couldn't turn him down flat. He could at least hear the guy out. Before he could respond, the line grew heavy with static, and the call cut out a second later.

"Hello? Caden, are you still there?" Nothing but dead air.

So much for reception in town. Austin plunked the useless phone in the cup holder while Josh suppressed a laugh.

He pointed a finger in his nephew's direction. "Don't even say a word."

"Who, me?" Josh held his hands up, the world's most innocent teenager. "Wouldn't dream of it."

Austin killed the engine, cutting off the supply of warm air, and opened his door. "Okay. Let's get those supplies."

For the first time all day, Josh grinned, and skipped ahead through the open door.

At least he was smiling. With any luck, that wouldn't change once they started the renovations. Austin pulled the long list of items from his back pocket and made a mental note—*find a replacement activities coordinator.*

He mulled over Caden's words as he stepped through the sliding double doors. As much as he might dislike the idea of hiring a stranger, he didn't have the luxury to be choosy. He had a little under a month to get the camp ready by the first week of June. No way could he find a replacement that quickly. He might regret this decision later, but he was running out of options and time. His grandfather might have been a wise man, but he hadn't been one for scrutinizing finances. If Austin didn't turn things around and get the camp up and running this season, he didn't think the place would survive much longer.

With half a bar of service, Austin typed out a quick text and sent it off to his friend. This plan had better work. He'd get the number for whoever it was Caden had thought of and go from there. It was far from ideal, but it was the best option he had.

A half-hour later, Austin unloaded their supplies at the front counter and didn't say a word when Josh slipped a few bags of Lifesavers candies behind the boxes of nails and sandpaper. Back at the car, he sent off another text to Caden and prayed this project wasn't doomed from the start.

Camp Kinnikinnick had been in the family for over a century, and most of his best memories took place during those summers in the mountains. Even his sister had loved the rugged lifestyle. Not that she'd spent much time here as a kid. But to him, this place was more home than anyplace else.

Now that his grandfather was gone, the responsibility fell to him. A blessing or a curse, he'd yet to decide.

CHAPTER

Two

MAY TWELFTH. THAT was the day the doctors had told her she could run again. Tess had circled the date on her calendar in permanent marker and held onto that hope like a lifeline. She had listened to the specialists, done her physical therapy and then some, kept her foot iced and elevated when she wasn't training. She'd even done every alternative treatment possible in hopes of speeding up her recovery.

Today was May sixteenth, and her ankle remained as swollen as a small cantaloupe.

Tess eased onto the treadmill and tested her footing before she bumped the speed up to a whopping level two. *Good grief.*

Dr. Kelly Buckner watched with a pleased expression as the machine hummed to life. She scribbled a few notes in her folder and reassessed Tess's progress. "Great. Take it nice and easy."

For the past month, it had been the same routine—physical therapy sessions three times a week, walk on the treadmill for fifteen minutes, listen to doctors croon over her progress. Today, she was stuck with Dr. Buckner, a sweet but misguided physical therapist who thought a bum ankle was something to celebrate.

Three months ago, Tess had been ambulanced to the UC San Diego Medical Center after falling at the Tritonman finish line. The x-rays showed she sustained a bimalleolar fracture, a clean break to both her tibia and fibula. The on-call orthopedic surgeon suggested immediate surgery. Three hours later, Tess had an intramedullary nail embedded into her shin and a series of internal screws to hold the joint together. Her only visible battle scars were two four-inch incisions on either side of her left leg, and a bruise the color of a tropical storm.

At least she was back home in Denver. But that was little consolation if she could barely walk.

"Okay, Tess. You can come down now." Dr. Optimistic beamed as if Tess had run a mile sprint. "Everything appears to be healing nicely. Do you have any questions or concerns at this time?" She sat in the chair opposite Tess and folded her hands across her clipboard.

How about when will I be able to compete again?

She should have been in Florida this week for the Vero Beach triathlon. She'd already missed over a dozen other races during her recovery, and she cringed, thinking about the others she'd yet to cancel. And the Olympic qualifiers? Her heart broke at the reminder that she'd failed yet again. At least her sponsors had understood. Tess wouldn't have been able to stomach it if she'd lost her sponsorship with TrailTec and her career in one fell swoop. They'd even offered to cover the cost of surgery and therapy, hoping she'd be back on the circuit as quickly as possible. Whenever that might be.

Tess pulled her limp ponytail over one shoulder and tugged at the loose ends against her caramel highlights. She shoved the other questions aside and voiced the one that rang loudest in her head. "When can I run again?"

Dr. Buckner's countenance dimmed. "Your ankle is healing at an expected rate, Tess. I know it might seem slow, but you're rebuilding bone and muscle strength, and that takes time. But don't worry. You're getting there."

Her forced optimism grated on Tess's nerves. Why couldn't any of her doctors give her a straight answer? Three months or four. Yes or no. Be able to compete again or...

Or what? She couldn't let herself think of that possibility yet. Racing was her life, her everything. All her friends were a part of that world, her trainers, Ryan. Okay, so maybe Ryan had been mysteriously AWOL the past month, but he was busy with his other athletes. He checked in when he could, which meant the odd phone call between meetings and races. Besides, he was due back from Florida at the end of the week, and they'd have the entire weekend to catch up.

At the end of the appointment, Dr. Buckner sent Tess home with a couple of new stretches and a prescription painkiller. Like that would ease the torture of sitting still for another month. Tess shoved the exercises and the prescription into her purse as she exited the building, the cumbersome ankle brace making her strides stiff and slow.

Outside, the Denver traffic zipped by. Highway noise drowned out the sounds of birds chirping in the trees, and a wave of heat radiated off the asphalt, melting the remnants of spring's final snowstorm. She hopped into her Prius and drove home from the hospital. When she'd finally parked, walked the half-block to her building and up the stairs, she collapsed onto the couch in her sparsely decorated Highlands condo.

Another look at her watch's step count reminded her how far she'd fallen. A few weeks after her first surgery, she'd sent her GPS watch back to her sponsors for repairs, and instead, they'd gifted her a brand new one a few days later, complete with all the latest updates. It was a thoughtful gesture, a sign of how much they believed in her recovery, but judging by this last appointment, she wasn't so convinced.

If only she could slip on her running shoes and get lost for an hour or two among the city's maze of streets. There wasn't anything a good run couldn't fix. And after three months of surgeries and therapy, she could do with an extra long one.

Tess fished her cell from her purse and sent a text off to her cousin Abigail. She flopped her head back against the cushion and stared at her textured beige ceiling. Her cousin had brought color and life to their little corner of Denver, but now that Abigail had moved back home last fall to live with their great-Aunt Josie, it felt decidedly empty. That, and the fact Tess had upgraded her renter status to owner six months ago, made her nearly grumble into the nearest pillow.

The phone rang almost immediately, the cheery ABBA melody loud in the small space, and Tess lunged for the semblance of human contact. She answered before the song could reach the chorus.

Abigail's cheerful voice sang over the speaker, brightening the otherwise dreary living room. "Have you tried therapy via Rocky Road yet?"

"Not even that sounds good right now." Her favorite ice cream would no doubt give her a toothache and a brain-freeze.

"Oh, that's bad. Maybe I should come down and stay with you for a while. I'm sure Aunt Josie could spare me for a few days."

"And what would Ben say?" It was a sweet offer, but it would be nearly impossible to tear Abigail away from her fiancé for more than a few hours.

"He'd survive." Tess could almost hear the smile in her cousin's voice. "We could make an entire week of it. Movie nights, popcorn, some of Aunt Josie's cinnamon rolls. Like old times."

"Thanks, but I'm okay. Must be having an off day is all."

"Okay, but let me know if there's anything I can do to help." There was a momentary pause before she spoke again. "Has your brother called you recently?"

"Caden? No. Why?" Tess's heart sank. Her baby brother had been out to visit a few weeks ago. What new mess could he have gotten into this time?

"Oh. Well, I guess it's not a secret or anything." Abigail drew out the last word as if weighing whether to divulge more before finally giving in. "He mentioned something about one of his old college buddies starting up a local summer camp. Caden was supposed to help for the season, but you know Caden, already off onto the next adventure."

One of these days, her brother's nomadic lifestyle was going to get him in trouble. Four years out of college, and he still hadn't settled down. Sometimes Tess felt like the only responsible adult between the two of them. But that wasn't saying much, since she made a living as a twenty-nine-year-old traveling athlete herself.

Abigail continued. "He knows he's left his friend in a bind, but he thought, seeing as you weren't working at the moment, you might be interested."

Where had her knucklehead brother gotten that idea? Her—a camp counselor? "No, in fact, my darling brother hasn't said a word of this to me. But don't worry. I'll set him straight if he brings it up."

Abigail laughed. "He was so excited about his brilliant plan, I didn't have the heart to tell him you probably wouldn't be interested. Don't tell him it was me who spilled the beans, okay?"

"You have my word. And speaking of news ..." Tess reached toward the coffee table and snatched up the bright yellow envelope from yesterday's mail. "I see you and Ben finally settled on a date. Took you two long enough."

"It wasn't that long." Abigail laughed into the phone.

"Oh, of course. What was I thinking? It's not like it took you guys over a decade to make things official or anything."

Abigail and Ben had been best friends since middle school. They just took the long road to realizing what the rest of their small town had figured out years ago.

"At least we finally got there. And I've never thanked you properly for convincing me to move back here."

Tess's loss was Ben's gain. She was happy for her cousin. If anyone deserved to find love, it was Abigail. Even if it meant she now lived over two hours away.

Tess readjusted the lumpy pillow beneath her foot, secretly missing the quilted throw pillows Abigail had taken with her.

"So, I was thinking ..." Abigail continued. "How about you agree to be my maid of honor, and we call it even?"

Tess snapped her attention back to the phone, pillows forgotten.

"I—I don't know what to say... I'm honored."

"Oh, good. It'll be so much fun, and I hear Ben has a few good-looking college friends he could introduce you to at the wedding."

Tess held back a snort. If by "college friends" Abigail meant preppy engineers who worked in Seattle, she'd make a hard pass. Ben was the exception to the Ivy League stereotype. "Maybe Aunt Josie can work her magic and find a nice girl for Caden."

"One can hope."

Their great-aunt's unmistakable voice filtered into the background. Tess couldn't make out her words, but Abigail responded before hopping back on the line. "Sorry about that. I guess the water heater sprung another leak, and Ben needs some help."

Tess rolled her eyes and smiled. "Go join your handyman. I'm sure he needs your expertise on wrenches and water pressure."

Abigail gasped in mock offense. "I've learned a thing or two since senior year."

"I'll believe it when I see it." Tess smiled. "Tell everyone hi for me."

"I will."

Tess ended the call and relaxed back against the couch. Even with the distance, their relationship was still as much a balm to her weary soul as it had ever been. And her brother? She was an expert at fielding his crazy ideas. From what Abigail said, this was no doubt one more in a long line of half-baked schemes.

Her phone pinged with an incoming text, and her heart rate sped up at Ryan's special ringtone.

How's the patient doing? Feeling any better yet?

The simple text brought a smile to her lips.

Not much different, but the thought of seeing you this weekend might be a good distraction. Are we still on for Friday?

Tess waited for his reply, but those infernal dots at the bottom of the screen disappeared. She was about to write him back when a new message filled the screen.

Have you checked your email recently?

Tess frowned. Curious, she navigated to her cluttered inbox and scrolled until she saw what must have been it. The subject line read, IMPORTANT.

Her heart rate sped up another notch. She clicked on it and waited for her internet to catch up. A few seconds later, the message loaded, and her breath hitched at the start of the second line.

TERMINATION OF CONTRACT.

What? Tess read further, and the rest of the air vanished from her lungs.

Tess, I'm sorry to tell you this, but your sponsors at TrailTec have decided to cancel your contract. You're welcome to keep the promotional watch and everything else they've given you to endorse over the past few years, but until you can race again...

No. Her stomach dropped to her toes, and she numbly scanned the rest of the email.

... I'm sorry to do this to you, but without the money from the sponsors, I'm afraid I can't afford to stay on as your coach, either. As soon as you get better...

The phone slipped from her fingers and fell with a thunk onto the rug.

This isn't happening. Tess sat in dazed silence, and the throbbing in her ankle pounded all the way to her eardrums. How could Ryan drop her like that? It had only been a few months, and the doctors said she'd started to heal.

They'd been through everything together. Even when he tore his ACL two years ago, she'd stayed by his side while his other athletes switched coaches for a season. She'd never given up on him, no matter how many races she'd had to run alone while he healed between surgeries.

Tess's phone lit up with another incoming call, and the plucky notes of Van Halen's "Jump" startled her from her horrified trance. Caden. *What now?* She reluctantly accepted the call and didn't even have time to gather her spiraling thoughts before his eternally cheery voice launched through the speaker.

"Hey, sis. Have I got some news for you."

CHAPTER

Three

TESS MUST HAVE suffered an injury to the head when she fell in San Diego. Delayed concussion, late-onset amnesia, slow intracranial hematoma. No way would she have agreed to her brother's crazy idea if she'd been in her right mind. Yet here she was, driving up the world's muddiest road to God knew where. She sped up at the straightaway, and the murky waters parted like the Red Sea.

"Oh, no!" Twin rooster tails washed over her car, and Tess lost sight of the road. She slammed her good foot against the brake and swerved. Her breaths came in stuttered heaves as she fought to regain control.

Desperate. That's what she'd been when she'd called Caden's friend and had him email her the contract. Still second-guessing her decision, the printed-out contract had sat for three days on the counter until she opened her mail and spotted the first medical bill. Never had it occurred to her that when her sponsors ditched her, they'd take her medical coverage as well. Tess gulped at the number and snatched up the contract in a reluctant heartbeat. It wasn't much, but between that and her savings, she might manage.

It was only for a summer, after all. The racing world wouldn't implode without her, but her finances would if she didn't swallow her pride and get a job.

She pumped the brakes to slow down and took the remaining curves at a more cautious speed. One last turn, and the dense forest opened to reveal a worn sign staked into the rocky earth.

"Camp *Kin-nik-in-nick*." She sounded out the syllables and shook her head to wake up from this ongoing nightmare.

Qualifiers were three months away, but instead of racing, she was stuck here. Wherever "here" was. Tess turned down the music, as if that would help her better read the sign's fine print: *Established in 1985*.

"Here goes nothing." She prayed for an extra helping of patience and directed her two-wheel-drive sedan up the rutted driveway.

The first cabin came into view, and her eyes widened in disbelief. This wasn't a summer camp. This was a ghost town. Had tumbleweeds grown in the Rocky Mountains, she would have expected one to roll across the road on the next breeze.

She was inching her car forward into the seemingly vacant property, a dozen questions zinging through her mind, when a large hand rapped against her window.

Tess jumped back in her seat and slammed on her brakes. She looked around for the person who'd startled her but saw only trees and the dirt road. *Oh, no.* In one leap, she threw the car in park and was out the door, scanning the grounds until she spotted a man standing behind her car by the side of the road.

"I'm so sorry. Are you okay? I didn't even see you there."

Cold mud squished over the tops of her old running shoes as she scrambled around the car, praying she hadn't maimed someone on her first day. Her foot slipped, and she clung to the rear door handle for support. Face flushed, she looked up in time to see the man's mouth tilt at the corner.

"Careful. One wrong step, and you'll be showering for a week." The man's deep voice would have been soothing had she not been standing in ankle-deep mud. Despite the mud, he stood nearly six inches over her five-foot-seven-inch frame. Dark wavy hair tossed about in the cool breeze, and it looked like he hadn't shaved in days. She wouldn't have immediately described him as classically handsome. His eyes and hair were both a deep brown, and there was a bump in his nose as if it had been broken at some point and not set correctly. However, there was something in the way he looked at her that made her almost want to trust him.

Almost.

Tess crossed her arms and stared at the man. It didn't matter if that smile of his made her want to drop her defenses.

She'd made that mistake before. "Well, I wouldn't have slipped had you not jumped in front of me."

A humorous light sparked in his otherwise dark eyes. "Are you angry at me?"

"Of course not." Tess took another steadying breath and stood a little straighter. "You startled me. What kind of person knocks on the window of a moving car?"

He nodded toward her vehicle, and his mouth tipped at the corner. "Is that what you call that thing?"

Mud caked the entire surface of the silver Prius as if it were the Creature from the Black Lagoon. *Don't let him get under your skin, Tess.*

He chuckled. "Sorry, don't see many of those around here. Most places require four-wheel-drive to get around."

He shrugged and extended a hand. The same one that had assaulted her window moments earlier.

She eyed his dirt-stained fingers, but her feet remained firmly rooted beneath her. There was still time to back out. Reverse her crazy decision. She could turn back right now and drive all the way home to Denver and spend the summer in her familiar condo in peace. How hard would it be to find another job?

His gaze dipped to her muddy running shoes, and a smile tugged at the corners of his mouth. "Don't worry. I won't bite. I'm Austin, by the way. Austin Wright. And judging by the look of horror on your face, you must be Tess."

Those eyes seemed to see straight into her soul, and all Tess wanted was to look away in case he could read her thoughts. She blinked against the bright sunshine and reluctantly took his outstretched hand.

"Tess Prescott. Nice to meet you, Austin."

"Likewise. Glad to have you here. It's going to be a busy season, and we can use all the help we can get."

She managed to peel her eyes from his intent gaze and noticed the tool belt and stack of shingles tucked under his other arm. She raised an eyebrow in question.

"About that. My brother told you about my, uh, situation?" She couldn't bring herself to say *injury*. The stiff support brace digging into her shin was reminder enough. Her face heated despite the brisk mountain air. "I don't think I'll be much help with a ladder."

He dipped his head in a nod. "No worries. There's plenty of work to be found."

Faint lines crinkled around his face when he spoke, as if friendly conversation were embedded in the tanned skin itself. He couldn't have been more than a year or two older than her, especially if he'd known Caden in college.

On second thought, he reminded her of that actor from some movie her cousin Abigail had made her watch a couple of years ago—*The Potato Peel Pie Society* or something? As it so happened, Tess had agreed to watch that movie solely because of the leading man, but she'd never admit that to anyone. Least of all to Austin.

"Care for a tour?" His deep voice broke the spell. Gravel crunched under his shifting feet as he edged toward the grass.

"You can leave your car here for now. I'll show you the camp, and you can take your things inside later."

Without waiting for a reply, he took off up the hill with long, smooth strides. It took her a moment to scrape the mud from her shoes onto the grass, and he was halfway toward the nearest of the cabins before she finally caught up. In his wake, she caught a whiff of—was that vanilla and butterscotch? Odd, but not altogether unappealing.

Without a word, Austin led her over the small rise. He dropped his supplies under the awning of the first cabin and turned to face her, stretching his arms toward a smattering of cabins and fields as if they were the grounds of Monticello itself. "Here we are. Camp Kinnikinnick."

He beamed with pride, but all Tess saw was a tired property with weeds growing through the cracks.

"It's, um . . . nice."

She couldn't tell a stranger his place was a disaster. Not when he was the one giving her a job, after all. But, oh, something needed to be done about the wheelbarrow and stack of old tires on the front lawn. Everything about this place screamed old, antique... forgotten. What could a single man want with such a run-down property, anyway?

"I know, it's a mess," Austin chuckled, a light hum resonating from his chest. "You should have seen it a few weeks ago. We had a tree growing inside one of the cabins."

"No. Really?"

"Believe it. Would have been the perfect Christmas tree too if we hadn't had to chop it down."

Tess didn't know what to make of this man and his odd sense of humor. The idea of a fixer upper made her stomach churn. Her gaze fell to the tool belt and nails at his feet. "And the shingles are for . . ."

"A hole in one of the cabin roofs. A family of birds had made a nest in it, so we relocated them before fixing it." He slid her a look. "You don't happen to speak *woodpecker*, do you?"

She couldn't tell if he was serious or joking.

The hum of a lawn mower buzzed in the distance, and the scent of pine mingled with that of freshly cut grass. Tess breathed in a lungful of spiced air and counted down from ten. What mess had Caden gotten her into this time?

"So." Austin interrupted before she reached *one*. "Ready to see the rest?"

Before she could answer, he swung open the door to the cabin. A musty smell assaulted her nostrils, and for some reason she couldn't fathom, she followed him inside. It took a moment for her eyes to adjust to the dim interior. Four sets of bunk beds lined the walls of the small cabin. The bare floor creaked with each step, and she noticed a single feather caught in a spider web in the corner. If Austin wasn't blocking the door, she would have been outside in a flash.

"We'll have ten students in a cabin. Boys in these four, and girls in the others. The facilities for the small cabins are located down the path, so they'll get the true camp experience." He propped his shoulder against the doorframe and seemed to gauge her response from beneath his long lashes.

Tess cringed. She'd never been one for camping herself. Maybe it was the silken bug traps or the dusty air, but she was beginning to feel lightheaded in the confined space. To her relief, Austin stepped back outside, and she followed close behind. The high-altitude sun warmed her face, despite the chill in the air, and she breathed a sigh of relief.

From there, they continued on with the tour. Upon further inspection, the other cabins looked identical, and they made their way to a two-story log house at the end of the field with a stone chimney and wrap-around porch. The building looked like it belonged in a German ski village, not in the midst of the Colorado mountains. She stepped over the threshold and was happy to see the inside was in much better condition than the cabins. Probably because someone was already living here, judging by the shoes propped near the door. Most likely, Austin's.

"What is this place used for? Staff housing?" *I hope.* Tess craned her neck toward the second floor and the open railing that circled above the entry room.

Austin propped the door open and joined her in the center of the open living room. "Welcome to The Lodge. This is where all staff members will stay. Plus, it has the dining room, a state-of-the-art kitchen, and indoor commons area for the campers to use. Your room is upstairs and to the right, above the kitchen, and Josh and I are to the left. The other staff members will join us later, and we'll divide up the rest of the rooms then."

Tess peered up at the landing and down the dark-paneled corridor that led to her room. Her ankle throbbed at the mere thought of climbing those stairs every day. Those single-story cabins sounded pretty nice right about now. She inwardly cringed. Okay. So maybe not including the birds' nests and all.

"Just think about how much this will quicken your recovery." Her doctor's voice seemed to echo in her ears. Tess took one more look at the warped steps and strengthened her resolve.

"So, Josh is your . . ." she prompted, hoping Austin hadn't noticed her earlier silence.

"My nephew. He's here for the summer while his mom's away for work."

Oh. So that explained the lawn mower she'd heard earlier. On closer inspection of the room, there were other hints of a teenage presence—an open box of Cheez-Its on the table, a pair of dirty socks wedged between the couch cushions. A couple of empty candy wrappers sticking out from under the sofa. Interesting that the kid was here and not with his dad.

Austin stood near the fireplace, an unreadable expression on his face as if he were studying her reaction. "So, what's the verdict? Ready to hightail it back to the city after seeing everything?"

Tess reexamined the old furniture, debating if she should tell him the truth. She stole a peek down the hall and glimpsed a couple of buckets and mops. "You really want to know what I think?"

"Give me your worst." He sent her a challenging grin.

She took a breath. "Well . . . the lawn looks like a jungle, I've seen three cabins that appear as if they've never seen a broom or a solid cleaning, the main house is in serious need of a new layer of paint, and don't even get me started on the road out front."

"Anything else?"

She smiled. "Yeah, apparently you have a tree growing in the middle of cabin three."

At that, he laughed. "*Had* a tree," he corrected. "And don't forget the birds in cabin four."

His lighthearted manner put her at ease. Maybe she'd been too quick to judge. She glanced around the room again, and her gaze eventually landed on the massive stone fireplace and the array of framed photos lining the mantle. A handful of black and white faces smiled back at her, as if inviting her to take a step into the past.

"So, what's the story with this place, anyway?"

Austin picked up a framed portrait of an older couple and peered down at the weathered faces. "This used to be my grandpa's. He purchased the property not long after he lost my grandma and decided to open it up to the public. It may not look like it now, but it used to be one of the best summer camps this side of the Rocky Mountains."

He was right. She did have a hard time believing that.

"I can appreciate that. It takes a lot to start over and pursue a new passion. So how did you end up with the place? Forgive me for being nosy, but it seems like an odd choice of profession."

"No apologies necessary. I was lucky in that I got to spend my summers up here as a kid. When my grandpa passed a little over a year ago, I was working as a paramedic out in California. I'd been gone so long, it sort of felt like a call to come home."

Tess watched as he placed the photograph back in its rightful spot and turned his attention to her once more. Something else seemed to simmer beneath the surface, another layer to the story he wasn't sharing.

Before she could study him anymore, he turned from the mantle and made for the stairs, where he showed Tess to her room, tossed her a pair of keys, and left to finish repairing the cabin roof near the camp entrance. Ten minutes later, she stood on the wide front porch and watched his retreat toward the bunkhouses. Austin wasn't anything like she'd imagined, and neither was his camp.

Tess took one more look inside the house through the open door and paused when she spotted a discarded sweater slung over the back of a chair, *Go Bulldogs* emblazoned across its back. The peanut butter stain on the sleeve hinted at its young owner, and she wondered again about the nephew Austin had mentioned.

She loved her family but craved her independence too much to spend an entire summer with any of them besides Abigail.

The lawn mower continued to buzz in the distance, scaring a flock of birds as it circled the overgrown lawn. In one great arc, they swooped over the house and settled in a grove of nearby lodgepole pine, squawking at each other like a race-day crowd. She nearly laughed at the comparison.

What would Ryan think about her working here? He was always teasing her about her aversion to nature, and all because she'd run off the trail during a race when she thought she saw a snake. Turned out it was only a twig, but three years later, he still loved to rib her about it. His jaw would hit the floor when she told him where she was standing now.

The smile died on her lips. No, she supposed she wouldn't tell him about this. If it weren't for that email, she wouldn't have even been here in the first place. She'd known him to drop athletes like flies before, but never had she imagined she'd be one of them. They were too close, had too much history. Or so she thought. His betrayal stung like alcohol on an open wound, except it didn't feel like a healing experience.

Tess's phone burned in her back pocket with the desire to text him. Maybe it was a blessing she didn't have cell reception up here. Made it all the easier to step back instead of begging for more time.

All things considered, there were worse places to be stuck for a summer.

She trudged through the mud back to her car, careful of her footing on the uneven road. Even with her brace, it was still a tricky process. After removing her mud-caked shoes, she slid into the driver's seat and turned on the ignition. Warm air spilled from the vents, and she sat in silence, staring through the windshield.

She'd pushed herself to the edge before, but she knew her limits in the triathlon world. Out here in the wild, it was a whole new story, and for the first time, she was on her own. Like that first swim along a new racecourse, she was jumping into the deep end without a clue what lay beneath the surface.

CHAPTER

Four

WHEN AUSTIN AWOKE the following morning, he went for his usual seven A.M. run and took a quick shower before grabbing breakfast. As he entered the kitchen, the floorboards creaked overhead, announcing that Tess was awake as well.

"Feet off the table." Austin swatted his nephew's feet, which earned him a grunt of acknowledgement. "Now." He grabbed the top of the chair and rattled Josh awake.

"What'd you do that for?" The boy stifled a yawn and yanked his hoodie down to shield his eyes from the morning light.

"Eat up. We have a busy day ahead of us." Austin grabbed a bagel and tossed it across the table.

A moan emanated from behind the hood. "You've been saying that for weeks."

"And I'm sure it will be just as true tomorrow. So up and at 'em. Those cabins won't clean themselves."

There was another grumble of displeasure. His nephew sounded about as pleased as a bear waking up from hibernation. Only in this case, the bear would have at least responded to the bagel.

Judging by last week's progress, he figured he had another ten minutes until Josh woke up enough to follow him outside. Austin washed down his own food with a cup of coffee and left the groggy teenager to join the waking world.

Outside, a faint mist clung to the treetops on the fringes of the clearing. Despite its being mid-May, the morning temperatures hung in the forties, and bits of snow still blanketed the shadowed portions of the property, a welcome reprieve from the humid summers of San Diego. Austin pulled a wool cable-knit sweater over his clean T-shirt and rounded the back of the house toward the shed. He passed Tess's car next to his black and white SUV under the ancient spruce and picked up his pace.

Had he been crazy to offer her the job? Caden had mentioned the accident, and it was hard to miss the hefty brace swathed around her lower leg yesterday. Her job didn't require the ability to run laps around the field, per se, but the amount of activity both before and during the summer would make anyone's feet tired. Injury or no injury.

She was feisty, though, he'd give her that. Ten minutes on site, and she'd given her hearty disapproval of the camp's less-than-stellar status. Oh, she'd tried to hide it, but there was no mistaking the criticism in those hazel eyes of hers. If he could channel that energy into something constructive and light a fire underneath his nephew, then they might be able to get this place ready for their June fourth opening after all.

Three weeks to go.

Austin unlocked the shed and retrieved a stack of five-gallon buckets, some rags, two bottles of vinegar, and Castile soap. Armed with his gear, he closed the door and set off to wage war on the dust and cobwebs.

He was about to head toward the first cabin when he noticed Tess on the front porch. He slowed and watched as she squinted across the field over the rim of her coffee cup. She had loosely gathered her long dark waves at the base of her head, and the hem of her sweater grazed the carved rungs of the porch railing. The sun glinted off the face of her overly large watch like a rescue beacon in the forest.

"If you're looking for Bigfoot, you won't find him there."

Her mug tipped, and a wave of coffee sloshed over the rim. Barefoot, she danced to avoid the hot liquid splashing around her feet.

Austin climbed the steps two at a time and offered her a towel. "Sorry about that. I didn't mean to startle you."

Her eyes connected with his as if he'd magically appeared out of the mist. She graciously accepted the towel and dabbed at a stain on her sweater. "I don't know where my head was. I didn't even hear you walk up."

She was bending to dry off her feet and the patio when he stopped her. "Don't worry about the wood. It'll rain tonight and wash it clean. Besides, we're surrounded by forest. This patio has seen far worse than a drip or two of coffee."

The tension in her face eased, and she cracked a faint smile. "I'll bet there's a story or two there." She took another sip of what remained of her coffee and leaned her forearms against the railing. The morning breeze played with the ends of her hair, softening her prickly exterior from yesterday.

In the quiet morning, he could better study her. The spray of freckles across her upturned nose, the coppery tint to her hair when the sun hit it just right. Her tight-lipped expression had relaxed, revealing a gentle nature underneath. He could see a lot of Caden in her complexion, but her eyes were unique, a mixture of gold, jade, and brown that reminded him of a sunny day in the forest.

In fact, she was downright pretty when she let her guard down.

Aware he was staring, Austin turned his gaze to the pine slats at his feet. "In fact, this whole place has enough stories to keep you entertained for years. My grandpa once told me he spotted a mountain lion by the back door when he was a kid. He scared it away with his bare hands before it could eat the cherry pie cooling on the windowsill."

Her eyes grew wide. "No. That really happened?"

He shrugged. "My grandpa may have been one to stretch a story now and again."

Tess swatted at him with the towel, and her laughter eclipsed her earlier seriousness. "You almost had me going there. Glad I didn't spot any animals in the trees before you walked by."

He rooted his feet into the patio like the lodgepole pine in the distance and gazed in the direction she'd been looking earlier. "So, what *were* you looking at when I snuck up on you?"

Tess sized him up from the corner of her eye. Her lips kissed the ceramic mug, and she took another sip. She shrugged. "Just a camp owner with a terrible sense of humor."

He caught her grin hidden behind the cup.

He chuckled and angled his body toward the steps once more. "Guilty as charged. Well, if you're ready to get started, I'll be next door cleaning out the cabins." He lifted the buckets and rags to aid his point. He had turned to walk back down the steps when she shouted back.

"Just as long as Bigfoot doesn't catch me first."

Austin shook his head. Should have seen that one coming. He continued down the steps until the door clicked shut as Tess dipped inside the lodge. Arms warmed up from carrying supplies, he strolled the rest of the way to the first A-frame cottage.

Ten minutes and a bucket of cleaning solution later, Austin heard the slow approach of two people in conversation. Tess's voice was unmistakable, the way it punctuated the air with energy and brightened the quiet morning. She chatted away, zinging Josh with questions, which the boy didn't seem to mind. She laughed at something, and Austin stilled. Less than twenty-four hours, and Tess had already managed to connect with his nephew.

Josh's familiar clomps echoed up the cabin stoop and froze in the doorway. "What is that *smell*?" He pinched his nose at the vinegar's pungent aroma and made a face. "Did something die in here?" He took a step back outside and drew in a dramatic gulp of fresh air.

"Hey, is that anything to say to your uncle?" Austin leaned back from his spot on the wood floor and plopped the wet towel into the water. He couldn't help but laugh at his nephew's penchant for the dramatic.

Tess waved a hand in front of her nose and made a face as well. "I think I might have to agree with Josh. Why don't you use one of those lemon-scented cleaners? At least those smell nice."

Josh rolled his eyes. "Don't even get him started on that."

"On what?" Her brows pinched together in question.

Austin intervened before his nephew could say anything else. "How about instead of questioning my methods, you start cleaning? A little soap and vinegar won't hurt you." He grabbed a couple of towels and tossed them toward the open door.

"Okay."

"Fine."

Tess and Josh spoke in unison, her amiable response contrasting with Josh's less than enthusiastic reply, and they set to work. Josh handled floor duty, while Austin wiped down the walls and rafters, leaving Tess to scrub the furniture in methodical circles. The three of them grew quiet while they scrubbed, and soon the sounds of sloshing water filled the space. Josh's headphones dangled from his ears, and he bobbed his head to some silent beat.

Tess hummed to herself while she worked, a contented expression on her face as her arm moved in rhythmic circles across the wood.

Austin couldn't help but smile.

The three of them worked in relative silence, save for Tess's soft murmurings, until the entire cabin smelled of vinegar.

"So, how's your cousin Micah doing?" Austin wrung out his rag and ran it over the rough wood. He'd heard enough from Caden's comments over the years to know his cousin and the ranch had gone through some tough seasons with the recent droughts. "Caden said he was having some issues with the ranch. Hope it's not too serious."

A woodpecker hammered outside the window, and its echoing cry reverberated through the four walls.

Tess wiped the cloth across the lower bedpost and along one of the dressers. "I'm sure it's nothing. Caden's always looking for an excuse to spend time on the ranch. Micah has never let anything stop him from working, not even when he got bucked off his horse and broke an arm. I'll bet you anything my brother's really there to see a certain girl." She swatted at a web and brushed it aside.

That sounded like Caden, all right. He always had been one to follow his heart instead of his head.

He chuckled. "Yeah, I guess that makes sense. Well, in any case, I'm glad you agreed to take his place."

"Is that because of my stellar cleaning skills?" She flashed a carefree grin, which made Austin's pulse skip.

"Actually, I was thinking more along the lines of, if Caden had been here, he would have started a soap war by now."

"You might be right about that."

Friendly silence wrapped around them once more before Austin spoke up again. "Speaking of other staff members, Trudy should be here the day after tomorrow. She used to work here when my grandpa ran the place, and she was the first to support me when I decided to reopen it. Trudy and Jefferson Hinshaw are some of the sweetest folks around. They're almost as much a part of this place as these cabins."

The couple went back in his memory to the first day he'd set foot on this forested plot of land as a boy. One day, he hoped to be as happy as the two of them. But he had too much to worry about with the camp and his nephew to throw any romantic notions into the mix.

Tess dunked her towel into the soapy water, and he caught a short whiff of lavender. "She sounds lovely. I'm looking forward to meeting her."

"She may be a bit eccentric, but she has a good heart. And," he added, "she makes the best biscuits and gravy this side of the Continental Divide."

"Well, then I'm sure I'll love her too."

By the time they started on the third cabin, they had their system down. Even Josh's gloomy attitude had shifted. He tossed jokes back and forth with Tess, and Austin listened in fascinated amusement. Josh didn't open up much, but he hadn't stopped talking since removing his headphones an hour ago.

Austin reached into the bucket nearest to him and found it empty. "Looks like we're getting low on cleaning solution. I'll be right back."

He grabbed the handle and carried the bucket outside and down the hill to the hose. Cool water trickled into the five-gallon container, and he took the time to think through his to-do list. If they could get all the cabins cleaned today, that would bring them one step closer to opening. One step closer to keeping his grandpa's legacy alive.

A dash of red caught his eye, and before he could react, a woodpecker buzzed past. He ducked, and the bird flew inside the cabin, followed by a screech and the unmistakable sound of water splashing across the floor. Tess raced through the open door as fast as her clunky brace would allow.

"What was that?" she cried.

She'd dropped her rag, and rivulets of sudsy water circled around Josh's feet by the upturned bucket. The bird zipped back outside and perched on the lowest branch of the nearby tree, chest puffed out in pride for scaring away the *intruders*.

Austin smiled and shook his head in amusement. "Looks like you've met Morty."

"Morty?" Her voice rose half an octave, and she glared at the offender.

Austin held his laughter in check, not wanting to feel the wrath of Tess on their first day working together. "You remember those birds I told you about that nested in one of the cabins? Well, I moved the nest and patched the roof, but this guy keeps coming back."

"So you decided to name him?"

He shrugged. "To be fair, he was here before us. It seemed rude to shoo him away when he obviously doesn't want to leave."

Tess muttered something and shuffled back inside.

Austin waited another moment before following. Best to give her a second to cool down. With a long exhale, he grabbed the stack of towels from the porch and left the extra water behind to clean up the new mess inside.

There wasn't enough ice in the world to stop the throbbing in Tess's ankle. She could chip away at St. Mary's Glacier and still find no relief. Of course, she wouldn't tell Austin any of this. She saw the way he watched her when he thought she wasn't paying attention. Pity with a touch of uncertainty. Well, she'd prove to him she was up for any challenge, even if it meant she had to ice her foot an extra hour every night.

She hobbled over to the dresser and plunked down the half-melted cool pack next to her book. She had a whole shelf back home full of books to finish one day. Even without the distractions of racing, travel, or the internet, she still couldn't focus on the black and white pages. If only she could go for a run, that would clear her head, but that wasn't an option.

The light from her bedside lamp bounced off the small mirror above the dresser, and she took a good long look at the person staring back at her. Same hazel eyes. Same square jaw and pointed chin. The patch of freckles on her nose had faded during her rehab, and her caramel highlights seemed to lack their usual brilliance.

"What are you doing here, Tess?" she whispered at her reflection.

With a heavy sigh, she turned and dropped back onto the quilted bed, the dim lamplight flickering from the movement. With any luck, she'd get a decent night's rest. Or at least better than last night's. And hopefully, a vengeful woodpecker wouldn't disturb her dreams like this morning.

She listened to the shuffling of chairs downstairs, evidence of the two other people in the log house. When she'd left them over an hour ago, Austin had been attempting to teach his nephew how to play a card game. The poor boy looked about as excited as a cat in water as he stared at the ancient cribbage board.

Thoughts of a certain camp owner flooded her mind, and she let them wander. The man owned an abandoned summer camp, made friends with animals, and seemed to have the same interests as an eighty-year-old man. He wasn't all bad, though. He was handsome—she'd give him that—in a rugged, unintentional sort of way. Nothing like Ryan and his whitened smile and flashy sunglasses. Austin was far more patient than Ryan. Even when she and Josh spilled an entire bucket of vinegar water over the cabin floor, he'd swooped in with a towel at the ready and cleaned it up without complaint or rebuke.

A faint acoustic melody snuck through the crack beneath her door. The sound rose and fell, slowing Tess's breathing to match the rhythm. Like magic, her shoulders relaxed, and she climbed under the covers. After a short while, the music stopped, breathing its last resonant notes on a somber exhale as if lulling the world into slumber.

For the next hour and a half, Tess lay wide awake, thinking about the music and fighting for sleep against the too-quiet mountain stillness. Every noise caught her attention—a twig snapping, the rustle of wind through the forest, Morty hammering against a tree in the distance. It wasn't until after midnight that she finally drifted off into a fitful sleep, the nightmares of her last race plaguing her dreams.

CHAPTER

Five

TESS WRESTLED A stack of life preservers next to a row of propped-up canoes. Dust motes spilled through the small windows of the lakeside boathouse, reflecting the sunlight across the building's raw timber and stone construction. Cobwebs adorned the thick rafters, and she was pretty sure that scratchy sound in the corner was from something larger than a mouse. When Austin had suggested she and Josh clean out the old storage building while he worked in The Lodge, she'd envisioned something a little less . . . rustic.

"How much junk is in here?" she muttered under her breath before dropping a yellow and orange flotation device at her feet.

Josh popped out from behind a canoe with a puzzled expression. "Um? Are you talking to me?" Dirt covered his faded Broncos T-shirt, and his headphones were nowhere in sight.

Tess hadn't realized she'd spoken out loud. She shook her head, dislodging a sprinkling of dust from her messy ponytail. "Sorry about that. I sometimes think out loud. Used to drive Ryan mad."

Josh tossed another paddle onto the growing stack and sent her a questioning gaze. "Who's Ryan? Your boyfriend?"

Her face heated. For a time, she'd hoped. "He's..." Tess paused and brushed the thought aside. "Nobody. He used to be my coach." She slung a pair of rubber waders over the wall hook, and they clattered against the wood panels.

"Uh-huh." He seemed to ponder that for a moment before resuming his work with the paddles. "So why does it look like you want to murder that inner tube? It doesn't have anything to do with Uncle Austin, does it?" He dumped a set of oars in a pile by the door with a grin.

She was *not* about to answer that question. Especially not to the man's fourteen-year-old nephew.

Josh smiled, seeming to understand her unspoken frustrations. "Welcome to the club."

Tess swiped a hand across her forehead and surveyed the half-organized shelves of bait and tackle. All that fishing line would take months to untangle. "I take it you're not too keen on this camp idea either?"

He shrugged. "It's not so much that..." A pebble bounced off the toe of his shoe and skittered across the planked floor. "I'm glad Mom can finally get back to what she loves. Really, I am. But her trip came together so quickly, and, I don't know, I kind of hoped I could've gone with her."

"To Cambodia, right?" Tess struggled to wrap her mind around the idea of this city kid traipsing through the jungle. "You know this place is probably way less remote than there?" Come to think of it, without cell reception, maybe it wasn't so different. But at least they were still in Colorado.

"Yeah, but I'll bet she gets to do lots of cool things, like see ancient ruins and ride elephants."

Tess shook her head. It was as if he thought his mom was living in a real-life Indiana Jones movie. "So, you'd rather be surrounded by pythons and poisonous frogs for three months?"

"Well, probably not. But it would have been nice if I'd had the choice, you know?"

Yeah, she knew. "Was there anywhere else you could have gone? Your dad's, grandparents' . . ."

"Nah. Grandma and Grandpa travel too much, and my dad left before I was born." He said it matter-of-factly, as if he'd told her the sky was blue.

"Oh, I'm so sorry." What else did one say to that? She didn't know what she'd expected, but not that.

Josh tossed another life jacket and watched it land with a thud atop the growing pile. "It's okay. Really. I love Uncle Austin, and this place isn't all that bad." His head shot up and spun toward her. "But don't tell him I said that."

"Of course. Cross my heart." Tess drew her finger over her chest in an 'X' and tried to keep her expression serious.

They were shuffling a few more items around the small building when an idea popped into her head. She set aside an armload of fishing tackle and turned to Josh, hands on her hips. "How about we take a break and do something fun, for a change?"

The crease between his eyebrows said everything. "What did you have in mind?"

"Ever been canoeing?" She grabbed a newly organized set of oars and tossed one to him. "Last one to get their life jacket on has to steer the boat."

"You're on." Josh lunged for the red one on top and had it buckled in place before Tess could say *Kinnikinnick*.

Leaving their project for later, they hauled the wooden boat down to the dock. Tess was careful to watch her footing along the silty shore, but they managed to get the boat in the water without incident. For the next hour, the two paddled in circles around the small lake. Josh came alive on the water, talking nonstop about music, school, and his friends back home. Tess listened and slipped in a few questions whenever he took a breath, glad to see him opening up more.

Austin was right. Josh was a good kid. And through his nephew, she was beginning to piece together glimpses of the man as well.

Trudy arrived later that afternoon, her cream and gold SUV rumbling up the road like an old diesel motorboat. The sound carried all the way down the hill to the dock as Tess and Josh put the last pieces of equipment away in the boathouse.

"Just wait 'til you meet Trudy," Josh said as they locked the door and trekked up to the house. "I've met her a few times over the years, and she is *not* what you would call boring." He didn't elaborate, and all sorts of images of a cranky camp cook took shape in Tess's head.

Austin had mentioned the rest of the staff would start trickling in by the end of the week, but it was hard to keep track of the days when every day consisted of more repair work and cleaning.

Josh led the way up the front steps, and the screen door bounced shut behind them. Austin's resonant voice floated from the kitchen, deep in conversation with an unmistakably thick southern drawl. Sounds of clanging pots and silverware joined the friendly conversation before Austin stepped into the living area, a wide smile on his face.

"Hey, you two." His arms hung relaxed at his sides against his clean navy sweater, very much unlike Tess's uniform of grunge and lake water. He spoke mainly to Josh, but his eyes flicked toward her. "How's the boathouse coming along?"

"Almost done." Josh peered around Austin to see what all the noise was about. "I take it Trudy's already settling in."

Austin's head dipped in a "yes" as a woman with salt-and-pepper hair bounced through the doorway.

"Josh, is that you?" She bustled over and gave him a once over. "My, have you grown. Last I saw you, you were—" she held her arm out at shoulder height—"knee-high to a grasshopper." She planted her hands on her ample hips and beamed up at him. "I'm sure you're quite the catch now with the girls at school."

Josh ducked to hide his reddening face and gave her a hug. "Nice to see you too, Miss Trudy."

At the sight of Austin's grin, Tess fought back a laugh. She already liked this woman.

"And this," Trudy released Josh from her grip and turned, "must be Tess. How wonderful to finally meet you." She stepped forward and wrapped Tess in a motherly embrace. "I've heard so much about you. I feel like we've already met."

Tess eyed Austin over the woman's shoulder, and he peered innocently up at the ceiling.

The woman stepped back, hands resting on Tess's upper arms. She gave them another pat and smiled. "If I'd known you were already here, I'd have come sooner. But you know how men are. Forgetting little details like that." She nodded toward Austin. "No offense, dear. But you failed to mention this beautiful girl at church on Sunday."

"None taken." He raised his hands in contrition.

"Good. Now how about y'all come help me find the cast-iron pot, and I'll make us a nice dinner. I don't know how you've been survivin' on bagels and cold cuts." She motioned to the group and sashayed back into the kitchen, her magnolia print blouse swaying with the movement.

Tess watched wide-eyed, as if a cyclone had rushed in and then left the room in the same breath. This woman had enough life and energy to power the entire camp with her smile. Tess looked toward the kitchen door and noted that neither Austin nor Josh had moved.

"Should we follow her?" she asked, unsure how to respond.

Austin swooped his arm forward. "After you."

The three of them filed into the camp kitchen, where Trudy was standing on tiptoe for a pot on the top shelf. Austin reached above her and retrieved the Dutch oven, depositing it safely onto the double-wide gas stovetop.

"Bless you, dear. Either I've shrunk, or someone rearranged things in here without my say-so." Trudy sent him a pointed look and began unloading the items from the grocery bags on the counter. With a handful of carrots in one hand and a bag of potatoes in the other, she turned to the three of them. She raised the carrots and pointed them toward the stove. "Well, what are y'all waiting for? Pull up a knife or spoon, and let's get to work."

"Yes, ma'am." Austin grabbed three cutting boards from the rack and passed them around. When he got to Tess, he leaned in and whispered, "Don't worry. You'll get used to her soon enough."

"I heard that," Trudy called over the clanging of pots and spoons.

He sent Tess a wink and got to work on the onions and carrots.

Following his example, she grabbed a head of cauliflower and began to chop florets. Josh begrudgingly grated the ginger in silence. Even with the four of them at work, the kitchen somehow felt spacious and inviting. Not that it would have made a difference if the kitchen were the size of a cupboard. Tess got the impression that one did not say "no" to Trudy Hinshaw. Even within minutes of arriving, she was in full command of her domain.

When the oil was hot and ready, Trudy added Austin's chopped onions to the pan. She spun a wooden spoon in the air while she talked and sautéed. "My granddaughter gave me this new cookbook for Christmas, and I've been dyin' to give it a try. But Jeff, my husband, doesn't take too kindly to anything particularly exotic. So, I thought I'd wait to test it on you three." Her crimson-covered lips spread in an innocent smile.

Josh wrinkled his nose at the yellow and red spices and tins of coconut milk on the counter. He took one whiff of the turmeric powder and cringed. "What *exactly* are we making?"

Her eyes twinkled with delight. "Tonight, we're having curry." She did a little two-step dance around Austin and twirled back to the stove.

Tess had to give it to the woman. She hoped she had half her energy and enthusiasm when she was in her sixties.

She glanced at Josh. When the others were busy, she leaned over and spoke loud enough for him to hear. "Looks like you get to taste a little slice of Asia, after all."

He rolled his eyes and went back to grating the ginger with an audible huff. The kid didn't know what he was missing.

When Tess looked up, she caught a look of appreciation in Austin's gaze, and for a split second, something seemed to pass between them. Understanding? Or maybe something else.

Trudy's chatter cut in and broke the connection like a warm knife through butter.

Austin ducked into the pantry, and Tess studied the bright and talkative woman before her. Her very presence exuded warmth, and it filled the house with unexplainable comfort. Tess relaxed, glad for the woman's sudden arrival.

"Trudy, where did you say you were from, again? I don't think I've ever heard an accent quite like yours. It's beautiful."

"Oh, aren't you a peach?" The lines around the woman's face settled into their familiar place. "As it so happens, I'm Georgia born and raised." She took her time on the word *Georgia*, drawing out the word like it was a thread of saltwater taffy. "If you keep talking sweet like that, we're gonna get along just fine, you and me."

She had a feeling Trudy was right. A swell of warmth washed over her, and it was almost as if she were standing in her great-Aunt Josie's kitchen. She couldn't remember a better time. No worries aside from which pie to bake or how many cookies to eat. Over the years, she'd accumulated a stack of recipes from her favorite great-aunt, but it wasn't the same cooking for only one person.

Trudy stirred the remaining ingredients into the pot and reduced the heat to a low simmer. "All right, now. I reckon this has got about a half hour until it's done. How about the three of you go relax, and I'll let you know when dinner's ready?" She shooed them out of the kitchen like a mother hen, relegating them to the sitting room while she returned to her post.

Josh plopped onto one of the upholstered chairs by the fireplace. He fished his music player and headphones from his pocket and slipped into his own world once again.

Glad for a few minutes of rest, Tess followed his lead and sank into the nearby sofa, propping her aching foot on the edge of the coffee table. She'd been careful to watch her step on the lake's slippery bank earlier that afternoon, but the past few days were taking their toll. A slight reprieve was exactly what she needed. Her eyelids slid shut, and she inhaled a long breath.

The cushion dipped when Austin sat down next to her. When she opened her eyes, he was watching her with an unreadable expression. The direct gaze made her want to squirm in her seat, but she wasn't one to back down. He studied her for a long moment before finally looking away.

"Care for a game while we wait?" He reached toward the coffee table in front of them and pushed an old cribbage board toward her. Before she could answer, he dealt out a deck of cards between the two of them.

She stared at the stack of cards in front of her, amused and intrigued. Aunt Josie had taught her the game when she was a kid, but she'd played little since. Card games were fun, but no one could keep the Prescott cousins indoors for long when they were young. Nine times out of ten, she'd opted for something active, but that didn't mean she hadn't picked up a thing or two.

"You realize our grandparents probably played this game before there was television?"

He chuckled under his breath and sent her a humorous look. "Call me old-fashioned, then." He finished arranging the board and flashed her a boyish grin. "Ready? Or do I need to go over the rules, since it's such an *old* game?"

She wasn't going to let him win that easily. It may have been years since she had played, but her family didn't call her competitive for nothing. She peeked at her cards and smiled. She plucked two from her hand and confidently discarded them in front of him. "I think I'll be alright."

Fifteen minutes flew by, and Tess matched Austin's progression move for move around the cribbage board. They were within ten points of finishing the game when Trudy's voice interrupted.

"Dinner's ready." The woman bustled out of the kitchen with a large serving platter in her outstretched arms. "Come and get it while it's still hot, or it'll be cold cuts and bagels next time." She placed the dish on a hot pad in the middle of the table and went back into the kitchen for another load.

Josh unfolded his lanky form from his spot on the couch and dragged himself to the table, leaving a teenager shaped indentation behind, along with his discarded set of headphones.

"Looks like we'll have to wait until after dinner to finish." Austin tapped his cards against the edge of the table and placed them face down beside the board.

"Or you could admit defeat before I win."

"I think I'll take my chances." Austin propped his hand against the armrest and rose. In one fluid movement, he scooped

Josh's headphones and music player from the nearby chair and moved them to the coffee table.

Trudy's sing-song voice echoed through the room once more. "The food will start gettin' cold if you keep dawdling."

Austin shook his head and smiled. "Another thing you'll quickly learn. You don't want to keep Trudy waiting."

In a few easy steps, he was beside Tess and offering her a hand. An invitation.

Less than twenty-four hours ago, she wouldn't have accepted the help. She'd have pushed it aside with some joke or bristled at what she thought was pity. She was proud of her independence, and the fear of being dependent on anyone other than herself terrified her. Other people let you down. They made promises they never intended to keep or walked away when you needed them most.

But she was coming to think Austin wasn't like most people.

Lowering her propped up foot, she placed her hand in his. Without a word, he helped ease her up from the sunken couch cushion as she leveraged herself upright. She held in a wince when her foot touched the ground, but the pins-and-needles subsided as she gently shifted her weight back and forth.

He kept a soft hold on her arm. The simple gesture spoke volumes, and she wished she could take back all the unfavorable thoughts she'd had since coming here.

She squeezed his hand, a silent *thank you* she knew he'd understand.

The sounds of moving chairs drew their attention back to the dining table where Trudy had Josh laying out the place settings. Steam rose from the two serving trays in the center, and the aroma of warm spices wafted toward them.

Austin dropped his hold on her arm and took a step toward their seats. Friendly conversation filled the room, and Tess relaxed even more as the evening progressed. Trudy shared stories about her grandkids, and Josh told a few jokes. Austin jumped in every now and then, defending himself when Trudy brought up an embarrassing story or two of when he was Josh's age, but he smiled good-naturedly all the same.

Tess couldn't remember when she'd last laughed so much or felt so welcomed. It was a refreshing change to the past few months, and the summer was only beginning.

CHAPTER

Six

LOW CLOUDS ROLLED in the next morning, and a heavy air draped over the camp. A loud noise shattered the peaceful quiet. The electronic beeping of an alarm drowned out the birds' early serenade.

"Up and at 'em." Austin tossed a pillow at Josh's seemingly lifeless form and turned off the alarm on his nephew's phone. He knelt and pulled a pair of pants and a long-sleeved shirt from the bottom drawer of the dresser and slung them over the footboard.

"Gotta get an early start if we want to finish by this afternoon."

Austin was all ready to go. In the half hour he'd been up, he'd already packed their bags for the day and gathered the necessary gear. The water bottles were filled, and he'd stashed some food and a few protein bars in their packs for later.

Josh finally stirred and shoved back the covers to reveal a serious case of bedhead. "Do we have to hike to the shelter today?" he mumbled, groggy with sleep.

"No time like the present." Austin had been meaning to fix up the old structure for weeks. With the rest of the camp on its way to being finished, today was the day.

The boy yawned wide, and without further protest, carried the pile of clothes to the bathroom down the hall.

Austin walked downstairs into the dark living room, careful not to wake Tess as he passed her closed door. She could probably do with the extra sleep. He'd noticed how she favored her ankle every evening after work. She might not welcome the sympathy, but he wasn't one to do nothing when he saw a person hurting. There were other ways he could help—if she'd let him.

Ten minutes later, Josh clomped down the staircase with steps loud enough to wake a sleeping elephant. Austin cringed, his hope of giving Tess a morning of rest long gone. He gave the boy a silent stare meant to say, *do you intend to wake the entire mountain this morning?*

On the last step, Josh looked up. He paused and held his hands out, palms up, a look of innocence on his face. "What?"

Austin blew out a measured breath and let his frustrations go. "You all ready, then?"

He didn't expect much of a reply from a teenager woken before dawn, so he shouldn't have been surprised when the boy shuffled past without so much as a nod. An empty candy wrapper fell from the kid's pocket and floated onto the floor behind him.

Lord, give me grace. Austin picked up the plastic wrapper along with his pack and handed a matching gray and blue bag to Josh. With two thermoses of steaming coffee in hand, they left and began the long uphill trek into the forest.

The sun had barely begun to creep over the horizon when they set out, lighting up the sky with a pastel glow of orange and pink. They passed the first mile-marker and turned left at the fork, continuing upward with every step. Here, the tree canopy grew denser, wilder. Patches of snow covered the ground like a knit blanket, mounds of pine needles and underbrush poking through the half-melted ground cover.

They walked in relative silence, like hiking across the back of a sleeping giant. The caffeine didn't appear to have kicked in yet for Josh, and Austin was content to listen to nature's music for the time being. They reached the second and third markers and passed through a small aspen grove.

He could still remember the first time he'd hiked this path with his grandpa. He'd been quite a bit younger than Josh, but just as reluctant to be there. "Son," his grandpa had spoken in that worn voice of his that seemed to command the centuries, "we're goin' on a walk. You and me." With shoes a half size too small from a recent growth spurt, Austin had followed, gangly limbs and all.

Nearly fifteen years later, Austin was still trying to follow in the old man's steps. If only he could ask him what he was supposed to do next.

Austin led the two of them through the split in the rock and paused on the other side. *It should be about here...*

"Is that it?" Josh's voice pulled Austin back to the misty trail, and the boy pointed toward a dark shadow through the trees.

Austin could barely make out the three-walled structure with its slanted aluminum roof and steel fire pit ring in the dirt a hundred yards ahead of him. Evergreen sprouts encircled the building, and moss clung to the log exterior, as if the forest were attempting to reclaim the hilltop as its own.

Austin pushed back the branch of an overgrown bush to reveal a faded wooden sign that read: Black Bear Ridge Shelter. "Looks like we're here."

He pulled out a set of short-handled clippers from the mesh pocket of his bag and forged his way through the overgrown trail. Face slappers and runaway roots aside, the trail was exactly as he remembered it. A particularly large raspberry bush blocked the end of the path, and Austin and Josh had to sidle around it to trim back the shrub to its base.

"Ouch!" Josh recoiled from the plant as if he'd been bitten and cradled his hand in his lap. An angry red line had already begun to pucker around his wrist, and he glared back at the offending plant.

Austin swung his backpack from his shoulders and rummaged around for the first-aid kit. It was only a scratch, but it never hurt to be careful. Every wound had a potential for infection, no matter how small it might appear on the surface.

"Here." He handed Josh a disinfectant wipe and some dressings. "I should have warned you earlier about the thorns. These raspberries tend to feed on the blood of innocent hikers."

"So, you're telling me *now* this place is booby-trapped?" Josh swiped a pad of alcohol over the wound and applied a thin layer of antibiotic salve.

This kid and his video games. "You never know. Gotta watch out for all those mountain lions, bears, and—"

"Raspberries, apparently." Josh slapped a bandage over the scrape.

"Exactly."

It was good for them to have this time together. Austin snipped the final offending branch and tossed the dangerous limbs a few yards from the trail. He brushed the dirt from his hands onto his jeans and stashed the trimmers and first-aid kit back in his bag.

"Come on. Let me give you the grand tour." Austin hiked a thumb over his shoulder and strode toward the simple lean-to.

They stepped over the level stump and stood in front of the structure. It wasn't much—three flat walls of stacked logs, a brown corrugated tin roof with a bowing smile, and a few wooden benches circled around a dugout fire pit—but it was theirs all the same. All they had to do was trim back the trees, secure the metal roof in a few sections, and it would be good as new.

"At least it's still standing." Josh peered around the corner, doubt creasing his forehead as he surveyed the simple structure.

It might not be anything special, but Austin had many fond memories here. Camping beneath the stars, roasting marshmallows until they blazed like fiery torches, learning to play the guitar under his grandpa's patient guidance. Whereas Josh saw an old and worn set of walls, it transported Austin back in time to the best summers of his life.

Josh wandered ahead of him and froze when he spotted a second structure through the trees. A single limb curved toward the forest floor, supporting a few dozen branches on either side to form a tent-like shape. At its highest, the entrance stood nearly six feet tall and tapered all the way to the ground.

Austin had been saving the best for last. "Why don't you go check it out?"

Josh didn't need any further prompting. He jogged over to the massive survival shelter nestled against the large pine and ducked inside.

With eyes like a trained architect, the boy scrutinized every notch and twig. He gave the support beam a little tug, and the thing hardly budged. "This is so cool. I wonder how long it's been here."

Austin doffed his coat and backpack and rolled up the sleeves of his sweater to join him. He righted a fallen branch, memories coming back to him, and he looked up at his nephew. "About ten years. I built it the last summer I stayed here."

"You?" Josh's eyes rounded in surprise.

Austin chuckled. Maybe there was hope of resurrecting his "cool-uncle" persona, after all. "Don't look so surprised. I was a kid once too, you know." He might be closer to thirty now than he would like to admit, but he sure wasn't old yet.

"How is this still here?" Josh motioned to the slanted roof around them.

"If you build something well, it tends to last." It was a lesson he'd learned that year, after plenty of trial and error. And it didn't only apply to forest construction. That truth had stuck with him ever since.

Josh pulled his phone from the front zipper pocket of his backpack and snapped a few dozen pictures. "Wait 'til Lee and Carson hear about this. They won't believe it."

Austin's mouth twitched at the corners, humored to see how his nephew was taking to the camp. One could always count on a good treehouse or rustic survival shelter to grab a teenage boy's attention.

"So, how about we make a deal?"

Josh paused between pictures to listen. Austin had thought over the idea last night, and if Josh's current attitude was any indication, it was sure to be a home run.

"If we get the shelter fixed up and still have enough time before we need to head back for dinner, I'll show you how to build your own."

Austin didn't have to wait long for a response.

"Deal." Josh agreed with the enthusiasm of a trout leaping at mosquitoes.

Austin hid his laugh behind a tight smile and scooped up both their bags. "Well, okay, then. I guess we should get started."

CHAPTER

Seven

TESS TOSSED AND turned all night, haunted by dreams of running through quicksand. With each movement, she kept sinking, kicking her legs against the pit that tried to engulf her until she awoke with a start, legs tangled in her balled-up sheets. It took a moment for the fog to clear from her addled brain before she finally realized where she was again.

Morty the woodpecker's hammering echoed in the distance, the bird no doubt intent on reestablishing his home in the wall of his favorite cabin.

With a long sigh, Tess swung her legs over the side of the bed and planted her feet on the cool hardwood floor. Still groggy, she rubbed her eyes until spots danced across her vision. Despite her eight hours of attempted sleep, she couldn't shake the weariness that settled over her. If anything, the nightmares had gotten worse over the past few months.

Cool sunlight filtered in through her window and pushed back the earlier darkness. She drew in a deep lungful of crisp air and held it for a count of three before releasing it back into the room. Despite what others thought, she had always been a bundle of nerves before her races. Only her coach, Ryan, ever picked up on it, but he'd persuaded her to focus that energy toward winning. That was then. What race was she focusing on now?

Her gaze drifted to her pink and purple Adidas. Although well-worn and nearly tearing at the seams, they had been with her for years. They were more than a pair of shoes. They were memories. They'd carried her to her first win and secured her a spot in the big leagues—her first step on a podium, her first glimpse of a possible future. They were a reminder of all that she was capable of.

And she'd be remiss to forget the man who'd given them to her the first week of training.

Time to move forward. No more looking back.

Tess rose and slung the limp covers across the mattress before rolling out her yoga mat. She worked through her habitual morning routine of stretches and isometric exercises. Ankle flexion, toe curls, heel raises. The stiff joints and muscles protested the simple movements, and her frustration mounted. Who was she kidding? She could do all the exercises in the world, but if her ankle never healed correctly, her career was as good as over.

She powered through the last set and finished with a series of planks and core strengtheners. After a warm shower, she pulled on a pair of fresh jeans and a light blue sweater, ready for another day of work.

Sounds of clanging cookware greeted her as she made her way downstairs. She entered to find Trudy already at it, reorganizing cabinets and drawers like a madwoman.

"What's going on here?" Tess maneuvered around the stacks of dishes, careful not to bump anything. Not that she could make much more of a mess if she tried.

The woman spun and greeted Tess with a cheerful smile that matched the brightness of her yellow blouse. "Good morning, Tess. I didn't wake you, did I?" She set down a large wok with a concerned look and slid a plate of scones across the counter.

Tess took one whiff of the heavenly aroma of cherries and almonds and selected a small pastry to nibble on. "Don't worry. I was already up. But what happened here? It looks like you overhauled every last drawer."

The woman laughed and returned to her project of sorting plates and baking trays. "Well, you wouldn't be wrong. Bless those boys for cleaning this place up, but they don't know a thing about proper kitchen organization." She motioned to the piles around her as evidence, as if her methods appeared any less chaotic.

"Speaking of those two, have you seen them this morning?" Tess hadn't heard them leave, but their work shoes were not in their usual spot by the front door.

"Oh, they got up early and hiked to the overlook shelter. Sounds like it was in pretty rough condition last time Austin checked. They're aiming to fix it up today, I believe."

A sense of relief mingled with her disappointment. Not that she would have been of much use trekking through the forest, but the non-invite stung all the same. "Do you need any help here?"

It would take a miracle to figure out how Trudy's mind worked in the kitchen, but Tess could try.

"Normally, I would love the help, but I've got a system here that needs reinstating." Her eyes lit with an idea, and she put down her stack of plates. "However, I do need someone to drive to town and pick up more supplies. In case you haven't noticed, this kitchen is sorely lacking in basic staples and some good produce."

Tess straightened, glad to have something to keep her busy. A mindless chore sounded like the perfect distraction. "I can do that."

Trudy reached for her canvas tote bag, and Tess repressed a laugh as she read the words, *Totes ma goats* emblazoned in bright pink across the navy fabric. Next to it was painted a silly caricature of a goat eating a flower. She should have expected nothing less from the woman standing in front of her with lime green earrings swinging from her earlobes.

Trudy caught Tess staring and angled the bag toward her. "You like it? My niece makes them. Aren't they the sweetest things?" She slung the strap over her canary yellow sleeve and absolutely beamed.

Bless this woman's heart.

Tess nodded. "It's very . . . colorful."

"That's exactly what my Jefferson said." Her smile grew wide, and she returned to rummaging through the bag. "Now, where did I put that list? Ah, there you are." Trudy withdrew a folded length of paper and handed it to Tess. "You might have to shop around a bit to find everything, but it should all be there."

Tess glanced over the page, her confidence buoyed by the simple task. "Was there anything else you needed? I could pick up more dish towels, dust rags . . . maybe a mop?" She cringed as a dust bunny scampered into the corner with the breeze.

Trudy waved a hand to dismiss the offer. "No need. I've got a stash in the pantry. I ran this kitchen for twenty years back in the day. I know all the tricks to getting it in tip-top shape."

"In that case, I guess I'll head out."

With the list in her pocket, Tess circled around to the back of the main house and climbed into her car. From her vantage point, the Prius looked as if it had been bathed in mud. Which, in this case, it had been. After her drive up here, the thing was due for a solid washing. Since arriving, she hadn't bothered to clean it, and it showed.

Maneuvering around rocks and a few sizable washboards, she directed the sedan down the curvy mountain road. Music spilled over her speakers, and she hummed along to the upbeat '80s tune. She passed only one other car before she finally merged onto St. Vrain Avenue and crossed over into the town limits.

The gateway to Rocky Mountain National Park, the town of Estes Park was abuzz with activity, unlike the sleepy camp she'd left behind.

Tess drove past a few campgrounds and the ornate golf course, and her phone lit up with a handful of missed messages. At the stoplight, she fished her cell from the side pocket of her purse and opened the first text from Caden. She smiled. It was a picture of him and their cousin Micah baling hay. Well, Micah was hauling bales while Caden sat back and smiled for the camera.

That boy wouldn't know a hard day's work if it bit him in the behind. It really was no surprise he'd jumped ship from the camp and left her to fend for herself against the mosquitoes and mountain wildlife. But he was her brother. She was obligated to put up with his antics.

She scrolled through the other messages from her cousin Abigail. Tess selected the first voicemail and put it on speaker:

"Hey, Tess. Just checking in to see how things are going. As my call went straight to voicemail, I'm assuming you have spotty coverage, at best. Either that, or your phone got eaten by a bear." Her delicate laugh trickled over the speaker.

"Anyway, I was hoping you'd be free to chat soon about the wedding. I've narrowed it down to two bridesmaids dresses, and I want your input as maid of honor. I know the purple is more traditional, but I adore the yellow one as well. I'll send you a picture so you can decide. After all, you'll be the one wearing it, along with Beth, and I want you guys to love the dresses too. Beth voted for the purple. What do you think? Is it too much?

Call me when you have some reception. We've got lots to catch up on, and I can't wait to hear all about your first week. Love you. Bye."

Tess smiled in amusement. That sounded like Abigail, always trying to make people happy. Even for her own wedding.

A car honked behind her, and Tess looked up to see the light had changed to green. She tossed the phone onto the seat and eased through the intersection. At the next light, she spotted the grocery store parking lot and turned in. Before going inside, she pulled up the pictures Abigail had sent her of the two dresses. The purple was elegant and flattering. No doubt Ben's mom had suggested that one, but the other was Abigail to a tee. Tess could already imagine sunflowers in the bouquets and daisies lining the aisle.

Tess hit redial and waited until she reached Abigail's voicemail.

"Looks like we're playing a game of phone tag here. And, no, a bear did not eat my phone. I got your message, and I think the yellow dress is so you. This is *your* wedding, and it should be about you and Ben. Anything you choose is going to be perfect. Reception is pretty spotty here, but I'm in town right now, so if you get this within the next hour, call me back, and we can talk more. Love you too. Bye."

Tess grabbed her keys and wallet and set out to find the items on Trudy's list. After throwing a couple of packages of Oreos and disinfectant wipes into the cart, she paid for the groceries and made the trip back up the mountain. Abigail didn't call back, and when Tess reached the turnoff for the camp, she switched her phone off and prayed for better luck next time.

Trudy was still busy organizing the cupboards when Tess returned, clearly having moved onto the next phase of the deep-clean. She decided it was best not to get in the woman's way, so she quickly hauled in the produce and dry goods. She sighed with relief when she managed to escape out back for some fresh air, away from the lingering scent of vinegar and detergent. In hindsight, maybe she should have purchased a few air fresheners while she was out as well.

Tess breathed in a lungful of crisp pine and juniper air and listened to the creaking of branches in the breeze. The clouds had burned off with the late morning sun, and she could almost make out a few of the snow-covered peaks in the distance. She thought about the crystal-clear waters from yesterday's canoe ride, the rush in her veins when her foot dipped into the glacial melt off. Invigorating.

With the rest of the camp staff due to arrive within the next couple of days, now was as good a time as any to test out the lake waters with a swim. She'd been remiss in her training regimen, and it was high time she dove in. Literally and figuratively.

Tess pushed away from the back wall and started toward her car for her wetsuit and goggles. The alpine lake was sure to be frigid with the early snowmelt, but she didn't mind, so long as she could get in a few laps before Austin and Josh returned.

CHAPTER

Eight

A RUMBLING CARAVAN thundered up the drive, Trudy's cream and gold Ford Bronco leading the pack like the *Maillot Jaune* in the Tour de France. Gravel crunched under the tires as they inched up the hill, close on each other's heels. The French Plateau des Glières didn't hold a candle to this rutted mountain road. It may not have been a bicycle race, but the effect was still the same.

Tess tightened her grip on her coffee mug and took a fortifying sip. Today was the first day of staff training, and she could hardly wait to get it over with. She had finally settled into a routine with Austin, Josh, and Trudy, but she'd known this day was coming. Summer camps meant camp counselors, which ultimately meant hordes of screaming campers.

The five cars stopped at the top of the drive, a cloud of dust billowing in their wake, and a handful of teenagers spilled from the swinging doors. Two girls, one blonde and tan and the other fair with red space buns, climbed out first, followed closely by another girl in soccer shorts. Behind them were two boys in sweatshirts and cargo shorts and a final teenager with a baseball cap turned backward over a mop of unruly hair. A head taller than the rest, he made quick time catching up with the others.

The six of them appeared well acquainted, their banter and laughter bubbling up the path to the main house like they were old friends.

Trudy joined the group last. Her husband, Jefferson, stepped down from the driver's side to open her passenger door. They smiled at each other, as if there wasn't an audience gathered a few yards away. He gave her a quick peck on the cheek before waving to the group. Austin lifted a hand in response before the man got back into the car and made a U-turn down the road toward town.

The energy of the camp tripled with so many new faces, reminding Tess of her old racing friends before an event. Friends she hadn't heard from in months. Her shoulders tensed. It seemed it wasn't only Ryan who'd forgotten about her. Her fingers cinched around the lukewarm mug, and she steeled herself for what was sure to be a crazy summer.

The epitome of calm, Austin greeted the newcomers with a wide smile and took that moment to make introductions.

"Tess." He motioned for her to join the group. "Let me introduce you all. This is Genevieve, Kyle, Harper, Skye, Sean, and Grayson. They've volunteered to spend their summer working here before they go off to college in the fall. Their teachers, including Trudy's husband, Mr. Hinshaw, gave them all glowing recommendations."

The teens beamed under his praise.

"Guys," he turned to the group. "You all know Trudy and Josh." He motioned to them over one shoulder. "And this is Tess. She'll be working with us through the summer as our special activities coordinator."

Genevieve and Skye shared a confused look, and the tall redhead timidly raised her hand.

"Yes, Genevieve?" Austin turned toward the girls.

"Mr. Wright, what happened to the other coordinator? Mr. Prescott." She looked younger than the rest, but that could have been from the twin buns and glittery daisy clip in her fiery hair.

The last thing Tess wanted was to listen to some teenagers swooning over Caden's charm. She'd had enough of that in high school to last her a lifetime.

Austin didn't miss a beat. "I'm afraid he won't be joining us. But don't worry, you'll all be in excellent hands with his sister, Tess."

All eyes turned toward her, and she could feel them sizing her up. Challenge accepted. With another fortifying gulp of coffee, Tess infused as much enthusiasm into her smile as she could muster and greeted the group. "Hi, everyone. I know you were expecting my brother, but I'm glad to be here, all the same." Mostly. "I may be new to this, but I'm sure we'll have a great summer together."

Austin smiled his approval. He brought his hand to her shoulder and gave it a reassuring squeeze. She relaxed at the simple gesture. His eyes sought hers for a fraction of a second, and she could have sworn she sensed something else pass between them.

Clearing his throat, he pulled back and addressed the group again. "Tess is actually a professional athlete. She's graciously volunteered to take time from her busy schedule to work with us this summer."

His praise seeped over her like a warm blanket, momentarily soothing the ache of the questionable state of her career. He gave the briefest of nods, as if understanding the effect his words had on her.

The kid in the CU Buffs hoodie, Sean, spoke first, breaking the spell. "What sport? My dad was a coach for the University of Colorado football team."

Skye rolled her eyes and interrupted. "I'm sure Tess doesn't play football, stupid."

"I'm just saying." He turned out his palms and shrugged.

The other guys didn't dare challenge the petite blonde.

The girl Tess was pretty sure was Harper chose that moment to chime in. Despite her size, she spoke with the energy of a midfielder at the sound of the starting whistle. "That's so cool. I'm going to Northwestern in the fall on a soccer scholarship. I'd love to pick your brain later if you don't mind."

Tess looked toward Austin and held back a laugh. "Sure, that sounds great."

"Really? Awesome." The girl's smile glittered as much as Genevieve's daisy clip in the sunlight.

"Okay, okay," Austin interrupted Harper's string of rapid-fire questions. "I'm sure Tess would be more than happy to answer questions later. But let's take care of a few business items first." He pulled a stack of papers from his backpack and passed them around the circle. "Here are your training packets and room assignments. Girls on one side of the lodge with Tess, guys on the other with Josh and me. Trudy will be commuting from town, but other than that, say hello to your neighbors for the next three months."

Their chatter swelled as the teenagers collected their packets and returned to their cars to start unpacking. Laden down with one duffle bag each, the guys made their way inside, their clomping footsteps fading behind them up the stairs. Harper, apparently as speedy off the field as on, was right behind them.

The opposite of minimalists, Skye and Genevieve took their time unloading the luggage from their trunk—two suitcases each, a couple of backpacks, and another bag full of who-knew-what. It looked like they were moving their entire bedrooms to the camp. How that sedan held so much stuff was beyond Tess.

Unusually quiet, Josh shuffled over to Genevieve and Skye and offered to help carry some of their bags. Skye leapt at the opportunity and handed him the heavier items.

Genevieve smiled her thanks, a look of apology on her face for her friend's reaction. She offered to carry her own luggage, but Josh swooped in to grab the box of pillows. He took it all in one load and waddled past Tess up the front steps.

She shook her head, holding back her amusement.

Trudy pulled up next to her, and together they slipped inside behind the others.

The house came alive with the new arrivals. The addition of six newly graduated seniors was as obvious as a herd of elk on Main Street. Thundering footsteps, shouts of laughter—it could have been elk bugling season, where hundreds of the town's four-legged residents flooded the valley, to the tourists' delight, for all the noise they made.

At least they'll scare away the bears.

Flipping through her own camp binder, she inspected the schedule on the first page. Fifteen minutes until orientation. From there on, the rest of the week would be packed with training, group outings, and camp preparations. Austin had even marked off meal times, as if a group of teenagers needed a reminder to eat.

She snapped the binder shut. So much for her workout schedule. Not that she had done much so far, anyway.

Looking for a way to pass the next few minutes, Tess went in search of Trudy to help with lunch prep.

CHAPTER

Nine

LIKE THIS?" SEAN punched down on the CPR dummy and sang out, "Staying alive. Staying alive. Oh, oh, oh, oh..." The others joined in, belting the chorus in a mixed bag of keys and volumes as they took turns *reviving* the Rescue Annies in front of them.

"Perfect. And don't forget the two breaths." Austin walked around the group, correcting people now and again as they practiced their compressions.

"That's right, Harper. Nice job."

After the initial orientation, they'd jumped right in with CPR training. As director, it was Austin's job to make sure everyone remained safe and as injury-free as possible. Working at a camp was about having fun, but a twisted ankle or case of hypothermia could ruin that in an instant. It was better to be overprepared than not at all.

Maybe it was the Boy Scout in him, or his years as a paramedic. Either way, he knew well that things could go south fast. Even for a trained professional. And he wasn't about to let these kids loose on the mountain without teaching them the basics. Not when it was in his power to keep them safe.

Gravel crunched under his feet as he made another circle around the group, smiling at their progress. Austin noted the time on his watch and called out when the second-counter reached zero. "Good job, everybody. Looks like you've all got it."

Even Trudy gave it a valiant effort, although he was certain he did not want to be lost in the forest alone with her as his sole caregiver. Unless she was foraging for wild raspberries to make a pie. That, he could get on board with.

"All right, people. So, we've gone over emergency response, how to make a splint, and now CPR. All that's left is wound dressing."

Genevieve's shaky hand poked out from behind Kyle's backward cap. The poor girl looked like she was about to turn green. "There won't be any blood, will there?" she squeaked out.

"Not for the demonstration. But in the likely event that someone injures themselves, there very well may be."

She gulped and gave a weak nod. Sean and Grayson snickered behind her, but Skye sent them a withering stare that had them quiet in seconds.

Over the next fifteen minutes, Austin walked them through the process of cleaning and bandaging an injury, emphasizing the importance of tourniquets and applying constant pressure to the site. To his delight, nobody fainted, although Genevieve came close when he talked about the time he had to perform an emergency tracheotomy. At least it wasn't one of the many stories involving snowblowers. If he'd done that, he would have been showing the other staffers what to do when a person passed out from shock.

By noon, they were done and ready for lunch—a simple fare of premade sandwiches and fruit salad, thanks to Trudy and Tess. Friendly conversation filtered over the patio tables, as natural a sound in these woods as birdsong.

Austin had handpicked each of the volunteer staff members, or program interns, as the job description stated, each perfectly tailored to fit with the group. He and Caden had interviewed the candidates back in April, spoken with their teachers and church youth pastor, and selected these six with high hopes they'd be a perfect fit for the camp's opening season. He hadn't expected Caden to drop out at the last minute, but from the looks of things, Tess was settling in nicely with the group.

Josh carried his tray, piled chin-high with food, and joined the guys at the far table. With two extra cookies in his free hand, he looked as if he hadn't eaten in weeks. The rest of the guys helped themselves to seconds, and the girls chatted away over their half-eaten plates.

Austin waited for everyone else to grab their share before selecting a sandwich for himself and sitting at one of the picnic benches. With a sweeping glance, he took in the smiles on everyone's faces, and a sense of rightness settled over him.

"Penny for your thoughts?" Tess slid into the seat across from him and sipped on a glass of lemonade. Her lips pulled up at the corners, but there was a look of question in her eyes.

"I think we're off to a good start. Singing while doing CPR always seems to get people in a good mood." He'd done similar trainings before, each revealing the talented, and not-so-talented, singers of each group.

Tess surveyed the new arrivals and shrugged. "It wasn't ABBA, but I guess the song was fitting." She took another sip of lemonade but not before Austin caught a glimpse of a smile behind her plastic cup.

"So, '80s music, huh? I thought there was something off about you." He couldn't help the grin hat spread across his face.

Tess flicked a potato chip in his direction, her green and brown eyes dancing like aspen leaves in the wind. "Look who's talking."

"Remind me later to show you what real music sounds like." Austin lifted an eyebrow in challenge.

She propped her forearms on the table, her watch glinting in the sunlight, and looked out over the freshly mowed field below. "Questionable music choices aside, I think today is going well. The kids are a hoot, and Trudy has been smiling nonstop. Even Josh seems to have settled in."

He couldn't help but agree. They still had a long way to go, and the first campers weren't due for another week, but God had seen them this far. Austin had to trust that He would get them through whatever came their way, be it stubborn woodpeckers or a hole in the roof.

"How about you? Already regretting your decision to come here?" He'd been curious ever since she set foot on his property, but he hadn't dared ask until now.

Tess took so long to answer, he was afraid he'd overstepped. She pushed her plate to the side and picked a few seeds from her bread to feed to the family of timberline sparrows roaming the patio deck. The musical trill of a nearby male lilted from the trees, a long song that drew the attention of the foraging birds. They flew to the nearest conifer and perched in the upper branches.

Tess tilted her head, and a loose strand of hair blew across her face. She kept her eyes on the dainty sparrows. "This place isn't what I expected, that's for sure. But it's growing on me, and the people are great."

"Don't forget Morty. I think he's your biggest fan."

She laughed and gave him a sidelong glance. "No worries there. He makes sure to greet me every morning at five o'clock. Someone needs to tell him he's not a rooster."

Was that the reason for the dark circles under her eyes? She had seemed a little tired the last few mornings. He'd chalked it up to the long days, but now he wasn't so sure. He wanted to ask more but figured it would be best to let it be for now. The staffers were finishing up with lunch, and they'd be on to the next activity in a few minutes. He still had three months to figure her out—time he was looking forward to.

As if on cue, Trudy bustled through the door with a towel and broom, ready to shoo people from their seats so she could tidy the patio.

Standing, Austin brushed the crumbs from his shirt and scooped up their empty plates.

"Looks like it's time for the real fun to begin."

If, by fun, Austin meant the blindfolded trail of death, he was spot on. Tess inched her toe in front of her, feeling every dip and pebble along the trail. Dirt and pine assailed her senses, all on high alert for the next low-hanging branch.

She couldn't check her GPS, but they'd been at this so long, they had to be halfway down the mountain by now. In two days, they'd run through the zip-line course, had gone over the basics of canoeing, and were now onto the team-building activities.

"Now lower your foot and take another step."

The chorus of "Stayin' Alive" pumped through her mind as she fought to heed Josh's instructions. The kid was trying his best to direct her, but Tess had never known such anxiety as trusting her life to a fourteen-year-old. She inched her right foot forward, feeling for the change in the ground. Earlier, he'd forgotten to warn her of a steep drop, and she'd nearly pitched forward when she walked off the foot-high step. One or one-hundred feet—it felt the same. Her cheeks still burned thinking about the scene she'd made.

"Just keep walking. Follow my voice." Josh beckoned her forward. In the distance, Harper shouted out commands like a seasoned professional, no doubt leading Kyle with perfect precision ahead of the group. Genevieve and Sky were paired off with Sean and Grayson, who could be heard stumbling through the trees on either side of her.

She didn't know where Austin was. No doubt watching the group from a safe distance, laughing at their foolish meanderings.

Tess took another step forward.

"Watch out for the—"

A cluster of pine needles smacked her in the face, and she flailed her arms to regain her balance. Before she fell backward, a pair of strong arms caught her from behind. She inhaled the warm scents of cedarwood and clove. *Austin*. Heat blossomed up her neck once again, and she hoped the blindfold covered her face well enough.

Josh rushed to her side and apologized for the tenth time that day. "Sorry, I should have told you to duck sooner. Maybe we should switch places. I'm sure you'd be better at this than I am." Tess could envision the slump to the boy's shoulders as he spoke.

It wasn't all his fault. She should have waited like a smart person instead of taking off without instruction. Story of her life. In hindsight, she couldn't remember a time she'd actually looked before she'd jumped. Every one of her coaches had praised that about her, a testament to her racing success. But life was not a race, and the more time she spent within these quiet mountains, the more the realization sank in.

Waving the branches aside, Tess peeked under her blindfold and gave Josh and Austin what she hoped was a convincing smile. If a group of teenagers could do this, so could she. "I'm fine, really. See? Not even a scratch."

The wrinkle eased between Josh's eyebrows, and his body visibly relaxed. Austin, on the other hand, appeared less convinced. He studied her with a steady gaze that seemed to see right through her, an entire conversation passing without a single word.

Fading voices echoed through the trees—shouts of victory as the first group reached the finish line. Austin turned to his nephew and handed him the clipboard. "Hey, Josh, why don't you catch up with Harper and Kyle at the next station? It looks like they're about finished. You can show them how to do the low-ropes course."

Josh watched the girls lead Sean and Grayson down the trail without incident. He scrunched his nose and turned back. "Are you sure? Not afraid I'll mess it up?"

Sometimes she forgot how young Josh really was. No doubt the prospect of leading a bunch of soon-to-be college students through the ropes course had him going from excitement to apprehension all in one breath.

Austin gave a confident show of encouragement. "Nah, you'll do great. Tess and I can take it from here if you want to go ahead."

Brightening as if he'd been invited to lead a treasure hunt, the boy raced off through the trees to join the others, leaving her and Austin behind.

She'd always subscribed to the tough love form of coaching, disregarding those coaches who handled their athletes with kid gloves. Watching Austin and Josh, though, made her question that. What would it be like to have someone support her like that? The thought warmed her despite the chill breeze.

The forest exhaled a slow sigh that played at the ends of Tess's hair and the bandanna wrapped around her head. Sliding the calico bandanna from her face, she tipped her head back and let the wind brush over her freed skin. Despite her well-intended plans, she couldn't help but wonder what it would be like to call a place like this home. Not that it was an option, but one could dream.

The breeze dissipated, and Austin and Tess stood together under the large evergreen. Dried pine needles shifted under his gray hiking boots, and he took a step forward. Paused. Tilting his head toward the trail, he picked up her discarded blindfold and held it out for her. "Care to continue the trust walk?"

Had he asked that two weeks ago, her answer might have been different. With a surge of energy, she grasped the piece of fabric and made a show of tying it back on. Maybe it was the thin mountain air messing with her brain, the lack of oxygen telling her this was a good idea, but she relished the thought of walking a little longer through the forest with him by her side.

"As long as you don't run me into any more trees, I think we'll be okay."

CHAPTER

Ten

HI, ABIGAIL. I got your last message." Tess's shoulders sagged as she spoke to her cousin's voicemail once again. One of these days, she would get through to Abigail, but it didn't appear today was that day.

"Sounds like things are really coming along with the planning. I'm sorry I haven't been of more help. Tell me what still needs to be done, and I'll do my best. Campers don't come until Sunday. I'm in town right now, so call me back, okay? Bye."

She pocketed her phone and slouched against the chair. Music filtered over the cafe's outdoor speakers, and tourists milled about the busy Main Street. Her iced latte sat melting next to a half-eaten blueberry muffin, and she squinted at the sun's reflection bouncing off her tablet.

A long list of names stared back at her, and she highlighted those who'd yet to RSVP. Only one month before her cousin's wedding. She might not have decent cell reception, but nothing was stopping her from emailing a quick reminder to the rest of the guests.

Tye and Beth would be there, and her brother, Caden, would come with their cousin Micah and his mom. Then there was the rest of the family and all of Ben's and Abigail's friends.

In Abigail's last message, she'd reminded Tess about her plus-one and teased again about setting her up with one of Ben's college buddies if she came alone.

Tess huffed and took another sip of her drink. Normally, she would have asked Ryan, and he'd have jumped at the invitation, but they weren't exactly on speaking terms. Even if she could forgive him, there was no way she was going to bring him to her cousin's wedding. Not now.

A string of messages from him waited to be opened on her phone. Every time she drove into town, another text from Ryan flashed across the screen. She couldn't bring herself to read a single one. No doubt checking up on her. Well, she didn't want to hear it.

The man had to take the hint eventually.

A muscle twinged in her ankle when she shifted in her seat, and she massaged it until the cramp subsided. She'd been feeling so much better the past week, despite the long hours on her feet. Why was it that as soon as she had a moment to herself, the throbbing started up again?

With a sigh, Tess copied the highlighted names into a new email and sent it off before powering down her tablet. Finishing her drink and muffin, she vacated the table by the river and made her way through a sea of pedestrians lining the sidewalks. The summer season was in full swing. Memorial Day decorations graced the historic downtown from the weekend's festivities, a reminder that this was her last chance at freedom before the real work began.

Tess waved her thanks as a car stopped at the intersection, and she crossed the narrow street. The town hummed with a palpable energy. People crushed into quaint coffee shops for their caffeine fix, day-trippers were busy perusing the shops, and a steady stream of traffic inched through town toward Rocky Mountain National Park.

She had just about gotten used to the place and its small town charm—the quiet, the stillness, the untouched beauty of a simpler way of life. Even the camp felt familiar and homey. But that was all about to change.

A block from the post office, her phone buzzed with an incoming text.

Caden.

Mind if I RSVP via text? I think I lost the invitation a while back, but I figured, with you being the MOH and all, you wouldn't mind.

The MOH? Where did her brother learn these things?

Sure, not a problem. I'll let the happy couple know you'll make their wedding.

Three dots blinked at the bottom of the screen until his message came through.

Sweet. See you then, Sis.

She shook her head. What would Caden do without her? At least she could count on Micah to make sure her brother made it there in one piece. The last thing she needed was him showing up late. Or, worse, not at all. He meant well, but would it kill him to own up to his commitments every once in a while? Maybe being around Micah would rub off on him if Caden didn't drive their cousin mad before that could happen.

Pocketing her phone, she sidestepped a large planter box of red and white petunias and continued down the sidewalk. How had Austin ever thought Caden could be responsible for a bunch of kids when he was still one himself?

Despite a few rough patches, the rest of the training had gone off without a hitch, all except for Sean getting a black eye during the trust fall. Tess should have felt more sympathy for the kid, but he wore his shiner like a badge of honor, convinced it gave him a dangerous air. It didn't matter that they'd all been there when it happened. No duel, no wrestling of bears, only an elbow to the face when Grayson panicked halfway into his turn.

But Skye couldn't have been more attentive. Her cool attitude toward him had all but vanished, and she'd been bringing him bags of frozen corn to slow the swelling ever since.

Tess could remember a few similar incidents involving her brother. How long would it take before boys learned—dangerous stunts and injuries didn't impress all girls.

Reaching the local post office, she mounted the steps and entered the building. A blast of air conditioning greeted her. Gooseflesh broke out across her arms as she stepped behind a mother and daughter in line. The queue moved at a steady pace, and before she knew it, she was at the counter. Fishing the folded delivery slip from her purse, she handed it to the clerk and waited as the woman vanished around the corner. Less than a minute later, she came back with a large dress box. Tess signed for the package and was about to duck out the door when a familiar voice called her name.

A woman waved at her from the back of the line, a pair of lime green earrings dancing with the movement. "Well, fancy running into you here."

Huffing, she readjusted her grip on the large box at her hip, and Tess stepped forward to help. Just as she caught one of the corners, something large and heavy rattled against the cardboard.

"Trudy, what do you have in here?" The thing weighed as much as a bunch of gym weights.

"Oh, a little something for my granddaughter's birthday." The woman wrapped an arm around the large box and hefted it back onto her hip. "Thought I'd get her one of those karaoke machines I keep hearing about and a box of CDs. She'll be the coolest eighth-grader this side of the Mississippi."

The line moved. Trudy shuffled forward, and Tess followed on the other side of the ribboned barrier. She picked her own package up as they went, the fabric inside rustling as she maneuvered it beneath her arm.

"From the sound of it, I'd say there's a dress in there." Trudy's smile beamed with girlish curiosity.

She readjusted the box in her arms and smiled. "It's a bridesmaid's dress for my cousin's wedding next month."

Trudy's crimson smile widened. "How wonderful. I'm sure all the men will be clamoring to dance with you. Are you bringing anyone special? Nothing like a wedding to fuel a romantic's heart." Her eyes practically glittered beneath the fluorescent lights.

"Actually, I think I'm gonna go by myself. It'll be better that way. I can devote my time to making sure my cousin has the best day of her life. Besides, I've already got the perfect excuse to stave off any unwanted dance partners. Not that anyone will ask." She wiggled her braced foot, but her laugh fell short.

Trudy's expression dimmed, and a slight frown creased her usually cheerful face. She laid a manicured hand on Tess's shoulder and gave it a light squeeze. "I think any man would be lucky to dance with you. But don't let one rotten apple ruin the rest."

Tess stiffened at Trudy's words.

"I'm sorry, dear. I didn't mean to upset you." Compassion softened the lines around her mouth. "Whoever this man was, if he couldn't see what was right in front of him, he ain't got the good sense God promised a billy goat."

"He . . . what?"

"You heard me." Trudy pushed a loose strand of hair from Tess's face and looked her in the eye. "The right man will stand by your side even when the road threatens to crumble beneath you. That's real love. Like the good Lord above."

Despite the arctic chill of the air conditioning, heat flushed up Tess's neck. This conversation was moving like a bike without brakes. When did she ever mention anything about love? "Trudy, I really appreciate the pep talk and all, but I think I might have given you the wrong impression. Ryan and I were never together. He was my coach. A friend."

"Mm-hm. Doesn't make the leaving any less difficult."

The woman ahead of Trudy finished her purchase and stepped to the side. The clerk waved for the next in line, and Trudy leaned toward Tess. "One moment, dear. Let me mail these real fast, and we can pick up where we left off."

While the two women chatted about the weather and town gossip, Tess held back and waited by the packaging station. She picked a card at random from the rack and stared at the couple in love. She blinked rapidly against the burning in her eyes. What was wrong with her? She would not cry. Not here. Not over Ryan.

A few years ago, she'd taken part in the Leadville ultramarathon—one-hundred miles of rugged off-road trail running through the Rocky Mountains. Only half of the contestants even finished within the thirty-hour time limit. She managed it in under twenty. If she could survive that, she could push through anything. Right?

For once in her life, she was free from the strain of constant racing, but she'd somehow turned her convalescence into a competition as well. If someone like Trudy could see it, a woman she barely knew, she wasn't doing as well as she thought she was.

Austin, Trudy, and Josh had been nothing but welcoming ever since she'd arrived. All she'd been able to do was repay them with guarded humor and superficial gratefulness. She wasn't the only one trying to deal with the consequences of another person's actions. Caden had been the one to drop out from the camp at the last minute, and Josh's mom had left him for the summer for Cambodia.

Tess hadn't even bothered to ask Austin how the plans were coming along for the camp.

Maybe there was some truth to Trudy's words, after all. Without realizing it, she'd built a wall around her heart. Sure, she could talk and joke with the others at the camp, but she had purposefully kept things light and simple to avoid baring her soul to another human being.

She'd been so busy trying to get through the summer and get back to racing, she'd lost sight of the bigger picture. The image of her Bible collecting dust on the dresser made her heart sink. When was the last time she'd even prayed?

Lord, I need Your help to get through this.

Returning the card to its rightful place, she turned at Trudy's approaching footsteps. The woman's cheerful smile pushed back the gray clouds in Tess's soul.

"I was thinking, it's such a lovely day out. What would you say to a nice cup of coffee? I know this wonderful little place tucked next to the river. Their scones can't compete with my mother's recipe—not enough sugar—but I suppose they'll do."

What had Tess done to deserve such grace from this woman? She smiled. A morning with Trudy was exactly what she needed, and a second cup of coffee couldn't hurt either.

"Sounds perfect."

CHAPTER

Eleven

AUSTIN LOOKED OVER the schedule for June and jotted another note on his growing to-do list. If there was anything he didn't care for about managing a camp, it was the paperwork. Release forms, bookings, insurance ... Grandpa never talked about this side of the business—and for good reason.

Austin compared the account information with the summer's calendar in front of him and massaged a kink from his neck. Their first group of families had checked in yesterday, reserving the cabins through the week. After that, the camp was booked for a family reunion, a Girl Scout troop, and a handful of church retreats in July.

He glanced over the rest of the calendar, and his breath caught in his throat. How had he double-booked the Girl Scouts with the church group from Denver? A quick flip through the binder, and he found the printed-out confirmation emails. He held them side-by-side and groaned.

Less than one week in, and he'd already messed things up.

He squinted at the clock above the fireplace. Six-twenty in the evening. First thing tomorrow morning, he'd have to drive into town and see what he could do to fix it. The last thing he needed was either of the groups canceling on him because of his error. He'd go over all the email threads tonight, do all he could to figure out a solution, and hopefully persuade both groups to keep their intended reservations. With a few schedule changes, of course.

As long as he got the camp out of the red by the end of the season, he could breathe a sigh of relief. The thought of letting his grandfather down ate at him every time he looked at the numbers or went to the post office to pick up another bill. This was the last thing he needed right now.

Light rain pattered against the windows, transforming the trees into an abstract picture of greens and browns. How was it they could have ideal weather all through May, only for it to rain opening week?

What started out as a beautiful morning had quickly turned dreary when a surprise rainstorm greeted their first round of campers. He'd thought all his carefully laid plans would go out the window the moment the skies broke loose, but the kids couldn't have been more pleased. The parents, on the other hand, had been trying to coax their children inside all afternoon, to no avail. At least the staff members were doing a good job of keeping them all entertained.

The door swung open, followed by the sounds of children's giggles. A group of soggy seven-year-olds tumbled inside. With a flick, Austin snapped the binder shut and pushed it safely out of harm's way. He couldn't help but smile as the kids untangled themselves from their jackets.

All he wanted was to create a safe space where kids and families could relax and have fun. And not just any place, either. He firmly believed his grandpa had given him the camp for a reason, and he would do all it took to see it come back to life. Even if it meant crunching numbers and putting out fires by the day.

Careful not to let his worries show, he leaned forward with his arms braced against his knees and put on a cheerful face. "Now, what do we have here? I thought you had a scavenger hunt to finish."

"We already found everything." The smallest of the four pushed to the front, unaware of the water dribbling down her legs onto the floor. She held up a soggy page and gave him a toothy grin. "And Tess said, if we asked nicely, Miss Trudy might make us some hot chocolate as a reward."

"She did? Well, you're in luck. Miss Trudy happens to make the best hot chocolate in town."

A chorus of cheers erupted, and the kids' ruddy faces beamed with excitement.

"Now, before we go ask her, though, how about we get you dried off real quick? Don't want to track mud into her clean kitchen." He walked a couple of paces to the downstairs closet and retrieved a stack of towels. He was about to hand them out when the door opened once more.

One by one, the others spilled into the room, shedding their boots and raincoats as they entered. The fresh smell of rain swept into the room on their heels. Kyle closed the door behind the last person, and a layer of humidity settled over the room like a wet blanket.

Austin handed the stack of towels to Josh and came back with another armload.

Tess greeted him with a smile before her gaze fell to the trail of water along the floor. "Sorry about that. I tried to catch them, but when I mentioned hot chocolate, they took off running."

Her chuckle was full of warmth. Damp tendrils of hair curled behind her ears, and he couldn't help but admire the rosy glow to her skin. The moment she walked into a room, it was as if some sixth sense announced her presence, and he was helpless to ignore it.

Best if he didn't let it go any further than that. Too many people relied on him to make this summer work. He didn't need another distraction. He had enough things to worry about already.

Tess was halfway through helping one of the girls out of her coat when Trudy bustled through the kitchen door.

In one look, she took in the group's varying states of undress, down to the discarded raincoats and stocking feet. "My, it sure is coming down out there. Who's ready for some cocoa?"

Four small hands shot into the air. Trudy propped her fists on her hips, and her eyes twinkled with laughter. "Goodness, well, come on in, then. I've got the perfect recipe to warm even the most rain-drenched of souls."

Like she was herding cats, she rounded kids, teens, and parents into the kitchen, where a pot clanged onto the stove. No doubt she was already fishing out the cinnamon and vanilla—her secret ingredients—to add at the end.

Austin hung back while the group slowly filed out of the front room. Turning, he scooped a discarded rain jacket from the floor and draped it over the others on a chair.

Tess finished unbuttoning the coat of one of the little girls and plopped it on top of the soggy pile. "Who would have thought such little kids could make such a big mess?"

He held back a laugh. If she thought this was a mess, he couldn't wait to hear what she thought about the church retreat in a few weeks. Four kids were nothing compared to fifty. That was, if he could find a way to resolve the booking issue before then.

"You haven't seen anything yet. Tell me what you think after a month of campers." He quirked an eyebrow in her direction, earning a smile in response.

"Are you questioning my abilities?" With a playful scowl, she flicked a wet sleeve toward him, and a spray of rainwater kissed his cheek.

"I'd never dream of it." He paused and sobered. "In fact, I think you're quite capable of whatever you set your mind to."

She wrung the last of the water from the end of her long ponytail and trained her hazel eyes on him for a long second. When she finally spoke, a peace seemed to settle around her, something he longed to feel for himself. Her slow smile warmed him more than any cocoa ever could. "I'm realizing I'm not as great with change as I thought I was, but I'm learning."

"I'm glad to hear it. And just so you know, I think you've been doing a great job here. I don't know if I've told you, but I really appreciate you stepping in for Caden. I'm sure you could be doing something much more exciting for the summer."

He knew enough about her to see how much her injured ankle bothered her. Not the pain, necessarily. She'd never once complained. But he figured it was the reminder that she couldn't do what she loved that stung the most.

Tess ducked her head as a slight flush crept up her cheeks. "It was nothing. Really. I—"

A small hand reached up and tugged at the corner of her sweater, cutting Tess's response short. Round eyes trained on Tess. The girl tugged again, this time with more conviction. "Come on, Tess. We're gonna miss the hot chocolate."

Tess looked back up at Austin and smiled her apologies. "Sounds like I'm being summoned."

Hands raised, he took a step back and nodded toward the kitchen. "Don't let me stop you."

The little girl grabbed Tess's hand and pulled her toward the smell of chocolate and cinnamon. Tess trailed behind her and looked back at Austin. "You're not coming?"

There wasn't anything he'd love more, but if the past hour was any sign, he had a long night of paperwork ahead of him.

Laughter trickled from the kitchen, carefree and innocent. How long had it been since he'd felt that free of worry? Of responsibility? The binder of work caught his eye on the edge of the table, and he shook the fanciful notions aside. The floor creaked as he took a step back.

"I should really get this work finished, but maybe later."

A crease formed between her eyebrows. "You sure?"

He nodded. Mugs and spoons clinked from the kitchen. Trudy would be serving up the hot beverage any minute now. "You'd better hurry before it's all gone."

Her gaze dropped to the stack of paperwork on the table and back to him. "Okay. But promise me you'll come up for air soon. Take a break and have some fun."

If only the paperwork and bills would oblige. "I'll try my best."

With a twinge of regret, he watched her disappear into the kitchen before ducking upstairs to retrieve the camp's checkbook.

He snatched the leather booklet from his dresser, and a few loose sheets of paper fluttered to the floor. Stooping, he gathered them up, and his gaze caught on the words at the bottom of a page. Smoothing the crease from the printed email, Austin straightened before perching on the corner of his bed.

Last time he was in town, he'd printed off his latest emails, but he'd had little free time to go through them until now. He skimmed over the first few lines of Meghan's last letter, smiling

at her latest *jungle story*, as he'd started to call them, and paused
when he turned to the second page.

> *... I know it's been your dream to restore Grandpa's legacy,*
> *but I'm concerned about you. This isn't one of your rescue*
> *patients. You don't need to perform CPR on a camp to*
> *bring it back to life if it means losing yourself in the work.*
> *Aren't you always the one telling me to try my best, and*
> *give the rest to God? Well, now I'm telling you the same*
> *thing...*

Even from halfway across the world, she couldn't stop
being the concerned older sister. More often than not, that role
usually fell to him. He'd been the one looking out for his big
sister and his nephew all these years. Couldn't she see, he wasn't
doing this for himself? It was for all of them. A chance at a fresh
start.

But her words haunted him, still ... *try your best, and give
the rest to God.* He'd used that line on her so many times, he'd lost
track. He'd seen her through some of her darkest days, losing her
job, raising Josh as a single mother.

The phrase unlocked an old memory, and he recalled his
grandfather telling him the same thing when he was a kid. It was
his first summer here, and he'd desperately wanted to prove
himself. No matter what he did to help, though, he made a
bigger mess of things. After two weeks, he was sure his
grandfather would send him packing, but when the old man
found him behind the woodpile with a broken birdhouse, he

laid a reassuring hand on his shoulder and said, "Just try your best, son, and give the rest to God. That's all we're asked to do."

That's all he'd been trying to do for years.

Austin refolded the loose papers and placed them back on the dresser.

This was different. He wasn't a kid anymore, and this wasn't a birdhouse he was trying to fix. He had a whole camp of people relying on him to make this work.

With the checkbook in hand, he returned downstairs and smiled at the mug of steaming hot chocolate waiting for him beside his stack of papers. As he approached, he noticed a square of paper wedged beneath it. He lifted the stoneware and read the handwritten message: *Everyone deserves some hot chocolate, especially the one who made this all possible.*

Tess. He smiled and tucked the note in his pocket. The spicy scent of cinnamon tickled his nose, and he let the velvety liquid warm him from the inside out. His eyes slid shut for a brief second, and he savored his next sip of the rich drink before the stack of unpaid bills called his name once again.

More than one person was counting on him this time, and he wouldn't let them down. Any of them.

CHAPTER

Twelve

SATURDAY MORNING, EVERYONE was back at work. With a reluctant farewell, they'd waved goodbye to their first round of campers earlier that day and were already preparing for the next group.

Despite her earlier misgivings, Tess had been sad to see them leave. Sure, the kids were loud, the days were long, and there was always some new emergency to deal with, but the people made it all worthwhile.

Together, the staff worked like a well-trained relay team. Every new challenge allowed someone to step out in their strengths. When one person struggled, the others stepped in. When one person excelled, the encouragement from the others was astounding. Affirming. The last time she'd felt this sort of camaraderie was during her high school track days, and she couldn't for the life of her remember why she'd stayed on her own for so long.

Thoughts of Austin skipped through her mind, and another prayer swelled in her chest. This past week, he'd seemed more than a little stressed. He never said as much, but his eyes had a way of straining at the corners that told her otherwise. If only there was something she could do to ease his stress load.

Now that she'd had time to think about it, her simple offering of hot chocolate seemed laughable. And the note? What had she been thinking?

Dust rag slung over her shoulder, Tess retired to the kitchen in search of her third cup of coffee. Beyond the door, she caught Trudy's sigh as she stood scrubbing the remaining dishes from breakfast.

"Everything alright, Trudy?"

Lines marred the woman's forehead, but she relaxed her gaze from the kitchen window to the dirty pot soaking in the sink. "Fine as a frog's hair."

That's a new one. Another phrase to add to the growing list of Trudy-isms.

"Care to talk about it?" She wasn't great at giving advice herself. Race-day pep talks were more her speed, but she knew when someone could use a listening ear. She grabbed the thermos from the counter and poured steaming hot liquid into her half-empty cup, waiting for Trudy's answer.

"It's just... I was hoping Austin might take the evening off, seein' as it's been a long week and all. But y'all are still working the day long, it seems. And today of all days." She shook her head, speaking the last bit to herself, and plunked a dirty dish into the sudsy water.

Tess wasn't sure if she was supposed to hear that, but the regret in the woman's voice piqued her curiosity.

"What do you mean, 'today of all days?'" Tess turned toward Trudy, who'd gone suspiciously quiet. Tess had been in enough scrapes with her cousins to know when someone couldn't keep a secret.

Unable to contain herself, the woman caved after a few beats of silence. She threw a hand in the air as if to surrender. "Oh, all right. It's Austin's birthday, but don't let it get out I was the one to spill the beans. Thirty is a big one, and he's never been one to celebrate much."

Thirty. Only a year older than herself. "Why would that be a secret?"

Trudy waved her hand, causing her bright pink bangles to clatter. "You know Austin, always looking out for everybody else. If I had my druthers, we'd be throwin' that boy a party rather than cleaning cabins all evening. I know he doesn't want to be a burden, but it would be nice if he'd let someone look out for him every now and again. It may not be my place, but I worry about him all the same."

Tess caught the motherly concern laced through her words. From everything she'd heard and seen, Trudy and her husband had always treated Austin like family. And now Josh as well.

Grabbing a clean towel, Tess reached into the sink and pulled out a soapy dish. A stream of water dribbled onto her foot, and she shook it off. She rinsed the plate, wiped the cloth over the dripping surface, and stacked it on top of the others. "Why don't we, then? Throw him a party, I mean."

Trudy gave her a pointed look that seemed to question whether Tess had lost her marbles. "Have you met Austin Wright? He'd sooner gnaw his arm from a bear trap than be the center of attention."

The truth of that statement brought a smile to Tess's lips. Three weeks under the same roof, and she still knew precious little about the man. Not that she had been much better. "But what about this camp? He leads the staff every day, not to mention the dozens of campers that stay here as well."

Trudy shook her head. "That may be, but when it comes to himself, that boy's about as good at opening up as a clam at low tide."

"Then maybe it's time someone pushed him outside his comfort zone." God knew he'd been doing that for her for weeks.

The woman laughed. "Honey, if you can convince him of such a thing, I would be over the moon."

"Leave that to me. I'll find a way." Ideas had already begun to percolate through her brain.

Trudy scrunched her nose. "I *have* been wanting to try out a new recipe. Mind you, it's a little extravagant for a normal dinner..."

"Then it's settled. We're throwing a party. Tonight." Tess swiped a blank notepad from the counter and began to jot off a to-do list. First thing would be to recruit Josh and the other staff members, and then they could get started.

If Austin's latest project took as long as expected, they'd have plenty of time to set a plan in motion. And he would be none the wiser.

Austin swiped the back of his hand over his sweaty forehead, grateful for the afternoon breeze that swept through the open door. During his final round of inspections, a few loose floorboards in one of the cabins had all but begged for some attention. A new panel and a dozen more screws later, he could gladly say they were ready for their next round of campers.

He had noticed little activity around the property the past few hours, but with the sun at its apex, it wasn't a far cry to guess that people had gone to the lake for the afternoon. He couldn't blame them. A dip in the icy water sounded mighty refreshing right about now.

Once he returned all the tools to the shed, Austin ducked inside, his sights set on a cool shower and a change of clothes. Halfway to the stairs, he froze when a loud cry pierced the air. Another yelp came from the kitchen, followed by a resounding chorus of, "No, no, no!"

"Trudy? Are you okay? What's wrong?" Images of a knife wound or burnt fingers flashed across his mind. His training kicked in gear, and he rushed through the open door, bracing himself for whatever emergency awaited him inside.

He passed under the arch and paused when he spotted Trudy by the stove. She stood poised beside a lopsided two-tiered cake, with what looked to be chocolate frosting coating her hands. The top layer had slid off onto the counter, and the bottom one was dangerously close to following suit. A mound of chocolate curls sat on a nearby cutting board, and a bag of peanut butter cups lay open, its contents scattered across the counter.

"What happened here?" Austin scanned Trudy for injuries, and his shoulders relaxed when he came up empty. Careful of the frosting on the floor, he sidestepped the mess and cautiously laid a hand on the woman's shoulder.

Trudy waved an arm in the plate's direction and glared at the offending mess. "Just look at it. It's gone all cattywampus."

He'd never seen Trudy like this over a cake before. Her sniffles about did him in. "Here, why don't I do that?" He plucked the damp towel from her fingers and took over, wiping down the countertop, much to her dismay.

She foisted clenched hands onto her ample hips, smearing the frosting into the once-white apron. "Now, when did I say you could help?"

"You didn't." He flashed a grin, relaxing her stern expression.

Working in wide circles, he scooped up the frosting and confectionary fragments and dumped them into the trash. He'd get to the floor later. He wiped his hands on his already dirty pants—what was a little frosting mingled with sawdust?

"What's the cake for, anyway? Did I miss something on the schedule?" Austin turned in time to see her give him one of those looks, the kind that conveyed he ought to know the answer to his own question.

She shook her head, green earrings dancing like a pair of birds in flight. With another towel, she wiped the frosting from her hands and tossed it by the sink. "You and that schedule. You know, it wouldn't kill you to take a break every now and again. Celebrate. Maybe throw a party . . ."

Austin looked from her to the cake, and it hit him.

"Not this again. I thought we agreed, nothing special." He moved around her to scrub at the counter, the pungent smell of vinegar water cutting through the sugary frosting.

He'd planned to sail through this year without any pomp-and-circumstance. Who cared that he was turning thirty? Nobody, that was who.

"You can't hide forever, you know."

"From what? The clock? I already have a few gray hairs to prove otherwise." He pointed out a sparkle of silver at his temple. Not that it bothered him. It wasn't the double-digit number that gave him pause but the stark reality that came with it. Clarity, as some called it.

By the time Meghan was his age, she'd already had a seven-year-old son and a thriving career. What did he have to show? A crumbling camp from his childhood that may or may not succeed?

A soft hand rested on his shoulder, and Trudy interrupted his spiraling thoughts. "I was talking about people. Like them."

She motioned her head toward the window, and he followed the track of her gaze. The staffers, all six of them, stood huddled around Tess and Josh, shrieks of laughter at some joke they must have shared.

"Your grandfather." Her voice had grown soft. "Do you know what he used to tell me?"

A few ideas came to mind. The man had practically been a walking fortune cookie with all his sayings and proverbs. Austin almost said as much but sensed Trudy was working toward something specific. Now was not the time to make more jokes.

He shook his head and let her continue.

She gave him a soft look. "He'd say, 'that boy's got a million things flying through that head of his, but not one of them is named Austin.' "

His grandfather's words sank in, calling to mind the summers they'd had together. He'd been a kid, and an awkward one, at that. Meghan was always off staying with friends or traveling to volleyball camps across the country. And him, he'd been dropped off that first summer to stay with a grandfather he'd hardly known. Ever since, this place had felt more like home than anywhere else.

More laughter carried into the kitchen through the open window, the sound a backdrop to his vivid memories.

"That was different."

"Yes and no." Trudy gave up on fixing the cake and turned her full attention to Austin. "Sooner or later, you're going to have to let someone behind that wall of yours. And I don't just mean me and Josh."

Opening up with others had never come easily to him. He'd rather be the person listening than the one to bare his soul—the first responder rather than the one needing help. But, of course, Trudy already knew that. Sometimes, he marveled at the way she could sum up a person with a single look. It was a gift, one he hadn't seen the last of yet.

Something tugged within his chest, begging to unfurl and be freed. It sounded simple. All he had to do was let it go. But after years of holding on, he wasn't even sure where to begin.

He looked at the vanilla sponge, which had stopped sliding, as if to prove there was hope after all. "How about I help you remake the cake, and I'll promise to think about it?"

Trudy gave him one of her smiles, sweet as honey, as she would say, and brushed a speck of frosting from his shirt. The action reminded Austin of a mother fussing over a child, but that had always been her way. The sentiment brought him a measure of comfort.

"I have a better idea. Why don't you and I whip up a new one together, and then you take the rest of the afternoon off? Relax. Do something for yourself, for a change. I can handle the rest from there."

For all her southern charm, there was no talking Trudy out of an idea. The best he could do was agree now and try to find a way to help later. "I guess that sounds reasonable enough."

She gave his arm another pat, and her eyes crinkled around the edges. "That's all I ask."

CHAPTER

Thirteen

LOOKING GREAT, YOU guys. He's going to love it." Tess watched while Harper and Josh tied off the last corner of the makeshift movie screen over the railing. Sean and the others were still busy rearranging the patio furniture, but from where she stood, it all looked perfect.

"Does the screen look even to you?" Harper asked over the sound of moving chairs behind them.

Josh stepped back and studied the white sheet, looking a little too much like his uncle. "Maybe another inch higher on the left, and it should be good." He stepped onto the chair Harper had vacated moments before and cinched the fabric tighter. "There. Perfect."

As soon as Tess had mentioned a surprise party, she'd hardly had to lift a finger. Trudy had the food under control, and the teenagers jumped at the chance to plan the rest. Kyle even drove into town to borrow a projector from Trudy's husband, with the promise to save him a slice of cake. And the rest was history.

With everything outside under control, Tess walked around back and pushed through the side door into the kitchen. The scents of vanilla, chocolate, and homemade lasagna washed over her. She could hardly contain the rumble in her stomach as she breathed in the heavenly aromas.

"It smells wonderful in here." She leaned against the cool countertop and inspected the decorated cake. With a healthy smear of frosting and a pile of chocolate shavings on top, the dessert looked impressive enough to grace the front cover of a cookbook. "Is there anything I can help with?"

Trudy's gray curls bounced while she stirred a fresh pitcher of lemonade. "Well, aren't you a peach? I'm just waitin' on the lasagna, but thank you for the kind offer." Her sweet southern drawl was heavy as molasses.

"Oh. Are you sure? I could carry out the plates or something. I don't mind."

"Actually..." Trudy paused as she tasted the lemonade. Puckering her thin lips, she poured in another cup of sugar and stirred. "Would you mind fetching a few tablecloths from the hall closet? They should be behind the folding chairs in a large storage box at the back. I'd grab them myself if someone hadn't stacked them a mile high."

Tess could take a guess who that someone might have been.

"Sure. Anything else?" She pushed away from the counter, eager for a chance to be useful. Not that planning a surprise party was simple, but she wanted to do more than supervise. Even if it was only to retrieve a few tablecloths.

At Trudy's shake of the head, Tess took a step toward the door.

"Give me a holler if you can't find them." Trudy's voice trailed behind as Tess ducked around the corner.

No sooner had she stepped from the kitchen than the soft pluck of a guitar drew her down the hallway toward the small office at the far end of the house. Something about the tune seemed familiar, but she couldn't quite place it. Curious, she ventured farther. She peaked through the open door, and at the sight of Austin's back, she froze.

All those nights she'd lain in bed and let the music lull her to sleep... It had been him. She listened for a few minutes, trying to puzzle out the ever-evolving man in front of her. When there was a beat of silence, she turned to leave. A floorboard squeaked, bringing the soft music to a halt. Caught. Reluctantly, she looked back over her shoulder, and Austin's eyes met and held hers.

She took a step toward the hallway, not sure whether to stay or duck out of sight. "I'm sorry. Trudy sent me to get something. I didn't realize you were down here. I'll be a second."

"Why don't you sit for a few minutes? I don't mind the company." He pushed the chair back toward the desk, making room for her to settle into the matching seat.

She darted a glance in the closet's direction. Trudy wouldn't mind if she lingered a little longer. From the look of things, dinner still had another ten or so minutes before she needed to get back.

Deciding to stay, she sank onto the chair and eyed the guitar propped against Austin's leg. "Did Trudy banish you from the kitchen, too?"

His chest fell with a single laugh as he repositioned the guitar in his lap. "Something like that."

Without the music of moments before, the room grew quiet. Somewhere, a clock ticked loudly as laughter trickled in through the open windows. Tess sank into the cushion and nodded toward the guitar. "Know any Journey or Simon and Garfunkel?"

Austin looked toward her with those dark eyes and tilted his head as if in thought. "Not sure about those, but..." He leaned back and plucked a few notes, seeming to test the strings. "Tell me if you recognize this one."

He played a few chords, his left hand sliding up the neck with sure, quick movements. He repeated the pattern and stopped after the third repetition. "Think you've got it?"

She laughed at the familiar melody. "Is that Van Halen?"

The acoustic rendition seemed oddly suited to this place and the man next to her.

"Only their greatest hit." With a boyish smile, he played the intro again and ramped up the speed to a rollicking dance. He bobbed his head to the beat, and a few dark curls fell around his face. His hands moved with incredible accuracy.

He wasn't okay—he was . . . good. More than good.

Austin played through the chorus a couple more times and finished too soon with a slow strum across the strings. The air vibrated with the energy of the final notes, and she held her breath for fear of breaking the spell. He laid his hand across the neck of the guitar, silencing the strings, and peered up at her with a sheepish look on his face.

Applause broke from the hallway, and Trudy poked her head through the open door. "My, I haven't heard music like that in ages." She slung a dish towel over her shoulder and beamed at him. "You've kept at it, I see. And a good thing too. Frank always said you had a genuine talent."

"It was nothing. Grandpa was the real musician of the family. Actually, you might remember this one, Trudy."

Austin plucked at the strings and returned to the simpler tune he'd been playing when Tess stumbled in moments before. The music rose and fell like waves on the lake. Not a cheerful melody, per se, but neither was it solemn. His hands hardly moved, as if the music flowed directly from the acrylic strings and resonated through the hollow wood straight to Tess's heart.

Her body stilled under the magic of the roaming melody, and she breathed it in like a sweet perfume.

When he finished, no one spoke, as if the music demanded its own holy reverence. A cool breeze from the open window brushed against Tess's skin, nature's own sigh of contentment.

"That was beautiful." Her words came out with a breathy exhale, the magic of the music still weaving through her mind like a fond memory. It was a paltry compliment, but that music had lulled her to sleep almost every night since she came here, and she couldn't find a better word to describe how it soothed her soul.

There was a faint sniff from the doorway, and Tess turned to see Trudy swipe a hand beneath her eyes. "I thought I'd never hear that song again."

"You know it?"

"Do I know it?" Trudy chuckled low and turned watery eyes toward Austin. "That was one of his granddaddy's favorites. Used to sit on the porch every night and serenade the campers." Her eyes grew misty once more. "Does the soul good to have music here again. He always said it made him feel closer to God. Something that sweet has to be a gift from heaven."

There was a long moment of silence before Austin spoke again. "My heart, O God, is steadfast. I will sing and make music."

"Mm-hm. Amen to that," Trudy hummed in agreement as if to a preacher's sermon.

Tucked in her chair, Tess studied the man with newfound curiosity. Despite their time together, Austin Wright was a puzzle she'd yet to solve. He could go from obnoxious and witty to mysterious and contemplative within a second. Although downright infuriating at times, he had graciously taken in his nephew for the summer—her too, for that matter. But while she'd come here angry and hurt, she'd yet to see his patience crack. He was as steady as the ground beneath her feet, and she was as wild as the mountain wind. Or at least she had been before coming here. She couldn't explain it, but the longer she stayed, the less she wanted to leave.

Before Tess could say something to that effect, a buzzer went off in the kitchen.

"Oh, that'll be the lasagna." Trudy drew in a deep breath, as if waking from a dream, and tugged the towel from her shoulder. "I'd best go check on it. Tess, do you need any help with those tablecloths?"

It was as if someone had flipped a switch, and gone was the moment's earlier calm. She'd been looking for something to do, but now all she wanted was to spend another minute tucked within that peace.

She braced her hands against her legs and stood as Austin closed the lid on his guitar case. She was halfway to the closet when he fell in behind her with long, easy strides.

"I can help with that. Don't want to keep the kids waiting too long for the big surprise. I've kept you here long enough. It's the least I can do."

Tess stopped in her tracks and turned. "What surprise?"

Passing her at the threshold, he slanted her a look full of innocence. "I suppose that would be the party I'm not supposed to know about."

Tess's eyes widened.

"Don't worry. I saw nothing." Austin grinned as he reached the closet and swung the door open.

Hands on her hips, she gaped at him while he hauled down the topmost box. "And I thought it was the kids I'd have to watch out for. You'd better put on a convincing show when we walk out that door in a few minutes. They'll expect you to be surprised."

He set the box on the floor with a thud and held up three fingers. "Scout's honor."

She gave him a wry look as he unfastened the plastic lid.

"We'll see about that." With a shake of her head, she plucked the fabric sheets from the box, but he swooped in behind her.

"I've got those." Before she could protest, he was already disappearing down the hallway with an armload of red and white checkered tablecloths.

"People celebrating their birthdays aren't supposed to do any work!" she shouted after him.

"Then it's a good thing I don't know it's a surprise party," he teased, tossing her a wink as he rounded the corner. She heard the unmistakable click of the patio's screen door as it shut behind him.

Tess shook her head at his hasty retreat. She didn't know which Austin she preferred—the easygoing friend she could joke with or the man who stuck up for his family and looked out for everyone around him. It was as if there were two sides of him, and all she ever got were glimpses.

But was she any different? It had been years since she'd truly let anyone behind her defenses, and her experience with Ryan hadn't helped matters. Her history of shallow relationships seemed to mock her.

Suddenly uncomfortable in the empty hallway, she gathered up the remaining napkins and followed Austin through the door.

CHAPTER

Fourteen

TESS'S STRESS OVER the past few months melted under the gleam of the star-studded sky. She wrapped the wool knit blanket tighter around her shoulders and sank deeper into the thick cushion. Once they were done with the cake, Trudy had gone home to her husband, leaving the rest of the group to indulge in their movie marathon. Sometime between *Raiders of the Lost Ark* and *Return of the Jedi*, most of the cushions and pillows had found their way to the patio deck, making one giant fort for the kids to spread out on in front of the makeshift screen.

Tess and Austin hung back on one of the bench seats, happy to observe the others and relax away from the noise. She rested her head against the cool metal frame and let her eyes wander from the drop-down screen. Even through the darkness, she could still make out the outlines of the cabins under the moonlight. Crickets chirped nearby, their songs mixing with the movie like a peaceful memory.

As kids, she and her cousins had spent many evenings at the local drive-in theater. It didn't matter what was playing, only that they were together with their bags of popcorn and fifty-cent licorice sticks. Time seemed so simple back then—carefree summers down by the lake and baking cookies after church with great Aunt Josie and Uncle Jack. Abigail had since moved back, but the rest of them had gone their separate ways.

She'd been all too pleased to abandon the small mountain town of her youth when she went off to college. Now, sitting here on a mountain watching an old movie in the woods, she couldn't remember why she had been so eager to leave all that behind.

The action scene moved ahead, but her mind remained rooted in the past. Tess sipped her hot cocoa and curled her feet in closer, savoring the feel of the night sky overhead.

Austin's knee bumped against hers, drawing her from her meandering thoughts. "How's the ankle? I know we've kept you fairly busy the last few weeks."

She rotated her foot beneath the blanket, content with the lack of swelling she'd grown accustomed to the past few months. "Surprisingly, a lot better."

"You're not saying that to keep me from prying, are you?" His broad shoulders filled up the space on the small bench.

"You got me. Looks like I'll have to come up with a better plan next time." She hid her smile behind the mug but not before she noticed the shake of Austin's controlled laughter beside her. The sound brought a few curious glances from the peanut gallery in front of them, but they shifted back to the movie with the next scene change.

Creases fanned the edges of Austin's eyes when he looked down. "Guess I walked right into that one."

"I guess so."

Calm silence followed. Tess found she learned more about him in these quiet moments than with a thousand conversations. The way his gaze kept a steady watch over his nephew and the kids when they weren't looking. How his face softened whenever he smiled. The selfless way he watched out for those around him. Austin Wright might be a mystery in many ways, but he was an open book when it came to the things that mattered.

His shoulder grazed hers as he leaned in, and his warm breath tickled her skin when he whispered. "Thank you for organizing all this, by the way."

The knot that had been in her stomach all afternoon relaxed. "What makes you think it was me?"

Austin turned and gave her that look he used on Josh whenever he'd been found out. "Trudy may be great in the kitchen, but she's not what you'd call a party planner. And she might have mentioned it was your idea."

"Did she, now? Apparently, she's not known for keeping secrets either."

"Anything I should know about?" His voice dipped low, causing goosebumps to break out over the exposed skin at her neck. Despite the innocent question, heat crept up her face at her unspoken thoughts.

"You really want to know?" She gave him the same challenging look she'd given him her first day at the camp.

His brow dipped and, as if on cue, a roguish smile crept over his face. "Give me your worst."

She didn't need to look around the property this time to figure out her answer. She'd lived by casual friendships and surface-level relationships for far too long. Trudy was right. It was time she started to let people behind her wall, even without the promise of them doing the same.

She took a deep breath. "Let's see..." She plucked at a frayed corner of the blanket, summoning the courage to step out on this limb. This whole vulnerability thing wasn't as easy as it sounded.

As if sensing her hesitation, Austin gave her shoulder another playful bump, and it was all the encouragement she needed.

She offered him a timid smile. *Start with something small.* "Well... Most people don't know this about me, but I talk to myself when I get nervous."

Austin held back a chuckle, and her worries melted to humored annoyance.

"What? It's true." She spun toward him and laughed when he raised his hands in concession. "You asked if I had any secrets. So there."

The corners of his mouth twitched, but he held his ground. "I'm sorry, but that's not a secret. I caught you mumbling on day one. You sing to yourself as well, in case you didn't know."

Tess threw her head back and searched the night sky for something else. "Okay, how about this? I think '80s music is the best, and anyone who thinks differently is plain wrong."

Austin let loose a laugh. The rich sound settled around her with more warmth than the wool blanket pulled up to her chin. Josh shifted on the blankets to face them. Raising a finger to his mouth, he gave them a loud *shush* before spiraling back to watch the movie with the others.

She tapped her foot in rhythmic motion to the music spilling out over the darkened patio, all the while fully aware of Austin's presence beside her. Somehow, she knew she could trust him. Being near him brought a calming presence she'd only ever found in her cousin Abigail and Aunt Josie. Perhaps it was time to let someone see the real her.

The last of her worry faded under the diamond-speckled sky before she spoke once more into the still night. "When they rushed me into surgery, I thought my career was over." Her fingers stilled their fidgeting with the blanket's edge. She didn't look up, but she could feel Austin watching her intently. "The doctors said I have a good chance for a full recovery, but I'm not so sure. For the first time in a long while, I don't know what the future holds, and that terrifies me."

Austin sat quietly beside her. He didn't say a word, but he didn't need to. His steadfast presence was enough. When he lifted his arm and wrapped it gently around her shoulders, she didn't hesitate to lean in. His chin brushed against the top of her head. "Anything else?"

She felt the rise and fall of his steady breathing and smiled. "Yeah. Despite my best effort not to, I think I love it up here."

He exhaled, and the motion tickled the skin around her ears. "Now, *that's* a surprise."

She pulled her head back and saw the amusement in his eyes. "I wasn't that bad when I first got here."

"Whatever you say. But you were awfully flustered when Morty chased you from the first cabin."

Tess wasn't sure if she wanted to punch him in the shoulder for teasing her or hug him for making her laugh. "I'll have you know that's not the first time a bird has attacked me."

"I can't wait to hear the story behind that."

"In your dreams. That secret goes with me to the grave."

A chorus of chirps and night sounds blended with the music of John Williams ebbing through the portable speaker. Austin didn't press any further, and she settled back against the warmth of his arm before he switched the subject. "Hey, Tess. I was wondering, are you free tomorrow?"

"I don't know. You tell me, Master of the Schedule."

His eyes crinkled at the edges. "I think I can make something work. How does tomorrow afternoon sound? There's something I'd like to show you, but it's a bit of a hike to get there."

"Don't you have work to do? Bills to pay and all that?"

He shrugged. "It'll still be there when we get back. What do you say?"

"How can I pass up an invitation like that?"

"So, is that a yes?"

Tess thought she heard a waver of uncertainty in Austin's voice. Good thing for him, when she made up her mind to do something, she was all in.

Her hand found his, and she gave it a slight squeeze. "Yes. I'd love to."

With that, they settled in to watch the rest of the movie. They laughed at the same spots, took turns quoting lines, much to the kids' chagrin, and when they weren't disrupting the movie for the teenagers, they leaned back and watched in comfortable silence.

The moon rose higher over the clearing as the movie came to its climactic end. With yawns and a few droopy eyelids, everyone grabbed a blanket and dragged themselves to their respective rooms. Tess followed, reluctant to leave her cozy alcove and the man beside her.

Austin made sure everyone was inside before he turned off the porch lights and locked the door. It wasn't until they reached the common room that they said goodnight.

Tess reluctantly peeled herself away before she said anything she'd regret and ruin the perfect evening. With a smile, she retreated up the stairs after the others and closed her door behind her.

When her head hit the pillow, the faint notes of a familiar sweet melody floated up the stairs as if to bid her goodnight. To the sounds of a gentle lullaby, she drifted off into a peaceful sleep filled with dreams of moonlit movies, licorice sticks, and tranquil rest.

CHAPTER

Fifteen

AUSTIN EYED TESS'S bare ankle for the hundredth time that morning as she strode ahead of him down the trail. To say he'd been surprised to see her without her brace would have been an understatement. At least she'd opted for a decent pair of hiking boots instead of those worn-out running shoes she typically wore. He thought ahead to the uneven path ahead of them, and hoped her ankle, and those boots, were stronger than they looked.

At a fork in the trail, they followed the path to the right, where he directed them up the slope and around a small outwash of rocks and debris.

"So, where are we going on this mystery hike?" Tess asked over the sounds of dirt crunching beneath their feet. Birds chirped overhead, and the gentle sway of the trees hinted at another mild summer day in the mountains.

He cinched the straps of his backpack snug against his chest and slowed his pace to let her catch up. "Well, I thought since our next group of campers arrives tomorrow, why not take advantage of the day and do a little exploring? There are dozens of secret waterfalls around here, and if we keep following this trail, we'll eventually run into the Continental Divide."

She gave him a sideways glance and raised a single eyebrow. "Had I known you were planning on crossing the entire Rocky Mountains, I would have brought more than some trail mix to tide me over."

"Good thing Trudy packed us each a lunch." He patted his backpack, where a box of sliced apples, cheese, and whole wheat crackers rattled against a thermos of coffee.

Golden sunlight glinted off her chestnut waves, and she shook her head in disbelief. "I should have known. The two of you think of everything."

They continued on up the trail, filling the tranquil silence with lighthearted conversation. For the first time since opening day, a weight seemed to lift from his shoulders with every step they took deeper into the forest. The air grew thick with the scent of pine and earth, and the sounds of road noise vanished behind the ridge.

Austin pushed aside a drooping branch, and his hand brushed against hers in the tight space. Austin's chest grew tight, and once forgotten words from his grandfather surfaced from his memory.

"Son," he'd said one summer when they were fixing up the cabins. "When you find the girl who makes you feel alive, hold on tight."

Last night's conversation with Tess had stayed with him into this morning. He could still feel her warmth beside him, the way her head had rested on his shoulder.

He tried to distract himself with the surrounding forest, but his grandfather's voice echoed once more in his mind. Austin shook away the thought. They were practically strangers, besides the fact that in a matter of months she'd be gone. However, he couldn't deny the effect she had on him even after such a short time.

They crested the next rise, and the notes of ABBA's "Super Trouper" shattered the calm quiet.

Tess stopped behind him and swung her backpack around to pull out her cell phone. "Hello?" She paused to listen, and her face lit with recognition. She smiled at Austin and turned to talk to the trees. "It's good to hear from you too. I can't believe it's taken so long to connect."

She went silent, no doubt listening to whoever was on the other end of the line. Caden, her cousin, or possibly that Ryan guy. Austin didn't like the way his gut tightened with that last thought. Tess was free to talk with whomever she wanted. He had no right to feel jealous.

But his chest and his head definitely were not communicating the same thing.

"I know. It's been crazy here too. No need to send out the search party. How are the wedding plans progressing?"

Austin unclenched his jaw at the mention of the wedding. He wasn't proud of the relief he felt, but something else took its place when Tess turned to him once more with her wide smile.

A few seconds later, her smile dimmed, and that little crease between her eyebrows deepened. "Abigail. Hello? You're cutting out. Hello?" Tess raised her voice as if that could clear the static. Austin heard muffled noises on the other end before the phone beeped with a failed call.

"Not again." Tess dropped her arms in defeat.

"Do you want to call her back? You can try my phone, but it probably won't be any better."

She pocketed her cell and started down the trail ahead of him. "No. I'll have to call her next time I'm in town."

He could fully understand her frustrations. "I know the feeling. Try running a business where you don't even have the internet to check emails." For as much as he'd wanted to run the place the same way his grandpa had, the camp could use some updating to stay current with the times. "Last week, I had a near heart attack when I thought I'd accidentally double-booked two groups for the end of June. Turns out, it was a simple fix, but it would have saved me a whole lot of stress had I been able to make a few quick phone calls."

Tess kicked at a pebble and watched it skitter across the trail in front of them. "I'll bet that was more than a little stressful." She reached for the branch in front of her and pushed it aside, her watch glinting in the sunlight.

His hand brushed against hers as he replaced her hold on the branch and let it swing behind them. "No kidding. Finding decent reception on this mountain can be about as easy as finding Bigfoot."

"We're back to that again, are we?" She sent him a wry look and sidestepped the large rock in the middle of the trail.

He laughed and followed behind, clearing the rock in one fluid stride. "Guilty. Are you holding it against me?"

She scrunched her face in thought. "I probably should, but no. I was convinced there was a ghost in our attic as a kid, until I caught Caden red-handed removing a walkie-talkie from behind the vent."

Austin remembered some of the pranks Caden had played on him during college. He had been a freshman during Austin's senior year, but they'd been fast friends ever since. "Yep, sounds like something he would do, alright."

Sunlight danced across her skin under the aspen canopy as she turned to face him. Her mouth tipped to one side, and she smiled. "That's not even the worst of it. Do you remember those little Furby dolls? Small, furry toys that looked like a cross between a hamster and an owl?"

He nodded, remembering how much Meghan had begged their parents for one when she was younger. Personally, he'd found them rather creepy, but she'd loved it even after it stopped working.

"Well, a few years ago, Caden bought me one for my birthday as a joke. I actually thought it was really sweet of him to remember, but little did I know he'd gone and programmed it beforehand."

"Uh oh. What did he make it do?"

"What didn't he do?" She threw her arms wide. "That thing was so possessed, Abigail and I had to take out the batteries so we could sleep. And even then, I'm convinced it haunted our condo for another few months until we got rid of it."

"Oh, man. I'm sure you two had some choice words for your brother after that."

"Let's just say we paid him back in full." She tossed him a mischievous smile and marched ahead.

He watched with appreciation as Tess led the way, her chestnut ponytail whipping back and forth between her shoulder blades. She could be a force of nature if she wanted to, yet she was still here. So far, he hadn't chased her away with his nearly hundred-year-old camp and a houseful of teenagers and campers.

She'd trusted him enough last night to open up about her fears. It was only fair he return the gesture. It wasn't his natural inclination, but the more time he spent with her, the more he wanted to share with her.

"Hey, Tess. Wait up." He jogged ahead. "Speaking of family, earlier... I'm sure you've been wondering why Josh is here with me at the camp."

"He told me a little. His mom is working on a project in Cambodia for the summer, and your parents were busy, so he's staying here with you."

"Did he say anything else?" He wondered how much Josh had revealed.

Tess nodded. "He did. He mentioned his dad was never in the picture, but he didn't elaborate, so I didn't want to pry." Her smile was kind but understanding. She was giving Austin a way out of having to explain.

"I'm sure he appreciated that. I'm honestly surprised he said even that much. If you haven't noticed, it can take a while for him to open up around new people. That's something he and I have in common, I guess."

A shower of aspen leaves danced on the breeze before settling on the dirt path in front of them, and they walked on.

He continued on ahead, suddenly needing to move. He didn't talk about it much, but something about Tess's friendly smile and the way she'd opened up to him the night before told him he could trust her with anything, including the thing that haunted him most from his past. In a sense, it wasn't his story, exactly, but the impact of it had defined his choices the past fifteen years. And for some reason, he wanted Tess to know the real him.

"My sister graduated with a degree in environmental science from UC Davis and immediately joined the Peace Corps. She had this dream of traveling the world, helping others wherever she could." He'd admired her dreams as a kid and still found inspiration in his sister's story. "However, during her first assignment, she met this guy, Brian Hughes. They hit it off right away. She even brought him home with her a couple of times. He seemed nice enough, and our parents loved him, but there was something off about him."

Austin kicked a pebble with his shoe and watched it skitter across the dirt. "I was in high school at the time, so I didn't think too much of it, but a few months later, Meghan called us in tears and told us she was pregnant. Brian had left to join another team, and that was the last we ever heard from him."

He slid a glance toward Tess, curious of her reaction. She'd gone relatively quiet, but he didn't see pity in her eyes.

"I imagine that was a hard time for all of you. I guess that explains why you and Josh are so close."

She couldn't be more correct. "Family comes first. It's taken me years to finally convince Meghan to get back to the work she loves. That's why she's in Cambodia this summer. It's not the Peace Corps, but she seems happy to have this opportunity again."

"She sounds like an amazing woman. Josh is lucky to have a mom like her." Tess stopped and bent to retie a shoelace that had come undone. She looked up from her squatted position on the dirt and talked as she worked. "You said Josh doesn't know the whole story. Does he know who his dad is?"

He nodded. "Josh doesn't know much about Brian. Only that he didn't stick around."

A stray leaf blew into Tess's hair, and Austin refrained from brushing it aside. Somehow, the natural adornment suited her. He smiled and decided to change the subject toward simpler things. "So, Abigail, she's your cousin who's getting married next month, right?"

Tess nodded and stood, laces secured. "I'm supposed to be her maid of honor, but Beth has been taking care of most of the planning. It's kind of difficult to coordinate vendors and a party when you have no reception." She stopped talking and chewed her bottom lip. "Speaking of next month ... what does the schedule look like?"

He waved a hand as if shooing the very thought. "Don't worry about a thing. We can hold down the fort while you're away. Like I said, family comes first."

"About that ..." She slowed her pace and picked at the zipper of her light jacket. "My cousin keeps hounding me about my plus-one, and I know she means well, but she's insistent, and I'm afraid if I don't bring someone, she's going to try to set me up with one of her fiancé's friends. So I was wondering, if you could spare a day or two, if you'd like to come with me. To the wedding, I mean. Caden will be there, of course, and knowing my great-Aunt Josie, she'll have made more food than an army of teenagers could eat."

"You mean, like a date?"

"I, um—" Her face reddened, and a flicker of hope stirred in his chest.

He didn't think he'd ever seen Tess Prescott lost for words. In the time he'd known her, he'd only ever seen her this flustered the day she rolled up that mountain road and took her first look at the camp. He'd seen the way she'd leaned toward her car door, ready to bolt, but this time, she held her ground and looked at him with questions in her eyes.

Austin chuckled and decided to put her out of her misery. "It's okay. I knew what you meant. I can talk with Trudy and see if she could hold down the fort for a few days. Wouldn't want you having to fend off any unwanted suitors on my account." He pushed aside a low-hanging branch and let her go first. She gave him a gracious smile and ducked under the overhanging brush.

A few yards ahead, a shadow passed through the trees, and Austin froze.

"Tess, whatever you do, don't move."

CHAPTER

Sixteen

TESS PAUSED HALFWAY down the slope and looked back over her shoulder at Austin. "What is it?"

Austin stared past her toward the grove of aspens below, eyes wide with concern.

She lowered her voice and looked around to figure out what had him spooked. "Austin, you're scaring me. What's wrong?"

He lifted his finger to his lips and pointed ahead. Leaves rustled behind her, and the hair on the back of her neck prickled.

Oh, no. Not a bear.

Tess had no desire to be eaten alive. She'd read about bear attacks in the newspaper, heard stories about unsuspecting hikers who'd lived to tell the tale. She'd even bought a can of bear spray last time she was in town—and it sat conveniently on her dresser back at the house.

Feet rooted to the ground, she readied herself in case they had to make a run for it.

Austin leaned toward her, and without a second guess, she grabbed his hand. His fingers wrapped around her clammy palm, and he helped her scale up the gravelly slope. Her boots crunched on the loose sand, and she cringed. At this rate, every animal within a one-mile radius would hear them.

The rush of blood pounded through her ears as loud as an elephant stomping over dry leaves, and she held her breath. At the top of the hill, she grew still and waited for Austin's instructions.

They watched as a giant animal pushed through the spiky branches, keeping mostly hidden, save for the edges of a furry silhouette. Like a ghost, the dark object shifted through the trees without a sound.

Were they supposed to make noise and run, or stay silent and remain still? She'd heard something about making yourself appear larger to scare off bears, but there was no way Tess could wave her arms wide enough to intimidate this animal, whatever it was.

Her fingers tightened around Austin's, and she leaned into him, ready for his direction. He held still, and so did she.

Leaves quaked under the passing movement of the shadowed figure, yet it made no noise. At the gap in the trees, it paused. Tess and Austin held their breaths as it stepped into the light. As if shooing a fly instead of a thousand needles, it pushed through the last branch with its five-foot-wide velvet antlers.

Tess released her breath.

"It's only a moose." A large one, she'd admit, but decidedly *not* a black bear. Her relief mingled with exasperation at Austin's overreaction. If he'd meant to scare her, he'd managed it with flying colors.

The creature nibbled at the peeling bark, seemingly unaware of their presence. Despite his size, he made hardly a sound amongst the dry leaves scattered across the ground and the low-hanging branches it nudged to the side with its large antlers.

Austin's hand squeezed hers, and he leaned in close enough to whisper. "I know they might look harmless, but they can be as dangerous as a grizzly . . . or more so."

"Now you're messing with me." She dropped his hand and took a step down the hill.

"Tess, what are you doing?" Austin whispered.

"Relax. I'm not going to pet him.." The animal might be larger than her kitchen refrigerator, but that didn't mean she had to be afraid of it. After all, she'd had more than enough experience with elk over the years to know they were only a threat to her great-aunt's flower gardens. A moose was no different, right?

A dry twig snapped under her shoe, and the harsh noise shattered the peaceful quiet. A low rumble reverberated through the trees, followed by a chorus of agitated grunts. The large bull flipped his head in warning and stomped its feet against the pine-encrusted earth.

Austin reached forward and grabbed hold of her wrist. His urgent tug brought her to a halt. Neither took their eyes from the animals in their retreat. Tess thought she heard Austin mumble a prayer under his breath but couldn't be certain.

Every crunch of gravel thundered in her ears. Tess bit back her unease enough to focus on the trail and the three animals only yards ahead.

The bull lowered his head, as if a knight bowing to an opponent, and took his first step in their direction. And then another. With alarming speed, he charged toward them.

"Run!" Austin pulled her forward, and they raced up the trail.

Instinct kicked in, and Tess's feet pounded against the ground. Branches smacked against their legs on the narrow trail before they plunged into the forest. The hoofbeats drew nearer, the deafening sound of splintered wood announcing the bull's quick approach.

Tess's foot caught on a root, and she nearly stumbled to the ground before Austin caught her. At the base of a large boulder, he swung left, pulling her against the cool rock.

When he stopped, she smacked into his solid frame. She caught herself and shrank into the shadow of the boulder. Austin's chest rose and fell in time with her own as they waited. She laid flat against the granite wall, and the rough surface bit into her palms like sandpaper.

Yards away, the crashing charge drew to a sudden halt, and the forest grew eerily quiet once more.

Confused, Tess peered around the rock slab, eyes growing wide the moment she spotted her. The moose caught her gaze and seemed to level her with a challenging stare. *Back off,* he seemed to say.

Not a problem. After that chase, she had no intentions of invading his privacy any further.

The bull kicked at the ground for a few seconds as if claiming his victory and retraced his path back down the hill. Branches racked against his antlers in a grim warning. When they could no longer hear the moose's retreat, Tess finally released a long exhale.

"That was close." Austin's shoulder brushed hers in the tight space, startling her once again.

Blood rushed down her limbs as if they had gone to sleep moments before. Her skin prickled, and her legs threatened to turn to Jell-O if she took another step. Adrenaline, pure and simple. But the fact was lost against the feel of her heartbeat skipping in her throat.

Tess braced her hands against the cool face of the rock, soothing her nervous energy. "Did you see how fast that thing could run?"

Austin shifted beside her, his breath tickling the loose hair at her neck. "That was nothing. A fully grown moose, if threatened enough, can outrun Usain Bolt any day of the week."

"But that would be . . ."

"Over thirty miles per hour. Yeah. People think it's the bears you have to watch out for. Unfortunately, they rarely think twice when they see a moose."

Tess was too embarrassed to admit that, until five minutes ago, she'd been one of those people. Wiping the sweat from her palms, she pushed away from their hiding spot and stepped over the uneven ground. She held back a wince as a dull ache twinged in her ankle. Why had she left her brace back at the house? Now that the adrenaline had begun to subside, she couldn't ignore the slow throb.

Another step, and she stumbled over an exposed root at the base of the giant boulder.

Austin caught her before she fell. "You're limping. Here, let me see."

"No, it's fine. Really, I—"

"I'm not taking no for an answer." Brow raised, he gave her a look that left no room for argument.

Begrudgingly, she hobbled back over to the rock slab. Once she was sitting, she toggled her ankle back and forth to say, *see, it's fine.*

Austin ignored her protests and knelt against the damp earth. His forearm boasted a few scratches of its own, but he waved them off. Without another word, he slipped a hand beneath her foot and unlaced the shoestrings. He removed her hiking boot, and Tess sucked in a sharp breath as a flash of pain shot up her leg.

His look of concern was enough to ground her once again, and she nodded for him to continue. Slower this time, he eased the boot the rest of the way from her foot and rolled her calf-high sock down to her toes. Her ankle now free, he inspected it for injuries. His strong fingers probed the puffy skin, every touch doing funny things to her stomach.

Startled, she shoved the feeling down.

This was Austin. Her boss. Coworker. A friend. They'd known each other for hardly more than a month. She couldn't possibly be having feelings for him. Not when it took years with Ryan, and even that turned out to be nothing. But she couldn't deny the way his gentle touch stirred something inside her.

"Everything appears okay. There's some swelling, but I can't tell if that's from before or after the moose decided to charge at us."

"It's been like that for weeks. It's actually a lot better than it was a month ago, if you can believe that."

Austin frowned. "Your brother mentioned the accident. What was it, two surgeries?"

"Three, actually. Plus a metal rod and a handful of screws. My ankle's like a regular ol' toolbox." She laughed, but the sound fell flat.

Austin brushed his thumb across the two small scars where the surgeons had placed the screws. Tess's breathing grew shallow. He took his time, and she could imagine him counting the stitches that had been there a few months before.

"It could have been worse." His tone was even. Clinical, almost, as he studied the puckered skin.

"Really? How, exactly?"

He continued to probe the rest of her foot, and she tried to hold back another wince.

"Sorry." He fished around in his backpack and unrolled an ACE bandage. He started at the arch of her foot and wrapped the woven material up the joint while he spoke. "When I was a paramedic back in California, I saw some pretty awful injuries. You wouldn't believe the things I've seen people come back from."

"Are you saying I'll make a complete recovery then, Doc?"

His dark eyes held hers, and all traces of humor faded from his face. He leaned in a little closer, and the forest seemed to suddenly grow quiet around them. "I'm saying anything is possible with a little faith."

His hand brushed against her hair. Tess's heart thudded in her chest, and for a fleeting moment, she thought he might kiss her. She stilled under his watchful gaze, reading the conflicting emotions simmering beneath those long lashes.

Was she ready for this? Was he?

Her breath grew shallow, and a second slipped into what felt like eternity. Tess wanted to run and to lean in all at once, but either fear or her common sense kept her firmly rooted against the cool stone slab.

ABBA music blared like a siren into the small alcove, startling Tess out of her trance. Her phone buzzed in the side pocket of her backpack as a series of text messages lit up the screen. Of all places, she had to get cell reception here? Now?

Austin pulled away, and a heaviness settled around Tess's shoulders. With distracted movements, Tess fumbled around her bag and withdrew her phone. She scanned her recent messages and frowned. Two texts from Abigail and a missed call notification from Ryan.

Austin cleared his throat, and she looked back up. "I should really finish wrapping your ankle. It'll only take a second." With quick movements, he wrapped the rest of the bandage and tucked the end in at the base of her calf. He gave it a light pat. "See? Good as new."

His quiet confidence did little to assuage the emotions settling in the pit of her stomach.

Austin took his time repacking the first aid kit while she fumbled with her phone, heat rising up her cheeks. What was wrong with her? If it hadn't been for the interruption, would she really have kissed him?

A gentle breeze sighed long and cool through the forest, toying with the ends of her hair where Austin's fingers had brushed moments earlier. She glanced at him as he threaded an arm through the straps of his backpack and wondered if she'd imagined it all or if she'd somehow already ruined their newfound friendship.

Once she'd finished adjusting her shoelaces, Austin offered her a hand and helped her stand. Tentatively, she tested her wrapped ankle with a little pressure, and when it didn't ache, she took another step toward the trail.

Austin stayed close to her side, ready to lend her an arm if need be. "Looking good. How does it feel?"

She tested it with a little more weight and sighed with relief. "Much better. Thank you."

"Don't mention it." He released her hand and hiked a thumb over his shoulder. "Now let's get you back to The Lodge so you can put some ice on that, Gimpy." He squinted his eyes in a teasing smile, and she knew she hadn't lost him yet.

Tess swatted a hand at his stomach. "It's not that bad."

He doubled over from the slight impact, feigning defeat.

"Oh, you're terrible."

He stood to his full six-foot-one-inch height and shrugged. "I try."

Tess laughed and shook her head. Only Austin could defuse her stress so easily. "Did anyone ever tell you your sense of humor stinks?"

"Who, me?" He laid a palm over his chest. "And here I thought you appreciated its subtle nuances."

She eyed him long and steady, noticing the sunlight playing across his upturned mouth. There was nothing subtle about Austin, much less his taste in jokes. As long as he was laughing, she knew where they stood with one another. Kiss or no kiss.

"Tell you what. How 'bout I promise not to make any more dad-jokes, as Josh so affectionately likes to call them, and you let me help you back to camp? Deal?"

Tess glanced toward where the moose had disappeared through the trees and to her wrapped foot. It was a good two miles back to the house, and despite her earlier claims, it would prove a struggle to walk it on her own. She'd hoped to impress Austin with her new hiking boots, and in a stroke of vanity had opted to go sans-brace as well.

Austin offered her a hand, the same one that had helped her up moments before. The one that had brushed against her hair before that. When she didn't respond right away, he wiggled his fingers and smiled. "I promise I won't bite. Don't worry. We'll take things nice and slow to start. Okay?"

A bit of the tension faded from her body at his reassurance. She slipped her arm across his shoulders as his hand came to rest on her waist. Her skin heated beneath his touch once more, but she ducked her head and said, "Lead the way."

Arms linked, they plodded through the forest in search of the trail. The longer Tess leaned against Austin for support, the less she noticed the throbbing in her ankle, and by the time they reached the camp an hour later, the pain was all but gone.

CHAPTER

Seventeen

SLOW DOWN, WILL ya? Not all of us are world-class athletes."

At the stop sign, Tess eased on the bike's brakes and waited for Abigail and Beth to catch up. A warm June breeze chased the ends of her loose braid, carrying with it the lively sounds of a Friday night in one of Denver's trendy neighborhoods.

Despite the complaint, Abigail's face was practically glowing. Beth, their cousin Tye's wife, pulled up the rear, and the three of them waited for traffic to clear before they crossed the street.

"Up next, bachelorette party stop number two." Tess readjusted the paper bag of beignets from the restaurant under her arm and pushed off from the asphalt.

Behind her, the sound of gravel crunching under their tires brought with it a nostalgic longing she hadn't felt in months. Lifting her feet from the pedals, Tess let her bike carry her down the gentle slope and imagined she was flying amongst a throng of other racers.

Free. Fearless. Invincible.

Abigail pulled up next to her, huffing as she cranked her feet against the pedals. "I had the slightest hope I'd be able to keep up with you now that your foot is in a brace."

Tess spied Beth a few car lengths behind them and offered an apologetic smile. "Sorry about that."

"Don't be. I'm glad to see you're almost back to normal." She chuckled between breaths. "I should have challenged you to a race two months ago, but Ben convinced me otherwise. He said it would be taking advantage of your injury, but I thought it'd be the perfect way to level the playing field."

The road flattened out at the end of the block, and Beth caught up to them in her pink cruiser, face flushed to match her auburn hair. She swiped a hand across her forehead, skewing her helmet to an odd angle. "Next time we agree to ride around Denver, remind me not to bring my single-gear bike."

"Don't worry. We're almost there."

They crossed Speer Boulevard and turned left at Zuni Street. Abigail's bike rattled down to second gear as she pedaled to keep up with Tess. Her head swiveled from the local bakery to the park, taking in the familiar street. "So where are we going, exactly? We're almost back to your place."

"You'll see."

They passed the coffee shop on the corner and turned down another street. After a few more blocks, Tess slowed and came to a stop at a busy corner. String lights bobbed in the evening breeze over an open brick patio, and the scents of fresh waffle cones wafted across the road. Families milled around in the open courtyard, where a projector and screen had been set up against the adjacent building's concrete wall. A man was fiddling with the settings of a projector as an old black and white cartoon played across the screen.

Tess took in Abigail's approving smile and beamed. "Here we are. It wouldn't be a party without ice cream and a movie."

A chalkboard sign out front advertised a movie starring Humphrey Bogart and Ingrid Bergman, starting in twenty minutes. Already, the metal chairs around the patio had begun to fill with the weekend crowd.

Abigail gaped at the setup and blinked back the sheen from her eyes. "How did you plan all this?"

Tess smiled. She should have started a tally earlier in the evening for all the times her cousin had been struck speechless. She clipped her bike into the bike rack and did the same with Abigail's and Beth's. "Friday Flicks, remember? And I may or may not have called in a favor or two and convinced the manager to play your favorite movie."

"With my help, of course," Beth interjected with a cheery smile.

"You guys, this is perfect." Abigail drew the two of them in for a group hug.

"Now, don't go getting teary on us. The evening's still young, and we have some ice cream to dig into."

"Which reminds me," Beth zipped open her purse and drew out a crumpled veil.

Abigail scrunched her nose at the tulle and rhinestone clip and shook her head vehemently. "I am *not* wearing that. I think the sash is quite enough."

"Come on. It'll be fun." Beth's bottom lip protruded in a pout. "Just for a little while. You can take it off when the movie starts."

Abigail was too nice a person to turn down the request, but Tess didn't miss the look of distress in her eyes. She looked from the cheap veil to them and the lingering crowd before she finally relented. "Oh, all right. But I'm taking it off as soon as *Casablanca*'s opening credits start to roll."

"Deal."

Beth clipped the accessory into Abigail's pale blonde hair and stepped back to admire her work. "Now we're ready for ice cream."

The line moved relatively fast for a Friday night, and within ten minutes, they were in front of the outdoor counter, where a teenager in a white apron greeted them. "Welcome to Farmer Joe's Ice Cream. What can I get you?"

Tess pushed Abigail to the front and motioned to the veil and bridal sash. Abigail blushed redder than a sunburnt beachgoer and sent Tess a murderous look.

Unaware of her discomfort, the kid's face split into a wide, toothy grin. "Congratulations. Order anything you like. It's on the house."

"Oh, that's really sweet, but—"

"I insist. It's not every day I get to treat a bride-to-be." He gave her a not-so-subtle wink and grabbed a large waffle cone from behind the counter. "What'll it be?"

Abigail's face grew dangerously close to matching her cherry red Vans, so Tess stepped in to place their order: mint fudge swirl for Abigail, raspberry hibiscus sorbet for Beth, and espresso brownie for Tess. She paid for their ice cream while Abigail awkwardly tried to fend off the boy's obvious flirtations before he handed over her cone.

Beth elbowed Abigail in the side as they found their seats. "See, we told you it would be worth it."

Abigail sent the two of them what she hoped was a scathing look. "Yeah, it almost makes up for that embarrassing incident and the catcalls I got between here and the restaurant. I bet Ben's friends aren't subjecting him to this kind of torture."

"You're right. Dinner at Chaurice's, ice cream, and your favorite movie. How terrible." Tess tried to hold back her laughter, and lost it when Beth snorted next to her.

Another strand of white lights clicked on above them in the fading twilight, and a swell of music filled the small courtyard, announcing the start of the movie.

"Shh, it's about to start." Abigail turned her chair to face the screen and motioned for the others to sit. Veil forgotten, she sank into her seat with her ice cream to her lips and sweater pulled tight around her shoulders.

If it was old, classic, or antique, Abigail was a goner. It was no wonder she'd found her place back in Buena Vista working in their great-aunt's antique shop.

Tess watched the pure bliss on her cousin's face. Ben was the lucky one. It may have taken half a lifetime for them to realize what they had, but there weren't two more deserving people.

Tess prayed she'd one day be as happy as the two of them.

Thoughts of Austin and the camp played through her mind like the flickering silver screen before her. It wasn't impossible to imagine a future there amongst the pine trees. For all the years she'd chased after the next victory, she'd taken little time to pause and reflect on the future. Yes, the Olympics had always been her goal, but life was more than accomplishments. It was people who made life worth living. People like Trudy, Josh, Austin...

She relaxed against the cool seat. Maybe someday wasn't as far away as she'd once thought.

Tess lifted the whistling kettle from its electric base and poured the water over two bags of peppermint tea. She breathed in the refreshing aroma and swirled a teaspoon of honey into each cup.

She balanced the mugs in one hand and a plate of beignets in the other on her way to the coffee table, then plopped onto the couch beside Abigail.

Ten-thirty and Beth was already fast asleep in the guest bedroom. Tess hadn't missed the drooping eyelids toward the end of the movie, and as soon as the credits began to roll, they'd picked up their bikes and rode the few blocks back to her condo. After a few more yawns and apologies, Beth bade them goodnight and was fast asleep within a few minutes, leaving Tess and Abigail with the living room all to themselves.

Aside from Beth's occasional snores, which floated through the open bedroom door, it felt like old times.

Tess dunked her tea bag up and down in the hot liquid and waited for a lull in the conversation. "You'll be happy to know I've invited someone to the wedding. You can tell Ben I won't need him to set me up with any of his college friends."

Abigail spun next to her on the couch and nearly spilled her tea. "No way. Who's the lucky guy? Anyone I might know?" Her face glowed with excitement.

"It's nothing, really. And we're friends. So, I asked Austin if he'd be my plus-one."

Her cousin's eyes grew wide, and she inched closer. "You mean *the* Austin? Mr. Wright, or should I say *Mr. Right*? The one you ran away to the mountains to work for?"

Tess nearly choked on her tea. "I did not run away. Caden pulled out of a commitment, and I needed the job, in case you don't remember."

"Mm-hmm. Right, so it has nothing to do with the fact he's single, handsome..."

"When did I ever say he was handsome?"

Abigail's eyes glittered over the rim of her coffee cup. "You didn't until just now."

Tess opened and closed her mouth. "I guess I walked right into that one."

"Works every time." Abigail polished off the rest of her beignet and followed it with a long sip of tea.

Tess warmed her hands around her own mug and smiled. "I see Aunt Josie has started to rub off on you."

Abigail's bright laughter filled the small room. "I learned a long time ago to stop trying to keep secrets from her. Somehow, I think she knows my own thoughts before I do."

"Now that's a scary idea."

They giggled as if they were still little girls, remembering the times their great-aunt had caught them goofing around in the antique shop after school. To any kid, The Glass Cottage was a treasure trove of untold mysteries. Who wouldn't want to experiment and play with all the old knickknacks? But she didn't reprimand them like their parents would have. Instead, their great-aunt always pulled out a tray of fresh-baked cookies and had a story at the ready to quell their childlike curiosity.

After a few minutes, Abigail's energy cooled to the temperature of their lukewarm tea. She shifted in her seat and tucked a platinum curl behind her ear. It fell loose in front of her face, and she pushed it back once more.

Tess knew better than to overlook her cousin's obvious change in attitude. "Oh, just say whatever's bothering you."

"What do you mean?" The hair fell loose again, and Abigail all but shoved it behind her ear.

If Tess didn't have a sinking feeling in her gut, she'd have laughed at the dramatic reaction. "I can tell something's up by the way you're fiddling with your hair."

Abigail flexed her fingers and anchored them around the ceramic mug in her lap. Tess knew that look. She'd seen it hundreds of times on her cousin's face when she was holding something back. Like the time Tess skipped their psychology lecture for a training session or when she covered yet again for another of Caden's misadventures. Tess never had to worry about Abigail telling anyone, but she knew her cousin well enough to see when she had something on her mind.

"Abigail, whatever it is, you can tell me."

Her cousin's gaze flitted to the contents of her half-empty mug. Reluctantly, she set the drink aside and released a slow breath. "Are you sure bringing Austin is a good idea?"

"What? A minute ago, you said..."

"I know. And I'm not saying he isn't a great guy. I'm sure he is, but have you thought this through?" Abigail pressed her mouth in a worried line and continued. "What happens at the end of the summer when you leave? It sounds like his camp is a full-time business, and you'll be back to training and traveling between races. I don't want to see you get hurt again. First your injury, then Ryan..."

"Why does everyone always bring up Ryan?"

Abigail leveled Tess with one of Aunt Josie's no-nonsense looks. If anyone knew the truth, it was Abigail. She may not have said it in the past, but they both knew how close Tess and her coach had been. Two people didn't work together for seven years without forming attachments.

Having lost her taste for the tea, Tess discarded her mug beside Abigail's on the coffee table. "Okay. So, maybe at one time, I thought we could have been more than friends. But he made it abundantly clear he didn't feel the same. I've moved on."

"Have you?"

Wasn't that exactly what she'd been doing the past few months? It was all so complicated, even she wasn't really sure of her own feelings. But there was one thing that was for certain . . . "Ryan is in the past. We'll always have that shared history, but that's exactly what it is. History."

"Good. I'm glad to hear it." Abigail reached for her tea again and took a long sip before continuing. "What do you think you'll do once your ankle heals? I don't imagine you'll want him as your coach again."

Did she? She'd been so focused on the summer and her recovery, she hadn't put much thought into the logistics of her comeback. "Why don't we go back to talking about your wedding? I liked that topic a whole lot more. Another beignet?" She grabbed one from the plate, held up the confectionary dessert, and hoped it would be enough of a distraction to end her cousin's unwanted questioning.

To her relief, Abigail relaxed and accepted the offering. "Fine, you win. But don't think this conversation is over." She took a bite, and a sprinkling of powdered sugar dusted the couch.

A slow smile crept across Tess's face. She took a bite of her own beignet and savored the sweet fried dough as it melted in her mouth. "Wouldn't dream of it."

CHAPTER

Eighteen

TESS BENT TO remove a twig from her brace. The warm summer heat hovered in the high-seventies, and not a single breeze whispered across the camp. A far cry from last weekend in Denver. A trickle of sweat ran between her shoulder blades as she hefted another branch onto the growing pile behind the house. The afternoon sun warmed her neck, and she felt a mild sunburn beginning to develop around her quick-dry shirt. The teal fabric clung to her moist skin, as if it didn't know it was meant to be athletic wear.

She pulled at another unruly branch before snipping it free. The earthy scent of juniper filled her nostrils, and she inhaled a deep breath. Ever since the bachelorette party, she couldn't get Abigail's warning out of her mind. For all her cousin's concerns, she was blowing this all out of proportion.

Tess and Austin were friends, and there was no harm in bringing a friend to a wedding. Right?

Squeals of laughter cut through her thoughts. Across the field, Genevieve danced around the spraying hose and ducked when Kyle aimed the water at her feet. Harper, Sean, and Skye egged them on from the sidelines, already dripping wet. Kyle took aim once more but soaked the bystanders once again.

"Watch it." Harper tossed a dirty towel in his direction, hitting him square in the chest. "You trying to drown us here, or what?"

He flashed them a lopsided grin. "I wouldn't have to if Gen would stop hiding behind you all."

Genevieve made a face. "What? Afraid you'll lose to a girl?"

"Watch out, Kyle. She's coming for you now." Sean and Grayson joined in the cheers.

Tess chuckled at the teenage banter. There was never a dull moment with this group. Abigail had at least gotten one thing right—she'd be sorry to leave this place come the end of summer.

A flicker of blue caught her attention, and she turned to see Josh crouch behind a nearby bush, wet sponge in hand. He stilled when he saw her and raised a finger to his lips.

She smiled. This kid. Hard to believe he was the same grumbly teenager from her first week there.

Josh's face alight with mischief, he pointed toward the nearby group. When the others appeared distracted, he made his move. Sneaking behind Kyle, he reached his arms as high as he could and wrung the sponge over his head. A cascade of soapy water splashed down Kyle's face and chest, and the others shouted out their whoops and hollers of victory.

Tess chuckled to herself. She tossed her hedge trimmers onto the pile of branches and brushed her hands against her jean shorts. Time for a quick break. Then she'd finish up the back hedges later and maybe go for a long overdue swim.

Footsteps crunched behind her, followed by Austin's deep voice. "Looks like they're having fun."

She turned to him and smiled. "Were you thinking of joining them?"

He leaned in, enveloping her in a familiar spicy aroma, and whispered. "Careful, they might hear you and come over."

"Is that so? Well, we wouldn't want that, would we?"

A roguish tilt played at his lips. "You tell me."

A twig snapped behind her, and a shock of cold water spilled over her head. She gasped and looked up into Austin's smiling face. His eyes danced with laughter, and she couldn't help but join in herself. Water dribbled down her shirt and pooled in her shoes, but she welcomed the surprise relief.

Breathless, she turned to face her attacker. Josh beamed at her with an innocent grin and an empty bucket tucked behind his back.

"Oh, it's on." Tess reached for the discarded sponge on the grass and pivoted toward Austin. He tried to sidestep her, and she collided with his chest. Soapy water sprayed up his nose from the wet sponge, and he sputtered and coughed.

"I'm so sorry. Are you okay?" She looked around for a towel but came up empty. She would have torn off her work gloves and handed them to him if she thought they'd help.

Austin swiped a hand down his ruddy face and bumped her shoulder in a playful nudge. "Serves me right for trying to pick a fight with a professional."

Warmth flushed through her body, and she shrugged. "What can I say? I play to win."

"This isn't a game."

Skye pounded against the bathroom door loud enough to wake the neighbors a mile down the road. She banged on the door once more, sending a sprinkle of dust from the rafters onto the open binder on top of Austin's desk.

Although it was still early, the faint wash of dawn tinted the sky with a golden hue. Trudy was busy in the kitchen, as was usual this time of morning, the smell of cinnamon and yeast spilling down the hallway whenever she opened the oven door to check on her cinnamon rolls. And the campers would trickle in for breakfast within the hour, if they weren't awake already from the ruckus taking place upstairs.

With the last of this week's paperwork finished, Austin had thought to slip in a quick morning run when the hammering of a fist on the bathroom door began. Never had it crossed his mind that four girls sharing one bathroom might pose a problem.

Skye's voice rose another decibel. "Gen. Open up. You've been in there twenty minutes already."

There was a pounding of footsteps, and a door swung open. The solid wood panel bounced against the thick pine walls with enough force to make Austin wince.

Closing the binder in front of him, he shoved it across the desk and reached for his cup of coffee—black, just like he hoped their finances would be by the end of the summer. He took a sip of the strong brew and hoped it would be enough to bolster his resolve before facing the day's struggles.

He glanced at the clock and sighed. Only 6:20.

This weekend couldn't come soon enough. Tess had made it abundantly clear it was a friend sort of thing, but he'd be lying if he said he wasn't looking forward to her cousin's wedding. Two whole days to breathe. Two days without paperwork and playing referee to a bunch of teenagers. Two days with Tess . . .

It sounded almost too good to be true. He'd been afraid after their moose encounter that he'd messed things up between them for good, what with that almost-kiss. But yesterday's little soap war seemed to prove his fears wrong.

Austin smiled at the memory. He could still remember the way Tess's eyes widened in surprise the moment Josh dumped that bucket of icy water over her head. The way she'd eagerly joined in and nearly drowned him in soapy water.

Yes. Two days with Tess would be an adventure—one he was greatly looking forward to.

Despite his excitement, though, a niggle of doubt slipped through. What if Josh needed him? What if something happened at the camp while he was away?

More voices upstairs cut through his spiraling thoughts, and Austin focused once again on the present.

No use worrying about the future. There's enough in the here and now to keep a man occupied for a lifetime. His grandfather's words came back to him as if he were sitting in the chair opposite the desk. Like all his other words of wisdom, they seemed to rise to the surface at the exact moments Austin needed them most. That, and Trudy's constant reminder that he wasn't alone in any of this.

Trudy had assured him she and her husband, Jeff, would be happy to keep an eye on things while he and Tess were away. Austin wasn't usually one to accept help, but Trudy had a way of sidestepping his reservations with her jovial smile and southern charm. The woman probably would have even agreed to guard a wild mountain lion if he asked.

Not that he was asking.

A door banged shut upstairs, followed by blessed silence.

Downing the last of his coffee, Austin grabbed his sweater from the back of the chair and made for the side door before any more unexpected interruptions could stop him. Outside, he pulled the gray hoodie over his head and jogged down the wooden steps toward the trail.

By the time he finished his three-mile loop, almost half the camp sat wide-eyed and bushy-tailed on the open patio, making short work of the freshly cut fruit and Trudy's cinnamon rolls.

The tempting scents beckoned like an alpine lake after a ten-mile hike. But first, a change of clothes was in order. Taking the steps two at a time, Austin ducked into his room and switched out of his sweaty running gear for a fresh T-shirt and jeans. In the kitchen, he refilled his coffee cup from earlier and joined the rest of the group outside. Two steps onto the patio, someone shoved a plate into his hands.

"There you are. I saved you the last cinnamon roll."

In a juggling act of hot coffee and cream cheese frosting, Austin deposited the items on the nearest table and turned to face Josh. "Thanks. I was sure they'd all be gone by the time I got back."

"They are. Which is why it's a good thing I thought ahead. Where were you, anyway?" Josh slid into the seat beside him and stacked his fork with pastry and scrambled eggs.

Austin held back his opinion of his nephew's odd taste and dug in, himself. His first bite nearly melted in his mouth, and he chased it with another sip of coffee to wash down the sweet icing. "I decided to go for a run before it heats up."

"Smart." Josh talked around a mouthful of food while loading his fork once again. "So you must have missed Skye and Gen's argument this morning, huh?"

"Unfortunately, no. I was in my office and heard the whole thing."

"Aw, man. That would have at least made the run worth it." With a final swipe of his fork, the boy cleaned the last of the food from his plate.

"You know, one of these days, you might come to enjoy running. There's a lot more to it than the physical exertion itself. It's a time of reflection, to process your thoughts and..."

"Boring. At least with soccer or football, you're running *toward* something. But running to run ...? Nope. Count me out."

"You don't know what you're missing. Running beats video games any day."

Josh rolled his eyes dramatically, as if the very idea were as interesting as watching paint dry. "I think I'll live."

Austin smiled and chewed another bite. This was nice. He'd been so busy running the camp, the two of them had spent little one-on-one time together since the first campers arrived. Once he and Tess were back from the wedding, he'd set aside some time for him and Josh. They could go back up to the shelter or take out one of the canoes. Any activity Josh picked would be fine, as long as they could do it together.

Austin dragged his fork through the icing pooled in the center of the plate and watched the way it slowly melted back together. "You sure you'll be all right with Trudy and Jeff in charge this weekend?" The last thing he wanted was Josh feeling abandoned once again.

Josh shrugged. "Sure. Trudy's cool, and Jeff promised to take us all fishing. Everyone's really excited."

"Really? Since when do you fish?" The closest Josh had come to a fish in years was dinner at Mr. Moto's Sushi back in California. And that had *not* been a positive experience. Josh had spent the entire evening poking at his spicy tuna roll and commenting about the restaurant's smell.

"How hard can it be? I *have* watched *Jaws*, you know."

Oh, boy. How Austin wished he could be there to see his nephew's reaction when he realized fishing was not like in the movies. "Well, if you need anything while I'm away, and I mean anything, ask someone for a ride into town and give me a call. Okay?"

"Nothing's gonna happen in two days." Josh started to rise, and Austin stopped him with a light hand on his forearm.

"Just promise. If you need to call…"

"Okay, *Uncle Austin*." Josh swiped their paper plates from the table and dumped them in the trash with a theatrical swoosh of the arms. "How about I send you a picture of the giant fish I'm gonna catch instead?"

Austin smiled. How was this the same city boy he'd nearly dragged up here a few months ago? Maybe things really were working out for the best.

"Can't wait to see it."

CHAPTER

Nineteen

GOT EVERYTHING YOU need?" Austin peered into the rearview mirror while Tess wedged her bag beside the dress box and closed the back hatch.

"All set." Ponytail swishing with each step, she circled the car and slung her backpack through the open passenger window.

The plan was to drive the half hour to Lyons, where they'd meet up with Tess's cousin Tye and his wife, Beth. The four of them would then carpool the last three hours to Buena Vista, where they'd spend the next two days going from one family gathering to another before the wedding.

He watched through the windshield as Trudy smiled and handed a smaller box to Tess. The woman said something he couldn't hear, and Tess nodded in response. Trudy wrapped her in a grandmotherly hug and waved at Austin as Tess dropped into the passenger seat.

Ever since he'd mentioned Tess's invite to the wedding, Trudy had been ready to shoo him out the door faster than she could say *skedaddle*.

Austin rolled down the window. "Don't forget to check on the cabins. Last night's rain was pretty heavy, and I think Harper mentioned something about a leak in one of the roofs. And Lighthouse Church left a message asking about scheduling a retreat in August. If you wouldn't mind giving them a call—"

"Austin James Wright. Stop your worryin' and try to relax. What do you think's gonna happen, that I'll let the whole place burn to the ground while you're away?"

"No, ma'am." He knew a scolding when he heard one, and he wasn't about to argue with Trudy.

"Good. Then I expect you two to have a wonderful time, and don't you dare call about work while you're away. In case you've already forgotten, we don't get reception up here, anyway." She turned her head and gave him a sugary smile. "Now have fun, you two."

Trudy waved a bangled arm as she stepped from the car, and Austin took that as their cue to leave. Tess waved back as he put the car in drive, and the camp shrank behind them in the distance.

Beyond the entrance, the road steepened, and Austin shifted into second. He eased around the first curve, careful to avoid the deep ruts along the shoulder, and slowed over the washboard surface. Something rattled inside the box on Tess's lap, and he slid her a glance. "What's in there?"

"Oh, this?" Tess tapped the large Tupperware. "Trudy's so sweet. She made us a few sandwiches for the drive, and I think I see some cookies in here too." She peeled back the lid, and the scent of buttery lemon shortbread filled the car.

He hiked an eyebrow at the couple dozen cookies wedged around the peanut butter and honey sandwiches. "It looks like she made enough to feed a small army."

Tess shrugged. "So she made a few extras. Anyway, we can share them with Tye and Beth when we meet up. I know for a fact Tye wouldn't say no to homemade cookies."

Austin eased up on the gas when they neared the highway intersection and turned north onto St. Vrain Avenue. Tess stared through the side window and hummed to the folksy tune that came over the radio. The air from the vents toyed with her hair as she watched the pine trees whoosh past them.

"So," he broke the silence. "Tye is yours and Caden's cousin, and his brother is Micah, the one with the ranch?" He'd learned a little of the family tree from Caden over the years, but the details were fuzzy.

"Right. It's me and Caden, Abigail, and Micah and Tye. Micah stayed at home after high school while the rest of us left, but I guess we're all sort of finding our way back to the mountains." She tossed him a grin and returned her gaze to the flashing wilderness outside her window.

It was impossible not to notice the way she'd changed in the past few months, as if she were slowly rediscovering herself after a long slumber. Whatever life she'd had before, the racing and the traveling, the highs of competition and the lows of defeat . . . did she miss it?

"You know there's nothing wrong with that. Returning to the things you love." Maybe it was a misstep on his part to assume, but he didn't have to know her well to witness the recent unfurling of her soul.

Her finger trailed the bottom of the window in mindless circles across the sun-weathered surface, and she looked up. "I think you're right."

Austin wished he could take his eyes off the road to see the smile he could hear in the lift of her voice, the soft way in which she spoke.

Her fingers stilled, and she relaxed in the seat beside him. "So, how did you end up here, of all places? I mean, you mentioned your grandpa left the place to you in his will and all, but what made you decide to quit being a paramedic and run a camp instead?"

Austin could feel her inquisitive stare as they dipped down into the narrow canyon. How could he explain it to someone who'd chosen to leave the very mountains he'd dreamed about as a kid? "Well, you already know my grandpa used to own the camp, and I'd visit during the summers. I grew up near LA, and this place felt as freeing as the city was claustrophobic. It was my home away from home, and, to be honest, I think I've always felt more at peace here than anywhere else."

"Did your parents come out here much, or was it mostly you and your sister?"

"Meghan usually joined her friends for trips or other summer programs, so most of the time it was just my grandpa and me. My parents were so busy with work, it seemed the best solution to keep us out of trouble."

Seven years older than Austin, and with a stubborn independent streak, Meghan had given their parents a run for their money on more than one occasion. Despite the age difference, he'd always felt the weight of their parents' worry, and he was still struggling to let it rest after all this time.

A crackle of static popped from the radio speakers. Tess fiddled with the dial until a local station came through. "So why come back here? Why now? I'm sure you could have waited to come back or hired someone to run the day-to-day things if you wanted."

She'd asked a similar question her first day there, and he'd given her a simple answer. But how did one explain something they were still trying to figure out? "Leaving California was probably the best thing that could have happened to me."

Tess turned in her seat and tossed him a funny look. "Is there some crazy stalker ex-girlfriend I should know about?"

Tess's lighthearted tease dissipated his tension. Austin laughed, "Actually, you're not too far off, but instead of a girl, it was more like a reminder."

"A reminder of what?" she asked, a note of curiosity in her voice.

"That life is precious, and living in the past can only prevent you from moving forward. I told you I used to be a paramedic, but what I didn't mention was how the job can eat at your soul. No matter your training or how prepared you might think you are for the impossible, some things are outside your control."

Tess grew quiet beside him. She seemed to mull over his words, so he continued.

"It was the last emergency call I responded to that told me I needed a change. You can only see so many people get hurt before you have to make a decision. Stay, and learn to deal with the pain, or get out."

"And you chose to start over."

He nodded. "I quit my job, bought a plane ticket to Colorado, and I haven't looked back since. Roof leaks and energetic kids are a walk in the park compared to 9-1-1 calls. I've learned there are lots of things I can't control in life, but it was here, in these mountains, where I really learned to trust the One who *is* in control."

For a moment, faint music filled the car until Tess spoke again. "You make that sound so simple." Her voice was soft, and a thread of doubt seemed to lace her tone.

"It is. It's the letting go that takes some wrestling with. But God is in the habit of building new things out of the broken and seemingly scattered pieces." A person's own fear was the one thing that so often stood between them and that peace. Even so, it was a laying down of oneself that demanded a daily commitment. One he sorely failed with, if he was honest with himself. The reality humbled him, and he vowed to do a better job in the days and years ahead.

Austin focused on the curvy road as they neared the bottom of the canyon. Houses and developments dotted the hillsides in greater density, announcing their departure from the mountains as they reached the small town of Lyons at the base of the foothills.

After turning at the light, he slowed, and they inched down the slumbering main street. Following the directions to the library on Tess's phone, they turned onto Fourth Avenue.

"I think I see Tye and Beth." She waved through the tinted window and unclicked her seat belt.

Austin turned into the parking lot. As soon as they parked, Tess hopped out and greeted the couple. Austin joined them as she was pulling back from Beth's embrace.

"What happened to the truck?" Tess peered around the hunter green Jeep parked beside them, as if another car might be hiding behind it.

"Nice to see you too." Tye chuckled. "I was driving back from a foaling when the engine gave out. Beth had to pick me up, and we had it towed to the nearest garage. Would've cost more to repair it than it was worth, so we decided it was best to get something new."

Tess frowned at the shimmery new paint. "Bummer. I always liked that truck."

Tye nodded his agreement and extended a hand toward Austin. "Sorry, we haven't met. I'm Tye, Tess's cousin, and this is Beth."

"Austin. Nice to meet you." He clasped the man's hand in a firm handshake and smiled at the couple's warm energy.

"Ready to get this show on the road?" Tye clapped his hands before he started transferring items from the back of Austin's car.

Among the four of them, they made quick time loading the car. Somehow, it all fit in the back of Tye's Jeep, and then they were off. Once out of town, they eased onto Highway 36 and cruised south toward the Denver metro area. Austin couldn't mistake the faint scent of hay and country air infused into the seat cushions, and he breathed in a deep lungful.

"So, Tye. Caden says you're a veterinarian. What's that like?"

"Oh, you know. Lots of cows and smelly barnyards." He smiled at the road, and despite his unglamorous picture, it was clear he loved what he did.

"At least you don't have to deal with patient complaints."

Tye chuckled. "You'd be surprised. The animals are great, but the owners make me want to pack up and change professions some days."

"You have my sympathies. I definitely don't miss working with human patients." He slid a glance toward Tess, and silent understanding seemed to pass between them. He hadn't planned on telling her about his time in California, but at the moment, he couldn't be more grateful that she knew more of his story.

Tye shot a look in the rearview mirror. "You a doctor or something?"

Tess watched Austin from the corner of her eye. A weariness seemed to pass over him at Tye's question, but he tried not to let it show.

"Paramedic, actually. I worked out in California until about a year ago, before moving back here."

"Where in California?" Tye's voice piqued with interest. "I studied at UC Davis, and I got to know quite a few of the local health professionals there. In fact, did you ever know a Dr. Langston? He always seemed to be the one on call whenever any of the veterinary students had a run-in with an animal."

"Tye." Beth laid a hand on her husband's arm. "I'm sure Tess doesn't want to listen to medical talk for the entire three hour drive." She gave her an apologetic look over the back of the passenger seat, and Tess nearly giggled at the look of horror on her own face.

"Oh, all right." Tye pretended to complain but smiled all the same. "Don't worry, Austin. We can talk more about this later. I've got some stories you'd love, and I want to hear more about your work."

Austin chuckled. "Looking forward to it, then."

They passed through Boulder and within forty minutes neared the exit that would take them to Buena Vista. Condos and large developments shrank behind them as they curved into the mountains and passed by the iconic Red Rocks Amphitheater in Morrison. Not a few miles beyond the first ridge, Tess's phone buzzed.

In the front seats, Tye and Beth chatted away in their own world as country music spilled from the speakers, and Austin seemed content watching the scenery through the window. Fishing her phone from her backpack, Tess clicked the home button to see a new text from Ryan flash across the screen.

She could ignore it like all the others, but something about being away from the camp and seeing the Denver skyline fading behind them in the rearview mirror gave her a newfound surge of courage. She couldn't run forever. And if she was going to start over, she might as well begin with Ryan.

Making sure no one else was watching, she slid her finger across the screen and opened the text message.

Hey, Tess. I haven't heard from you in a while, despite all my attempts to call, but I hope you're well. I don't blame you for shutting me out, but believe me when I say I'm sorry for the way I acted. It was a misunderstanding, that's all. We've been friends for so long, and I'd hate for something this trivial to come between us. Come back home, and we'll figure a way past this.

Tess blinked. She re-read his text as the tension grew in her shoulders. *A misunderstanding?* That's what Ryan called abandoning her after the accident and subsequent three surgeries? Perhaps she'd been right to ignore his calls all this time. If a few months weren't enough time for him to see reason, could he ever change?

Beth's laughter trickled into her thoughts—carefree and lighthearted.

Tess's eyes slid back to her phone, and she sighed. It was time to let go.

Honestly, she should have done this months ago, but she'd been too raw to see the unhealthy balance between her and Ryan over the years. He wasn't a bad guy. Only he wasn't the right guy for her. Or coach, for that matter. She would have to make some major changes if she ever got back to the competitive training world, and that started now.

Tess flexed her fingers and counted down the seconds before responding.

I appreciate all you've done for me over the years, but I've had a lot of time to think these past few months. I still haven't decided what I'm going to do next, but whatever I decide, I need to do this on my own. I need you to let me move on.

She shoved her phone back in the bag and blew out a controlled breath. For so many years, she'd let herself believe the lies that she wasn't good enough. One more race, one more win, and he would finally notice the real her. They all would. All it took was a broken contract and a medical leave of absence for her to realize the truth.

"Hey, are you okay?" Austin's deep whisper wrapped around her, concern evident in his voice. He shifted beside her and rested his hand over hers.

She hadn't noticed her hands were shaking, and she instantly relaxed under his silent strength. Feeling his intent gaze on her, she turned and looked up. A host of questions passed across his features, but he remained silent.

"I am. Just taking care of something I should have done a long time ago," she said, already feeling more like herself around Austin than she ever had around Ryan. The warmth of his touch seeped into her, and she knew she'd made the right decision.

CHAPTER

Twenty

TWO HOURS LATER, they passed through town and pulled up to a quaint yellow Craftsman, the open front door welcoming in the warm July breeze. A small shed barely hid the red classic truck parked out front, and pastel pom-poms flanked the yard on all sides. Hydrangeas, maybe? He couldn't tell through the hazy windows of the car, but there appeared to be an entire hedge of them beneath the base of the wrap-around porch.

Austin rolled down his window and inhaled a deep breath of mountain air. The spicy scent of sagebrush tickled his nose instead of the rich pine of back home, reminding him how far they'd driven in under three hours.

Tye put the car in park beside a silver pickup as a petite woman with short blonde hair came skipping from the house.

"Aunt Josie, they're here!" she called behind her. A shaggy black and white dog barreled down the porch steps and trailed after her across the lawn.

Before Austin had one foot out the door, Tess was halfway across the lawn with Beth hot on her heels. While the three of them chatted away, an older woman with silvery curls joined them, along with a second woman with graying blonde hair who had to have been Abigail's mother.

"Looks like it's up to you and me to get the bags." Tye chuckled as he shut the driver's side door. He rounded the car and shielded his eyes against the sun when he reached the back end. "Oh, look. Here comes Ben."

Sure enough, a tall man wearing a tattered ball cap emerged from the house. After stopping to greet Tess and Beth, he ate up the grass in a few long strides toward the parked cars, where he and Tye greeted each other with a quick hug and a slap to the back.

"Glad to see you all made it in one piece." Ben turned and offered Austin a hearty handshake in welcome. "You must be Austin. Nice to meet you. I've heard a lot about you, between Abigail and Caden."

Austin shook his hand. "And you must be the lucky guy getting married."

"Guilty as charged." Despite the threat of wedding day nerves, Ben appeared completely at ease. The dog shoved a nose in his hand as if to join in the conversation, and he ruffled its unruly fur.

"Speaking of Caden, where is he?" Tye pressed a button on his key ring, and the back hatch of the Jeep popped open.

"He and Micah are already at the house, along with a few friends from Washington. I assume you'll both be joining us there? I've pulled out all the sleeping bags I could find, and there's a guest bedroom and couch as well for people to fight over. It'll be a squeeze, but the more the merrier." Ben scooped up Tye's and Austin's bags and tossed them into the back of his pickup without a moment's hesitation. "If you don't mind sticking around for a bit and helping load up the rest of the boxes, then we can get going after that."

It was then Austin noticed the cardboard boxes and wooden crates of supplies beside their bags. At last, something he could do to stretch his legs.

"Sure thing. Wherever you need me, I'm here to help." Without being told twice, he swiped up two of the empty crates and made for the front door. The dog raced ahead of him and disappeared into the house.

"Hey Tess, I think he's a keeper." Ben called out as he crossed the yard behind Austin.

They passed her and the other women still talking on the lawn, and Austin caught her slight blush and silent nod of thanks. A subtle movement, but after two months of working together, he knew her mannerisms as if they were her own language. He returned the gesture and followed her cousin and soon-to-be cousin-in-law through the foyer, where a heavenly smell of something in the oven wafted toward them from the kitchen.

Ben led the way, talking as he went. "The girls have practically emptied Josephine's antique shop of every plate and crystal glass they could find. And I'm pretty sure the other half of the shop found its way here in the end, too. You'd think they were preparing for their own episode of *Antiques Roadshow*, by the looks of it." He chuckled, and Tye joined in as if he, too, knew what to expect.

Despite the warning, Austin was wholly unprepared for what greeted them around the corner. Across every available surface sprang up an explosion of mismatched dishes, glassware, and countless other items. Swaths of fabric hung in bows over the chairs, the yellow and white tulle gathering in puddles on the hardwood floor. An old wooden frame sat propped against the dining table, where dozens of photos lay scattered across the surface. There was even what looked to be a gramophone tucked behind all the decorations. But what they planned to do with that was beyond him.

"We're packing up *all* of this?" He did a rough calculation and wondered if they wouldn't need to make a couple of trips to move everything.

Diving right in, Ben grabbed the first glass and began to wrap it in brown paper. "Believe it. When it comes to a Prescott event, there's no holding back. Last year, Josephine and Abigail held a dinner for the whole town for helping with some repairs on the shop after a nasty snowstorm."

"Based on this, I could believe it." The initial shock faded, and Austin placed his box between Ben's and Tye's and got to work.

Halfway through the first stack of dishes, the notes of feminine voices filtered into the kitchen as the girls finally made their way inside. Tess broke from the group and joined Austin at the table, where she plucked the first of the bows from the chairs and got to work folding the billowy fabric into submission. "I see they've put you to work already. Got any other fun plans with Caden and the guys while we girls chat over last-minute wedding details?"

"Not that I've heard about, but knowing Caden, he's got something planned." Austin continued to talk while he worked. "I was actually thinking about maybe popping in on my aunt and uncle for a bit when we're finished up here. They don't live too far off Main Street, and they'd kill me if I came all the way up here and didn't say hi."

Tess dropped the bow, letting the tulle float toward the floor. "Wait, you have family here? How did I not know this?"

Austin chuckled. "Yep. And they're probably doing the flowers for your cousin's wedding." He reached for a bud vase and watched in amusement as Tess's face lit with recognition.

"No. You mean Erin and John Wright?" She gave him an incredulous stare.

He couldn't help but laugh again. "Those would be them. Small world, right?"

A loud knock interrupted them, and they looked up in time to see Charlie bolt toward the door.

"Hello, anybody home?" Caden's loud voice sailed through the open door. Dual footsteps echoed down the hall, and Austin turned in time to see Caden and someone who must have been Tye's brother step into the kitchen. Clad in their mud-streaked boots, they looked as if they'd come straight from a day in the fields. All that was missing was the cowboy hats.

"You guys made it." Abigail rushed in to give them each a hug, the top of her head barely brushing their chins.

"And just in time too." Ben pushed an empty box across the floor for them to join in. "I thought we'd be here until midnight, but maybe now we can at least finish before it gets dark."

Finally releasing her cousins, Abigail spun around and gave Ben a playful swat on the shoulder. "There isn't that much here."

"Of course. My mistake. I must have been thinking about another room full of assorted knickknacks and thingamajigs…" His lips curved, and she waved her hand as if shooing a fly.

"Just go back to your boxes."

Eyes twinkling, he dipped his head in a nod. "Yes, ma'am."

Ben ducked as a small throw pillow bounced against his side. He plucked the plush projectile from the floor with a grin and tossed it into the box at his feet.

Caden took in the stack of lace doilies and made a slow scan of the room. "Had I known being in the wedding party would be so much work, I'd have gladly given the position to some other unlucky guy."

"Don't make me throw a pillow at you too." Abigail raised a small lumpy cushion in his direction, but a giggle escaped before she could deliver on her threat.

Austin reached for another glass tumbler and slid a smile toward Tess. "Now I see why you're so good with all the kids at camp. Compared to this, they must be a piece of cake."

She handed him another sheet of paper and watched the group from the fringe of the room. "They can be a bit much, but I love them, you know? They're family."

He didn't need her to elaborate. "I get that. Not the whole large-family thing, but my sister and I are pretty close. Growing up, it was the two of us, and that had always been enough."

Taking care with the crystal, he nestled it against the others, the paper crinkling gently with every adjustment. Like the glassware safely tucked in that box, family was something to be protected. Cared for. It might require time and patience, but it was all worth it in the end. Whatever the cost.

Tess's arm bumped against his as she leaned across him for the next glass, her slender fingers working to fold the paper around its delicate edges as she repeated the same process he'd done a minute before. "Not having second thoughts about coming yet, are you?"

He smiled at the close-knit group around them and back at Tess. "Not even for a second."

A flash of humor glinted across her eyes. "Really? I know you're friends with Caden, but I thought you'd be ready to hop on the first bus back the minute you saw how crazy the rest of our family could be."

If it meant getting to see this carefree side of Tess all weekend, he'd welcome a hundred more lively family members. "If I can handle a houseful of teenage volunteers and middle-school campers, I figure I can handle pretty much anything."

CHAPTER

Twenty-One

TESS WATCHED FROM the photo wall as Beth and Tye raced off toward the dance floor. A new country song blended into the last, and they were swept into the arms of a rollicking two-step alongside a dozen other couples.

Not a single smile could compare to her cousin's on her wedding day. Never had Tess seen Abigail so happy, and she knew this was only the beginning. Ben had a way of bringing out the best in her, of capturing that effervescent energy of hers and letting it shine for all to see.

A chorus of cheers erupted around the room as Ben dipped Abigail over his knee and planted a kiss on his bride. Face glowing, she kissed him right back, and the sound of clinking glasses grew to the point that Tess was sure something might shatter.

Smiling, Tess turned from the rowdy group and studied the pictures she and Beth had hung earlier that afternoon. Framed in reclaimed wooden slats, the Polaroids dangled in rows from a collection of antique clothespins, courtesy of Aunt Josie's antique shop. Since the bride and groom had known each other since grade school, there were few pictures where the two of them weren't together. There had been a few years after graduation where they'd lost touch, but Aunt Josie insisted their love story had been written from day one.

Leave it to their great-aunt to still believe in fairy tale endings.

Tess unclipped a photo of all the cousins and thumbed the worn edges, the fond memory playing through her mind. If she closed her eyes, she could almost hear the waves lapping against the lake's pebbly shore, feel the silt between her toes as they raced across the beach the day after finals. She could even smell the wood smoke as Ben and Abigail fueled the bonfire and Caden passed around a bag of marshmallows and graham crackers to celebrate the start of summer.

She breathed in the memory as the warm scents of cedar wood and clove wrapped around her in another familiar embrace. Opening her eyes, she tilted her head to see Austin beside her with a plate in each hand.

"You look like someone who could use a piece of cake." He offered her the bigger of the two, and she gladly accepted.

Austin sliced his fork through the dark sponge and took a bite. No sooner had he swallowed when his eyes grew wide.

"Wow, what is this?" He stared at his plate like a kid in a candy store and speared another bite.

Tess savored the combination of sweet cinnamon and buttercream and smiled. "Spiced pear and caramel. It's one of Aunt Josie's specialties." Not to mention her favorite, as well. She and Abigail had tried making it once or twice, but nothing came close to their great-aunt's baking.

"I wonder if I could get the recipe from her, if it's not a secret, of course. I know for a fact Trudy and Josh would love it."

"I'm sure she'd be more than happy to share. I keep telling her she needs to write a cookbook someday. She has more than enough cakes and scones to fill at least a few volumes." Tess thought back to her box of handwritten recipe cards back home, remembering the Christmas Aunt Josie had gifted them to each person in the family. There was more sugar in those three-by-five notecards than Tess hoped to consume in a lifetime, but there was no mistaking the love baked into each one.

"Although," Tess leaned in as if sharing a secret. "If it were one of Aunt Josie's award-winning pies, that would be a different matter entirely."

Austin chuckled and swallowed another bite. "If she's anything like Trudy, I could believe that. She keeps her biscuits and gravy recipe under lock and key. Not even my grandfather knew her secret."

"Trudy? She's so sweet, she couldn't scare a fly if she tried."

"Believe it. You don't want to get between her and her skillet. I learned that the hard way once and barely made it out of the kitchen alive."

"I'm sure there's a great story there."

"There sure is," he said with a knowing grin.

He didn't elaborate, which made her even more curious. "Come on. You can't say something like that and then *not* tell me."

Tess waited for him to take the bait, but his annoyingly placid smile was all the response she got. Tossing her head back, she stared at the ceiling and tried to imagine a young teenage version of Austin and the sort of hijinks he would've gotten into.

"Let me guess, you stole the skillet and made mud pies in it with your sister. Or maybe you shot bottle rockets inside of it." She scrunched her face and frowned. "No, wait. That was Caden who did that last one."

He rewarded her with a deep laugh that warmed her to her toes.

"Let's just say I may or may not have used it to build my own smelter."

She gasped. "You didn't."

"I was ten. I thought cast iron was indestructible, and my grandfather had recently told me about the abandoned gold mines in the region. I was going to return it as soon as I'd melted down a few rocks I'd found by the river and found my fortune."

Tess blew out a slow breath. "I'm surprised she didn't tan your hide right there and then."

"She definitely thought about it, that's for sure. But she caught me before I'd made it out of the kitchen."

"Now I see why you're friends with my brother. That sounds exactly like something he'd do."

He reached for her empty plate and stacked it on top of his. "I had good intentions. When I became rich, I was going to buy her a whole new set of cookware."

"Ah, perfectly reasonable, then." Her face ached from trying to hold back her smile but not before an untamed snort escaped. Luckily, the music drowned out the worst of it, or at least Austin pretended not to hear it.

Comfortable to spend the entire evening on the sidelines with Austin, Tess relaxed and watched as the other guests mingled over cake and drinks. One song blended into the next. Twinkle lights flickered from the rafters like fireflies dancing above the room as if they too couldn't help but celebrate such a beautiful evening.

"So, what do you think so far?" Austin asked over the music. "About the wedding? Is it everything your cousin hoped for?"

Tess watched Abigail and Ben glide across the dance floor. "I think she could have worn a second-hand dress and gotten married in a field and been happy. So long as Ben was waiting for her at the end of the aisle." For the girl who'd wished on flower petals as a child, nothing could have been more perfect.

There was another round of clinking glasses, and somewhere on the other end of the room there rose a loud cheer. The country song wound to a close, and there was a moment of dead air as Caden abandoned his dancing partner to switch the music over to the next playlist.

Tess immediately recognized the familiar '80s intro the second "Footloose" came over the speakers. Tapping her foot to the beat, she barely missed Austin shifting beside her until he cleared his throat. He'd discarded their plates and nodded to the group crowding onto the dance floor. "You're already almost dancing. How about we show them how it's done?"

She hiked an eyebrow in his direction. "Sure you can keep up?"

"I guess we'll find out." He smiled and offered her a hand.

She kicked off her heels and slid them beneath the nearest table. Taking Austin's hand in hers, she joined the rest of the group with him and fell in step with the music.

As soon as those first lyrics began, they were off. Tess leapt into the dance, as if at the start of a race, and Austin was right beside her, looking like a pro doing the country grapevine. When it was time for the guitar lick, everyone jammed out on their air guitars before rushing into the kick lines for the chorus.

Ben and Abigail must have been practicing all week. Without misstep, they led the group through the fast line dance, Ben shouting out instructions like a well-trained square dance caller.

By the time they reached the bridge, Tess was breathing heavily. She looked over her shoulder and saw a bead of sweat roll down Austin's temple. Despite the quick choreography, he was doing an admirable job following Ben and Abigail's lead. Before she had time to look away, his head popped up, and he caught her gaze. His wink was nearly as fast as the footwork, and they were spinning once again.

Tess hadn't felt this alive in weeks. Feeding off the energy of the group, she sang out the lyrics to the final chorus between breaths, thankful for this moment and all the people here in this room.

The final notes of the song ended with a punch, and applause erupted throughout the room. In the quiet seconds between songs, people paused to catch their breaths before the music switched and a soft melody sighed through the speakers.

Caught in the center of the dance floor, Austin extended his hand once more to Tess, and she took it. She should have declined, gone in search of one of her aunts, or offered to help refill drinks or something. She most definitely did not plan to be slow dancing to any romantic songs this evening. But the way he led her in a gentle sway, one hand wrapped around hers and the other barely touching her waist, melted her doubts like the sea mist.

He seemed just as at home on a dance floor as he did hiking through the woods. The dirt floor was his stage, and the wind through the treetops his melody. Whether it was in a cathedral of dappled greens and sunlight or beneath a sky of twinkle lights in a converted barn, she and Austin had been silently dancing the same two-step all summer. Only now, she could finally hear the music.

"What's that look for?" Austin's warm breath tickled her neck, drawing her back to the dance floor.

She looked up, surprised by their closeness when she had to tilt her head back to meet his eyes. "What look?"

The slight pressure of his hand on her waist propelled her into a spin until they faced each other once again. The dim lighting shadowed his face, but not enough to cover his smile.

"You get this little crinkle between your eyebrows when you're deep in thought. Like you're trying to figure out the square root of pi or something."

Tracing a finger through the air, he brushed it against her forehead, and she felt the muscles there relax. Austin had a way of understanding people before they even said a word.

She studied the curl of dark hair above his right ear, unsure if she could trust her face not to show her every thought. "I'm still trying to piece you together."

"And what have you come up with?"

A simple enough question. If only she knew the answer.

Too soon, the music ended. Not wanting the moment to end, Tess waited for the next song to begin. She could continue this dance all evening, and, judging by Austin's hand still entwined with hers, he felt the same way.

Maybe she did know him, after all.

She was about to say as much when a deep voice popped their personal bubble of two.

"Mind if I cut in?" It was more a request than a question, like a bucket of ice water down her spine.

The slicked back hair and perfectly tailored navy suit immediately set him apart as one of Ben's groomsmen. She stifled a cough from his overpowering cologne and bristled at the abrupt interruption. Jonah *had* to take this exact moment to butt in. Not that she'd have welcomed his company any other time that evening. All weekend, she'd done her best to avoid any unwanted attention from Ben's old college buddies, but apparently Jonah hadn't taken the hint. They weren't all bad, but she couldn't stand another minute listening to them behave like they were still living in a fraternity.

Before she could voice her protest, Austin took a step back, the steadying warmth of his hand quickly vanishing from her side. Without a word, he ducked his head as if passing her off to her new partner.

Mouth agape, Tess watched as he disappeared into the crowd as another upbeat country tune came on. A wall of dark blue blocked her sight, and she looked up as Jonah cleared his throat.

"I think this is where we're supposed to start dancing." He flashed what was surely meant to be a disarming smile.

Around them, couples two-stepped to the familiar tune, carefree and without the weight of decisions looming over their heads.

How had this evening shifted so quickly?

Tess weighed her options. She could be rude and leave this man to run after Austin. That would involve her cutting through the crowds and drawing unwanted attention to herself. And who knew how he'd respond to such a move? Or she could choose the more reasonable option, finish this last dance, and give her emotions time to settle instead of making a fool of herself.

A couple bumped into Tess from behind, knocking her straight into the man's waiting arms. *So much for that decision.*

He drew her closer to speak over the loud music. "Did you say something?"

Great. One of these days, she'd have to learn to keep her thoughts to herself.

Shaking her head, she forced a smile. "I was thinking, if we stand here any longer, we might have another collision."

Taking that as an invitation, his hand tightened around hers. Without pause, he swept her into a series of steps and spins, and she tried to forget her disappointment for the next three-and-a-half minutes.

CHAPTER

Twenty-Two

HE SHOULDN'T HAVE walked off the dance floor like that. A few minutes ago, Austin had been holding Tess in his arms, her delicate hand fitting perfectly in his as they swayed to the music. Every second felt right, as if God were looking down on two halves of the same whole. And that's when the questions began to creep in. The fear of letting down another person he cared about. One day, he would. Judging by his track record, it was inevitable.

There was also the nagging fear that told him a workplace relationship could never work. His sister was living proof of that, and the last thing he wanted to do was cause Tess more pain.

After all she'd been through, she deserved so much more.

The moment Jonah interrupted them, Austin had made for the far end of the room to put some distance between his desires and his doubts. He couldn't think straight when she looked at him with those hazel eyes. The way they sparkled when he spun her beneath the chandelier and she tipped her head back with a laugh like liquid silver.

The song had since ended, and he'd lost sight of her retreat from the dance floor.

Austin pressed his palms against his eyes, but Tess's rosy cheeks and look of confusion played across the backs of his eyelids. He should have stayed. Ever since she'd set foot on his property with those purple sneakers of hers and her unbridled energy, he'd felt something between them. Only then, he hadn't realized what that was.

Spotting Caden by the soundboard, Austin pushed away from the far wall and wove his way through the throngs of people. He tried his best to avoid the twirling bodies around them and sidestepped a group of women to greet his friend.

Caden set aside the headphones and slapped him on the back in a brotherly hug. "What do you think of the music? Too much country or old-timey stuff? I suggested a little more EDM and a little less line dancing, but you know how brides can be."

He cast Austin a funny look, but his smile was unmistakable. Having already preset the songs for the evening, Caden's sole job was to make sure the music continued to play. Not too demanding a task when all it meant was hitting start on the playlist and letting it run.

Austin shook his head and had to raise his voice to be heard over the booming speakers behind them. "People seem to be enjoying it."

A loud cheer went up from the group as they started in on a new line dance. Angling his body away from the crowd and noise, he tried again. "Have you seen Tess? Beth thought she saw her go outside, but I couldn't find her."

Caden finished fiddling with the sound controls and turned a slow smile his way. "Keeping tabs on my sister, are you?"

Austin flicked a glance toward the open patio doors, instantly regretting his decision to come over. The last thing he needed was a ribbing from Caden. "I thought I saw her favoring her ankle, and I wanted to make sure she was okay."

Caden gave him a look that said he didn't believe him. Upon hearing his own excuse, he wouldn't have believed it either. "You don't have me fooled for one second. I saw the way you two were dancing." Caden backed away from the table, pretending to dance with an invisible partner. A few guests sent him odd looks, but he didn't seem to notice. Instead, he hammed it up with a dramatic sway of his arms and a final dip.

Austin thumped Caden on the shoulder, embarrassed enough for the both of them. "Okay, okay. I get it. You can stop now."

With a final bow, Caden stood, a wide grin plastered across his face. "Come on. How about you and I grab some drinks?"

Leaving the laptop to manage the music, Caden stepped to the fringes of the room. Sure he was in for a lecture or another round of teasing, Austin followed until they were behind the line of fire from the blaring speaker. Rarely did he ever give Caden room to razz him. That shoe was usually perfectly at home on the other foot.

At the back of the room, they stopped beneath a garland of ivy and twinkle lights where, a few hours ago, they had helped unload the boxes of mismatched glassware.

Caden reached for the nearest glasses. Ice cubes clinked against the punch bowl as he filled their cups. "Don't worry, I won't go all overprotective brother on you or anything. I think it's great that she's finally happy. She deserves it."

Caden poured out another lemonade and offered it to Austin, who gladly accepted. Condensation slipped down the outside of the cold glass.

Austin stared at the antique crystal as if it had all the answers. "You think so?"

"Yeah, man. I mean, you're no Justin Timberlake or anything..."

"Gee, thanks. Glad I have you around to keep my pride in check." He took a sip of the tart liquid and relaxed under their light banter.

"What are friends for?" Caden laughed and popped him with a light fist to the arm, sloshing a bit of Austin's lemonade onto the floor. "But seriously, Austin, you're a good guy. My sister could do a lot worse than you."

It felt odd discussing this here, especially when he hadn't so much as spoken a word to anyone else about it. He'd always thought of Caden as family, in a broad sense of the word, but this... This was different. "I enjoy having her around. We all do.

Trudy and she have become best friends, and even Josh has opened up a ton with her there."

"Not exactly what I was referring to." Caden waved at a group of girls walking by and turned his charming smile back toward Austin. "Can I give you one word of advice, though?"

"Sure. Anything."

Sobering, Cade swirled the drink in his hand before he spoke. "Just be honest with her, and be patient. She may act tough, but she's more sensitive than she looks. She doesn't need another person leading her on."

A barb against her old coach, but the warning brought Austin's own fears to the surface once more. Caden knew enough of Austin's family history to know he'd do anything to protect those he cared about, but even he didn't know the complete story of him, Meghan, and Josh.

Shaking his head, Caden downed the rest of the drink in one swig and placed the glass on a nearby table, as if doling out relationship advice was a regular occurrence. "Look, we've been friends for a while, man, and I know you'd never intentionally do anything to hurt someone. But Tess? Let's just say she has a history of people letting her down."

Something akin to regret flickered behind Caden's eyes, and the mask went back up. "So, are you two picking out china patterns yet, or what?"

"How about I start by asking her out on an actual date?" And apologize for walking away earlier. Both things required him finding Tess and talking with her.

"Well, you better hurry before another groomsman swoops her up." Caden plucked the half-empty cup from Austin's hand and downed the rest of his drink. When Austin tried to stop him, he grinned. "You're welcome. Now you're free to go after her."

Austin was about to give him a hard time when a flash of yellow caught his attention.

Caden clapped him with a solid slap on the back. "Good luck, man." He traipsed back toward the soundboard, leaving Austin to go in search of a certain woman in a yellow dress.

A crisp evening breeze rustled through the cottonwoods, their earthy aroma spicing the air like a cherished memory. String lights gently bobbed over the patio as the branches swayed overhead. Tess stood there looking out across the lake, music filtering through the open doors into the night air.

With a sigh, she leaned against the cool railing and fiddled with the clasp of her bracelet. For the wedding, she'd swapped her watch for the delicate silver chain, and her wrist had never felt more free.

Mindlessly, she stared across the lake. Even in the evening light, she could still make out the faint shadows of the mountains, dotted with flecks of late summer snow. The gentle lapping of water was accompanied by chirps and clicks of crickets and cicadas nearby, forming their own mountain lullaby that instantly calmed the racing thoughts buzzing around inside her head.

She didn't know what to think. Her heart was still thrumming from her and Austin's dance. She hadn't felt so alive since... She frowned. The energy of that race was seared into her memory, but even that couldn't compare to the rush she'd felt when Austin swept her into his arms and carried her across the dance floor. It was reckless, foolish even, but, oh, how her heart had soared for those fleeting moments with his hand at her waist and his breath caressing her skin.

Not even a sore ankle could have dampened her spirits. But Jonah's interruption had done a good enough job by itself.

She looked out over the dark waters, and a whisper of caution blew through the trees. Out here, alone, she could breathe. A few more minutes, and she would return to the group inside, but for now she could let her thoughts run wild.

Those last few minutes played in her head like an instant-replay after a race. She saw her fingers cradled in Austin's, the brush of her yellow skirt against his shoes, the way they'd practically floated across the floor. She could even feel the warmth of his breath against her skin in the wake of the evening breeze.

"Pull yourself together, Tess."

She turned halfway toward the patio door and sighed. Every time she put herself out there, she seemed destined to fail. All her life, she'd shoved aside her insecurities, forcing them deep beneath the surface in hopes of preserving herself. Sure, she lived a life full of risk, but the body was far easier to mend than the spirit.

Run, and you might fall...

She'd already done that, even had the scars to prove it. And despite her complaints, she knew she'd survive. So why was she so afraid to try again?

Walk by faith, not by sight.

The heavenly words seemed to whisper straight to her soul.

She looked out over the calm waters, remembering what it felt like to place her trust in the One who watched over her every step. And when she fell, He would be right there beside her, kneeling in the dirt to help her back up again.

Music spilled through the patio doors, growing louder as the dancing portion of the evening cranked into second gear. Turning her back to the water, Tess looked on from afar. How freeing would it be to leave her fears behind and learn to walk by faith?

Dancers twirled beneath a glowing canopy. An image of Austin, Trudy, and Josh popped into her head, and this time she didn't push it away.

Was that where God was leading her? The idea thrilled and terrified her all at once. How different her own plans would have been for this summer, but none of them would have led her to such a special group of people.

"I don't know where the road is going, Lord. But I'm trusting You to lead me every step of the way. Help me lay down my fears and listen to Your guidance, for once in my life."

The cottonwoods rustled overhead, and a breeze as fresh as a mountain stream rushed over her skin. The sweet-scented air filled her up, and with one invigorating breath, she felt as if she were flying. The sensation was so strong, she could have sworn she'd been swept up in the arms of the Creator Himself, if her feet weren't still firmly planted on the wooden deck beside the water.

With a lightness she hadn't felt since she was a kid, Tess pushed away from the splintered railing and stepped through the open door.

CHAPTER

Twenty-Three

IN A SHOWER of leaf confetti, Tess waved as Abigail and Ben drove away, the clanking of tin cans against the gravel like a final round of applause. By this time tomorrow, they'd be on a plane headed for Cancún, and she couldn't be happier for them and their new life together.

A solid shoulder bumped against hers. Caden stood beside her. Somewhere between the ceremony and cake cutting, he'd lost his tie, and his shirt hung loose and untucked at the waist. She was surprised he hadn't changed into jeans and a T-shirt by now, but maybe her baby brother was starting to grow up.

"Just wait 'til they see their luggage. I made sure to wrap it in as much plastic wrap as I could find in Aunt Josie's kitchen."

Or maybe he still had a little way to go.

"You realize you were only supposed to decorate the car, *not* the contents, right?" She could imagine the couple's surprise and horror when they went to unload their bags at the airport.

"Where's the fun in that?" He poked her in the ribcage like he was still ten.

She swatted at his hand. "One of these days, you're gonna grow up and find someone that will change your tune. Mind you, she'll have to be the most patient woman alive. If she doesn't go running for the hills first."

Stepping out of reach, Tess pulled up the closest chair and worked to unfasten the fabric bow from its back.

"I can be mature. Just say the word." He swooped in and grabbed the next bow, mangling the edges as he forced the wild tulle into submission.

Tess raised an eyebrow at the crumpled mess on the table. Caden, mature? She'd believe it when she saw it.

Footsteps echoed over the hardwood floor, and Austin joined them. "I don't know about you, but the adults here are going to help clean up." He aimed the teasing comment toward Caden, all the while seeming to gauge Tess with caution from behind those hooded eyes.

"Who says I can't talk and clean at the same time?" Caden threw them a devilish grin and swept the nearest two chairs into his arms, bows and all. "See? At this rate, I'll be finished with my side of the room before you can say, 'Flibbertigibbet.'"

"Flibbertigibbet," Tess and Austin said in unison.

Caden tossed back a laugh as he added a third chair to his stack. "Okay, so maybe not *that* fast. But nice timing. Have fun, you two." And with a wink, he was gone.

The minute Tess was alone with Austin, her doubts rushed in with abandon. It was one thing to trust God on quiet shores, but standing on the doorstep, she found it immeasurably more difficult to convince her foot to take that next step.

"Austin, there's something I—

"I'm sorry about earlier—"

They spoke at the same time, and their shared awkwardness set her more at ease.

"Sorry, you go first," Austin said.

"No, you."

He rubbed a hand across the back of his neck and looked at the floor. "I'm sorry I walked away after our dance. I thought, when Jonah cut in . . . maybe I'd been overstepping."

"No, not at all." She worked to school the flutter in her stomach. "I mean, you don't need to apologize."

"Yes, I do. The last thing I want to do is make you feel uncomfortable."

The sincerity in his voice was obvious, and Tess believed every word. She folded the bow in her hands with care and released a slow breath. "That text I got earlier, the one in the car? That was Ryan."

Austin took the chair in front of her and stacked it with the others. "Ryan, as in your old coach?"

She nodded. It might be a horrible idea to be talking about this here, with Austin, at a wedding no less. Letting him into her struggles could very well scare him off for good, if she hadn't done so already, but this time, she was finally ready to step out in faith.

"It's taken me a long time, far longer than was probably healthy, but I realized I was done letting him control my life. Done letting my anger and fear get the better of me."

Lowering the swath of fabric in her hands, she took a step toward the open patio doors. Austin followed her until they were standing side-by-side at the railing. This wasn't a moment to be shared with a roomful of people. In fact, there was only one person on her mind at the moment, and he'd gone surprisingly quiet.

She reached for the forgotten bouquet at her feet and fiddled with the yellow ribbon as she worked up the courage. Her fingers stilled over the sunflower-shaped pin. "You asked me once what happened, and the simple truth is, I trusted someone, and they let me down." She could talk all day about the hours of close training, Ryan's broken promises, how their relationship had bordered on something more … But when she boiled it down, all that mattered was she'd given her heart to someone who hadn't deserved it.

Tess waited as Austin leaned against the railing and peered at the stars that winked overhead. Only the rustling of the wind through the nearby trees interrupted the silence before he finally spoke.

"I know what it's like."

"What, having your coach drop you from his contract?" She tried for a joke, but her smile failed to reach her eyes.

His eyes didn't waver from the dark waters swirling beneath them. "To feel like your entire world has been turned upside down."

The mountain's nightly serenade filled the void. Tess followed Austin's lead and studied the soft reflections on the water.

"You know none of it was your fault." She broke the quiet but kept her gaze on the lakeshore. "I'm sure Meghan would tell you the same thing." She'd known too many people who played the blame game, and she couldn't stand to see it eat away at Austin as well.

Austin's sigh felt loud in the night air. "I know. But I can't help but wonder what would have happened if I'd stepped in sooner, spoken up about Brian before things went too far. Before he broke her heart and left her to raise their child on her own."

Tess joined him against the railing and bumped her shoulder against his. "But then she wouldn't have Josh. And I, for one, think he's a pretty great kid."

Austin rubbed a hand across the back of his neck and nodded.

Tess studied the man beside her, the way he carried the weight of an entire mountain on his shoulders without complaint. "I see a lot of you in Josh. Always looking out for others, not afraid to get his hands dirty... A little too charming for his own good." She laughed, and the last trace of worry faded from his face. "That kid's got a pretty great uncle to look up to. And I'm sure his mom agrees. All we have to do is walk by faith."

Austin sent her a curious look before a slow smile pulled at his lips. "There was something else I wanted to talk with you about." His hand brushed against hers in the dark. It was so soft, but the action resounded inside her like someone knocking against the door to her heart.

"And what might that be?" Despite her increased heart rate, she held her ground and plucked once more at the ends of the bouquet.

"I wanted to thank you. Not only for bringing me here, but for coming to the camp in the first place." He raised a hand to stop her protests. "I know I've said this before, but I'm forever grateful God brought you to us. To me."

"You are?" Hope tinged her voice, spurring him onward.

The sounds of laughter and conversation filled the intimate outdoor setting, and something like a mountain shifted inside him. Aside from being welcomed into this group of family and friends, it was the woman beside him who made this moment complete. There was a rightness to it he couldn't place. He couldn't explain it even if he tried, but it didn't make the truth of the matter any less real.

"Truly."

Tess dipped her head as if unwilling to trust the sincerity of his words. Her silver bracelet glinted in the dim lamplight as she distractedly toyed with the ribbon on her bridal bouquet until the end began to unravel. She tipped her nose toward the bundle of sunflowers and daisies. "Your aunt did a wonderful job with the flower arrangements."

"She always does." Austin picked a sprig of blue delphinium from the bouquet. "May I?" Careful of the long stem, he tucked the flower behind her ear and marveled at the way it brought to life the flecks of green in her hazel eyes. Warning bells went off somewhere in the back of his mind, but he shoved them down. This wasn't like his sister and Brian. That relationship may have ended in disaster, but Austin found he'd do anything to make things work with Tess. He didn't know how yet, but he'd find a way.

His fingers brushed a loose curl from her face and lingered against the warm skin of her temple. "Beautiful." It came out so quiet, he hardly heard himself say it. But the minute the word escaped his lips, Tess's eyes grew wide in surprise.

This was uncharted territory. No guides, no compass, only the Holy prompting that urged him onward.

Heart pounding, Austin waited for Tess to pull away, hoping and praying that she wouldn't. He moved in closer, gauging her every response as she held his gaze. His hand dropped to her shoulder, and with a gentle tug, he pulled her in to lay a feather-light kiss on her forehead. She closed her eyes, and he placed another on her nose.

Smiling, she peered at him through long lashes. His gaze dropped to her lips, the desire to pull her close fighting against his better judgment.

He meant to drop a single chaste kiss to her lips, but the minute he pulled back, she drew him closer. He was falling. Soaring. All other noise faded, save for the rustle of her skirt and the pounding of his heartbeat. He wanted to tell her how much she meant to him, how beautiful and special she truly was. How he'd do anything not to let her down.

Dropping the bouquet, she grabbed onto his collar and deepened the kiss.

Footsteps echoed across the wooden planks, and someone cleared his throat behind them.

Tess was the first to pull away, and she cast a sheepish smile toward her cousin. Micah stood in the doorway, hands in pockets, and seemed quite intent on staring beyond them toward the trees. He rocked on the heels of his cowboy boots and raised an eyebrow at the bouquet lying on the ground.

"Um, Aunt Josie was asking for you. Something about the centerpieces?"

"Did she, now?" There was no mistaking the giggle that escaped Tess's lips as she scooped up the fallen flowers. "Did she also send you out here to check up on us?"

A few inches taller than Austin, Micah could probably wrangle a bull, but right now he looked about as comfortable as a bear caught in a thornbush. Clearing his throat once more, he finally looked up from his perusal of the pine slats. "I'm only the messenger."

Tess seemed to be enjoying his discomfort. She slid Austin another glance that said she fully intended to continue their conversation, then looked back at her cousin. "I'll bet you're regretting that decision right about now. You can go back inside, though. We'll be right behind you."

"You have no idea," Micah muttered under his breath as he clomped back inside, leaving the two of them to find their way after him.

Once they were alone, Austin dipped his head and whispered, "Poor guy."

Tess shrugged. "He'll get over it. Besides, he needs to learn there's more to life than ranching and being so serious all the time."

"Such as..."

"I can think of a few things."

Austin couldn't help but smile at her infectious energy. And he quite agreed with the glimmer in her eyes.

"What do you say? Ready to face the music?" She reached for his hand, entwining her fingers with his.

Laying one last kiss against her forehead, he breathed in her lemony shampoo and smiled. "After you."

CHAPTER

Twenty-Four

COULD YOU HAND me another nail?" Austin's deep voice interrupted Tess's wandering thoughts.

She craned her neck and shielded her eyes from the blinding sunlight above her. He stood on the second-to-top rung of the ladder, the fresh panel of metal flashing in his hands glinting down at her. On tiptoes, she passed off the box of nails and watched him secure what she hoped was the last of their roof repairs for the day.

The past week had passed in a blur. Despite Tess's greatest intentions, she and Austin had hardly been able to find a moment's quiet. If it wasn't a camp-related emergency or making daily trips to town, it was dealing with parents or sorting out the next activity to keep the group of middle-school campers entertained.

On top of it all, one of the cabins chose that Tuesday to spring a leak. A real gusher, as Josh called it. After an hour of rearranging the room assignments, they finally had all the kids squared away in dry bunks. Genevieve and Skye were the first to volunteer to head into town for supplies, leaving Tess and Austin elbow-deep in wet rags dealing with the mess.

Maybe not one of the most romantic of situations, but as long as Tess got to spend her days working beside Austin, she couldn't have been happier.

"I distinctly remember you working on this roof the day I arrived." She chuckled at the memory. If she'd known how things would change in only a few months, she might have approached that first day with a little less dread.

"Right. Remind me, was that before or after you nearly hopped back in your car for a speedy escape?" He passed her the hammer and extra nails before climbing down the ladder.

Tess opened and closed her mouth. He wasn't wrong. "I think sensible caution is the word you're looking for."

"Is that what you call it?"

She didn't miss the warmth in his smile. Not even a pair of soggy shoes from traipsing through the floodway could dampen her happiness in this moment. She'd be wise not to rush into another relationship, but then again, she wouldn't feel so alive.

"What's got you smiling?" Austin bent to grab the ladder and laid it beside the other tools on the grass.

Tess took her time wrestling the plastic tarp as Austin gathered the last of the supplies. "I was thinking. Now that you've fixed the roof, why don't we take a break? Josh and the others have things under control for now. I'm sure they wouldn't miss us for another hour or so." She'd been eyeing the canoes all week, and now seemed the perfect opportunity to take one out.

The plastic sheet billowed in the breeze, and he caught the opposite corner before it could take flight. Tarp raised, he walked toward her, and their hands met over the folded drop cloth. "What did you have in mind?"

She took his end, and they changed sides in their evolving dance of fabric and folds. Ballgowns and spotlights were one thing. They lasted an evening and were gone the next day. But this . . . this was a dance she could imagine herself doing the rest of her life.

"I was thinking—"

A herd of tiny footsteps crunched up the drive. Tess turned, and a small troupe of third-graders marched past with Josh, Kyle, and Harper at the rear. Startled by their noisy steps, a blue jay darted from its perch, and every pencil scribbled to cross off the next line of their nature scavenger hunt.

"I saw it first."

"Nuh, uh."

"Did too."

Two boys bickered back and forth until one of them spotted Austin and Tess by the cabin.

"Mr. Wright!" the younger of the two shouted. With the paper clutched in his hand, he waved it over his head like a white flag. "Josh has been teaching us bird calls, but he said you're the expert."

"Did he, now?" Austin peered at his nephew, who sent him an apologetic smile.

"You're the one who taught me. I figured I'd give credit where credit was due."

"How thoughtful." He uncrossed his arms and turned to face the kids. "Well, every good birdwatcher needs to know this one." Austin cupped his hands and blew through his knuckles to make a two-toned whistle.

"Whoa, I wanna try." The boys tried to mimic him and made what sounded like a chorus of spitting sounds. One of them frowned at his hands in disappointment before his head snapped back up. "How did you do that?"

"Can you show us?"

"Please?"

The entire group gave a unanimous cheer, Josh and the other leaders included.

Austin slid Tess an apologetic look and chuckled. "Looks like I've been summoned. Another time, perhaps?"

"I'll be here."

Austin smiled as Josh flopped onto the couch like a bag of rocks. The nature walk had turned into more of a wilderness adventure, with the kids chasing down every bird and squirrel they spotted off the trail. It had taken all four of them to keep track of the dozen easily distracted kids. If it hadn't been for Austin's promises of bird calls and whistles, they very well might have wandered into the forest and never looked back.

"Thank goodness you stepped in when you did. If I had to come up with one more bird call…"

"You'd have what?" Austin smiled down at his nephew's sprawled limbs and exaggerated grimace. "From the look of things, you were doing great."

"If by great you mean ready to throw those two in the lake if they didn't stop talking, then sure." He plopped another candy in his mouth and crossed his feet over the armrest.

"Feet off the furniture." Austin pinched his nose as if Josh's feet stunk.

Smiling, Josh swung his legs over the couch cushion, and they landed on the hardwood with a thud. "I'm just saying. I don't know how you put up with it. It's like you've got this superhuman patience or something."

"Well," Austin slid off one of his boots and set it by the door, "I guess I learned it from being around you for so long."

Josh grabbed a pillow and aimed it at Austin's head. "You're not such a catch yourself."

Austin took the pillow to the face and threw it back at him.

With one hand, he caught the pillow, and a Cheshire grin spread across his face. "Although it appears Tess thinks otherwise."

Austin paused halfway through unlacing his other shoe. "How did you—?"

"What? You didn't think you could really keep that a secret, did you? I mean, for one, have you met Trudy? And secondly, I'd have to be blind not to notice the way you're always making googly eyes at each other."

Methodically, Austin loosened his shoelaces while he figured out his reply. If only the two of them could have had a little longer to figure out what was going on between them before the entire world knew. Especially Josh. He'd already upended the boy's world by bringing him out here for the summer. The last thing he wanted was to throw him another curveball.

He dropped his muddy boot beside the other and proceeded with caution. "So, what do you think? Is that something you would be okay with?" This was unfamiliar territory for all of them. And while it wasn't necessary, Austin wanted the approval from his nephew, all the same.

Josh stretched his lanky limbs and shrugged. "I like Tess. She's cool. Maybe if you spend enough time together, she'll rub off on you."

His teasing tone was enough to put Austin at ease. "Are you saying I'm *not* cool?" He reached down to ruffle the boy's hair before he could pull away.

"Hey, not cool." Josh ducked and flapped his hands like a bird protecting its nest. "Case in point."

Satisfied, Austin lowered his attack and chuckled. "You know, I've got an idea, but I'll need your help. What do you say? Interested?"

Josh finished fixing his hair and sent him a cautious glance.

"As long as it doesn't involve more bird calls, I'm in."

Sunday morning, Austin led the group down the winding path away from The Lodge until the forest opened up to a small clearing. Even at this early hour, the sun was already high overhead, bathing the trees and grasses in a warm glow.

Guitar case slung across his back, he stepped into the sunlit sanctuary and knelt at the base of a large evergreen, where Josh soon joined him. After talking over the idea, they'd found an old hand drum buried in the storage closet, and with a little practice, were all set.

Tess looked at him quizzically as he drew a small stack of papers from the front zippered pocket of his case and handed them to her. One look at the first page, and her eyes widened. "Church music?"

He slid the woven strap over his shoulder and nodded. "You seem surprised."

Ever since she and Trudy had stumbled upon him and his music a month ago, he'd felt drawn to follow in his grandfather's footsteps and resurrect this humble tradition. Trudy's words had reignited in him something he thought he'd lost, the reminder that he had more to give than his work and his worries.

Tess thumbed through the pages, and her face seemed to relax at the titles of the old hymns. Reaching the last page, she flipped back to the front and peered up from the stack of papers. "Not at all. I think this is a wonderful idea."

Her approval shouldn't have meant so much, but he found himself smiling up at her from the dirt. "Good, because I was hoping you'd agree to help lead."

"Me?" Her voice squeaked. A single page slipped from her grasp before she regained her composure. "In case you've forgotten, I'm not a musician."

"Don't have to be. I've heard you sing to yourself, remember?" He gave her a playful nudge. "You're far more talented than you give yourself credit for."

That familiar crease formed between her eyebrows while she studied the music once more. Maybe it was too much to ask. He had, after all, sprung his impromptu idea on her with zero notice. But if she said yes . . .

After a few drawn out moments, her forehead finally relaxed. She nodded once. Twice. "Okay. Lead the way." When she looked at him with that smile of hers, it was as if everything clicked into place.

"I was hoping you'd say that."

Trudy clapped from the other side of the clearing to get the group's attention, and all heads turned her way. Taking her cue, Tess moved toward the gathering circle and distributed the music between the groggy staffers. Five minutes later, and a few dozen pages of paper lighter, she reclaimed her position beside Austin and nodded that everyone was ready.

Head bowed, he led them in a simple prayer before they started in on the first song. With a few strums across the acrylic strings, Austin looked toward Tess, who smiled her encouragement. He took a deep breath and exhaled the first few lines of "How Great Thou Art."

He led the group in worship for an hour, and a sense of peace seemed to settle deeper within his soul with every song. Austin poured his heart into the music and let it move him as surely as the wind moved through the trees.

God was in this place, their own chapel of the woods. In the mountain soil and rough-hewn cliffs. Even the light breeze seemed to come alive with something other than wind and air. Despite all his misgivings the past year, Austin could see where the Lord's hand had been moving. Shaping. Directing him to this moment. This life. These people. And God willing . . . to Tess.

It was more than he'd ever hoped to ask for and far more than he deserved.

They finished the last song, and Trudy closed them out with a few lines of scripture. The pages of her Bible crinkled beneath her fingertips as she read. "One thing I do: Forgetting what is behind and straining toward what is ahead, I press on toward the goal to win the prize for which God has called me heavenward in Christ Jesus."

Tess went still beside him, soaking in the message like someone hearing the words for the first time. Never had he seen her so transfixed. So moved. So . . . at peace.

Her toes traced in a slow, mindless arc through the dirt as she listened. Back and forth. Back and forth.

Was she thinking about her career? Her life back home? It wouldn't be a far leap to get there from the race-themed phrasing of the passage, nor could he blame her if she had. Tess Prescott knew what it meant to press on toward a goal, probably more so than most people there. An athlete trained for years to get to that level. Did she regret her choice to come here when she could have easily stayed in Denver and worked through her rehabilitation there?

He hated the idea that it had taken her getting injured for her to come here in the first place, but he couldn't imagine what this summer would have been like without her.

If only he knew what thoughts were rolling around behind those eyes of hers.

Trudy closed the leather-bound Bible on her lap and drew Austin's attention once more as her voice dipped in prayer. "Father, God. How great You are. We thank You for the blessing to gather here together on this beautiful morning and sing Your praises, and for all You are doing in the lives of the campers who come through our doors and the staff You've equipped to be here. I pray we will hold on to the promise of Your truth and persevere through this season You've placed before us. For You have not given us a spirit of fear but of love. Let us love one another as You'd have us and turn our hearts to Your will. And all God's people said, amen."

"Amen."

The murmured chorus echoed around the circle. Lifting his head, Austin caught Tess watching him with a curious expression.

"What? Do I have dirt on my nose?" He scrunched his face, and her mouth tipped in a smile.

"Sorry. Lost in thought, I guess." Straightening her spine, she readjusted her light sweater and rose as the others gathered up their belongings. She reached for her packet of music and all but spun toward Kyle, Harper, and Josh.

Austin held back a chuckle and took his time placing his guitar in its case, watching from the corner of his eye while Tess flitted around the group to collect the remaining sheet music. Was there a slight flush to her cheeks, or had the sun tinged them pink through the loose canopy?

Whatever it was, it suited her.

There was a faint hammering of a woodpecker in the distance that faded with the wind through the overhead branches. Austin checked his watch and noted the time. Less than an hour before the next campers were set to arrive. Zipping the case shut, he slung it across his back and hurried to catch up with Josh and Tess as they made their way up the winding trail with the others toward The Lodge.

By the time the group had made the hike back and had lunch, the first of the campers began to arrive. One look out the windows revealed a few cars already dotting the circle drive, kids and parents mingling on the freshly cut lawn, laughing and exchanging hugs.

Austin watched from inside and smiled at the kids' excitement, how their eyes went wide at the tall trees and open field. It was moments like this that made it all worth it. All the hard work and questions and uncertainty he'd faced to get here.

He may have questioned God's direction more than once along the way, but that was squarely in the past.

Taking the steps two at a time, Austin swiped the sign-in form from the patio railing and set off to welcome the newcomers. After last week, he was glad to host a smaller group this time. Fifteen kids were much more manageable than thirty, even with the parents and chaperones they sometimes brought with them.

Halfway across the gravel, he stopped as a dark green SUV pulled up the drive and parked a few spaces away from the other vehicles. A man in his late thirties emerged from the car, his light brown hair brushed back as if he'd come straight from the city.

There was something familiar in his gait that had Austin slowing in his steps. Brown hair, commanding strides ... the man turned to open the side door, and recognition slammed against Austin's chest.

CHAPTER

Twenty-Five

THE AIR LEFT Austin's lungs. This couldn't be happening. Not here. Not after all these years. He nearly dropped the clipboard as his past collided with the present.

Brian Hughes.

For a moment, Austin's mind went blank. All the words he'd practiced for this moment vanished as his greatest fears came to the surface. The man who'd ruined his sister's life fifteen years ago, who'd abandoned her and Josh without a backward glance . . . now he was here, standing a few yards from his doorstep, holding the power to shatter the safety of this peaceful mountain with a single word.

A girl with matching brown hair leapt from the back seat with a teddy bear clutched in her arms. She couldn't have been more than seven. In one movement, the man swooped her into his arms, her girlish giggles sprinkling over the lawn. She squealed with joy as he swung her in a circle before setting her gently back onto the grass.

What was the man doing here? Austin had triple checked all the names on the check-in form, and none of them included the last name Hughes.

He looked around for Josh, not sure what to do. He hadn't been around to protect his sister before, but he could still shield his nephew from the ugly truth. The need to confront the man or run to find Josh warred inside him while Brian traipsed across the property. The sound of his heartbeat thudding in his ears grew more rampant, and he ground his teeth to will it back into submission.

Where had Brian been to twirl Josh when he was that little girl's age? And what about all the long nights when he had been sick with croup as a baby? All the birthday parties. The soccer games. A father should be there for his child, no matter what. Whether or not he thought he was ready.

God. What should I do?

The plastic clipboard bit into Austin's palms, and he slowly unclenched his fists from the crumpled pages. A cool touch brushed against his arm, and he snapped his head up to see Tess standing beside him.

"Are you okay?" Concern edged her voice. Gone was the wistful expression he'd seen there this morning, replaced by a tight-lipped frown. If only he could turn back the clock, go back to their moment beneath the trees where the world felt right and whole.

Austin tried to clear the tightness from his throat and failed. After all Tess had gone through, she didn't deserve to be pulled into his mess too. At least not until he had it firmly under control. But in order to do that, he needed space to think. And fast.

"Can you handle the check-ins?" He'd apologize later, but he couldn't stand to spend another second out here with that man around.

"Of course. If that's what you need." Her eyebrows drew together, but she didn't question him further.

He nodded. "Thank you. I'll, uh ... go check in with Trudy and see if she needs any help in the kitchen."

Anywhere that wasn't here. He didn't trust himself to say more than a few words without his emotions taking over. A healthy distance was his best option right now. At least until he'd had time to process his own thoughts.

With a fleeting glance, he handed the clipboard and sign-in sheet to a confused Tess and made a beeline back up the steps. He didn't dare look back. Not to see Brian, or the little girl who'd been enough for him to settle down and be a real father. And Tess...

He shouldn't have dumped his responsibilities on her like that, but any longer in her presence, and he feared he wouldn't have been able to keep his emotions in check.

Inside, a handful of voices mingled with clanging dishes and silverware came from the kitchen. Trudy's unmistakable southern drawl spilled through the open door, followed by Josh and Genevieve's laughter.

Some of the tension eased from Austin's shoulders at the sound. Josh was inside. Safe.

He glanced at the clock over the mantle and noted the slow tick of the second hand. As long as Josh stayed inside for the next few minutes, until all the kids were checked in and the parents had driven off, it would be okay. He could push off the inevitable for a little while longer. At least for a few more days.

Stepping back from the fireplace, Austin turned and walked with heavy footsteps down the hallway. Once inside his office, he closed his eyes and pressed his back against the rough wood. His fingers dug into the splintered pine, and he welcomed the sharp sensation.

Brian is here. God, why is he here? Of all the places for him to show up, and the one time when Meghan wasn't around to defend herself and Josh. After all he'd done, a lifetime wouldn't have been long enough to keep the man away.

Arms like lead, Austin peeled his hand from the wall and massaged the back of his neck. The taught muscles screamed their protest, and he eventually gave up.

What would Meghan say about all this, or their grandfather, for that matter? They were the gentle souls of the family. They were the ones who always saw the best in people, believed in them even when no one else could. But that had also been the problem with Brian. Meghan had trusted him with her whole heart, and he'd crushed it the first chance he got.

Austin replayed that summer in his head. Meghan's internship, her fledgling romance, her months of heartache. No matter that he'd been in high school at the time and Meghan was a year out of college. If he'd stepped in sooner, or somehow learned the man's true nature before it was too late. . . . But Tess was right. Then they wouldn't have had Josh, and he had proven to be the greatest blessing of all. No matter the kind of man Brian was, at least something good had come of the whole ordeal, despite all the pain it took to get there.

Austin stared at the ceiling, listening to the sound of laughter that trickled down the hallway. At least Josh could remain innocent in all of this. There was no reason he had to be dragged into it. Not when he was finally settling in. And especially not while Meghan was still overseas. Maybe one day, when he was older, he'd learn the truth about his father, but not now.

A heavy sigh escaped. This was a nightmare. He might have been able to run from the man today, but in less than a week, Brian would be back to pick up his daughter. And when that day came, Austin would have to be ready. Next time, he wouldn't hide. He'd face the man like he should have fifteen years ago. He'd face him and pray he didn't make a bigger mess of things in the process.

Tess waved to the last of the parents as their cars disappeared at the end of the gravel drive. When the dust cloud settled, she glanced down at the check-in sheet and scribbled a few notes beside the list of names. For her first time coordinating the student hand-offs, she thought it went rather well. Or at least as smooth as it could have gone, considering the circumstances.

If today wasn't a lesson in flexibility, she didn't know what was.

She drew a line through the first tabbed number, and a splotch of blue ink smudged across the page of names and cabin numbers. "Of all the..." She dabbed at the mess with a tissue, which smeared it further. Leave it to her to find a way to mess up the schedule in under an hour.

As always, Austin had the weekly schedule down to a tee. He'd normally handle the parents one by one while she and the other staff took turns showing the kids to their bunks. Then it was off to the first round of activities, and then dinner shortly after that . . .

She frowned at the dark blue ink staining the page. In all the months she'd been there, never once had she seen Austin hand over his responsibilities like that. Which made his sudden disappearance this afternoon all the more concerning. Normally, she would have joked that he'd seen Bigfoot hiding in the trees or something, and he would have laughed right alongside her. He surely wouldn't have disappeared into the house without a backward glance. The only other time she'd seen him that spooked was during their surprise moose encounter, but even that paled in comparison.

No. Something was wrong. And if Austin was rattled, it had to be something serious.

With the clipboard tucked under her arm, Tess glanced around the field once more before turning toward the house. Childlike voices and giggles spilled out of the open cabin doors lining the path, the excited energy mounting from one cabin to the next. A smile tugged at her mouth as she drew near the end of the row, memories of the past week flooding her mind with each step. The leaky roof. Working side-by-side with Austin. Their few stolen moments together . . .

With a fire in her step, Tess hurried up the front stoop and across the expansive patio. Last she'd seen, Austin had disappeared inside. For what, she couldn't say, but she had an idea where she might find him.

The clanging of pots and pans reverberated through the open screen door, and Tess slipped inside. She blinked, her eyes taking a minute to readjust to the harsh contrast from the high-altitude sunshine. For a moment, she was taken back to that day in San Diego. The flash of sunlight on the water, pavement under her feet. And then the falling. The pain.

Snippets of conversation and Trudy's southern lilt mingled with the clattering of dishware, and Tess continued on toward the kitchen. She had taken one step through the door when a silvery object swung dangerously close to her head. Tess ducked to avoid the cookie tray in Trudy's grasp.

"Good heavenly days." Trudy dropped the tray on the counter with a crash, and her free hand fluttered to her chest. "I didn't even see you come in."

Tess looked around the room. Dozens of cookies lined the cluttered countertop, and a giant pot of something simmered away on the stove. The smell of fresh baked bread teased her nose, competing with the scents of chocolate chip and oatmeal raisin cookies already cooling on the sheets of brown parchment paper.

"It looks like you baked enough for a small army. Didn't Austin tell you it's a smaller group this week?" The temptation to sneak one or two cookies from the kitchen crossed her mind, but she kept her hands firmly wrapped around the plastic clipboard instead.

"My motto has always been, if you bake it, there'll always be somebody to eat it. You'd be surprised how much food a bunch of second-graders can go through. Why, when Austin was their age, he could out-eat his granddaddy and me put together."

Her chuckle was soft and tinged with fond memories. Tess could very well imagine a younger version of Austin running through this house and the woods beyond. He'd no doubt have had grass stains on his knees and a smile to match the crescent moon.

"Speaking of . . . Did Austin come through here earlier?" She lowered her voice when her gaze caught Josh and Genevieve stationed at the sink.

A mountain of suds rose from the stainless-steel basin where Josh handed the dripping dishes over to Genevieve to dry. They appeared deep in conversation, miles away from the chaotic little kitchen and Tess's simmering concerns.

"Can't say as I've seen him. Have you checked outside?" Trudy edged around Tess and pried open the cupboard door behind her.

Tess stepped aside and handed Trudy the clean baking tray from the counter. "That's where I came from."

"Hm," the woman returned the tray to its rightful spot. "You know him. He probably got caught by a few parents and their questions."

Tess frowned. So Trudy knew even less than she did. The papers crinkled as she tucked them under her arm. Should she mention Austin's hasty retreat? She wasn't usually one to worry, and it could be nothing. A simple misunderstanding on her part. No need to cause Trudy any unnecessary concern as well.

"Well, if you see him, can you tell him I'm looking for him?"

A knowing glint sparkled in Trudy's eye, and Tess had half a mind to tell her the truth. As much as she wanted to see Austin for more personal reasons, what she really needed was to check in on her friend.

"Tess?" A door closed down the hall, followed by rapidly approaching footsteps. A few seconds later, Harper stepped into the kitchen, her long ponytail swinging against her back. "Tess, there you are."

Tess stilled herself at Harper's sigh of relief. A few minutes ago, the kids were still getting settled in their cabins. No way something could have gone wrong already. "Is there a problem?"

"No problems. It's just," the girl paused, her fingers toying with the ends of her hair. After another tug, she let her hands fall to her sides. "Kyle, Grayson, and I are supposed to start the kids on the ropes course in ten minutes, and we were wondering if you could give us a hand? I told Grayson you were probably busy, and I know you don't usually do this, but I can't find Austin, so..."

Tess sighed. There never was a dull moment here at the camp. That was for sure.

Trudy's bangle bracelets clinked behind Tess, and a flour-dusted hand came to rest on her shoulder. "Don't you worry, dear. I'll let Austin know you're looking for him. Now go have fun." Her tone was pure sunshine. Full of hope and reassurance.

Things Tess could really use right about now. Her conversation with Austin would have to wait. Another hour couldn't hurt, could it? Tess unclenched her fingers from the clipboard and turned again toward Harper. "I guess I have some free time."

Harper all but leapt into the air. "Thank you. You're a lifesaver. I'll go tell the others, and we can get started." In a heartbeat, she swiveled on the hardwood floor and sprinted out of the room.

For another moment, Tess remained rooted to her corner of the kitchen, torn between her duties and wanting to find Austin. The front door closed, and she watched through the window as Harper bounded down the patio steps to round up the group of kids.

"Best not keep them waitin'." Trudy hummed behind her, reaching for the next clean plate.

Josh and Genevieve continued in their task with the dishes, the three of them working at a relaxed pace to match the languid summer day. No matter the chaos going on outside, they somehow had managed to turn the kitchen into a peaceful hideaway. One Tess was sad to leave behind.

With a half-hearted smile, she waved to Trudy and the others and hurried outside, where shrieks and squeals shattered the peaceful calm.

CHAPTER

Twenty-Six

SUNDAY ROLLED INTO Monday, and Tess still had yet to find time to talk with Austin. Not that he was outright avoiding her. At least, that's what she kept telling herself.

When she finally spotted him later that evening, his mind seemed anywhere but at the camp. At dinner, he mostly kept to the sidelines while the students and staff had fun, and as soon as he finished, he slipped away with hardly a sound.

No one else seemed to notice much as they kept busy with the campers. Already, the staff was bonding with them faster than any other group of campers yet. Even Harper seemed pleased to entertain the group of girls with a few stories while they munched on Trudy's cookies.

All other worries aside, it had been a lovely evening. What would have made it even better would be if Austin had stayed. If things were back to normal, he'd have regaled the kids with a few stories of his own, and maybe with enough convincing, he would have even agreed to serenade them with a few of his grandfather's songs. Everything would be as it should, and the undefined unease would soon be forgotten.

Tess picked up her pace across the field toward the bunkhouses, where Genevieve and Josh had already set up the craft table for that afternoon. Tempera paint and brushes lay scattered across the white plastic tablecloth, ready and waiting for the kids to get started on their wooden birdhouses.

"Have I missed anything? Where's Grayson? I thought he was scheduled to help with crafts today."

Josh finished handing out the paper plates for the kids to begin and offered an extra one to Tess. "He was, but I asked if we could switch for the day. I figured I had enough of the ropes course yesterday, and he was more than excited to change with me."

Tess accepted the plate but not without looking between Josh and Genevieve. She tamped down a smile. Despite the age gap, the two had grown inseparable over the last couple of months. "You sure that's all it was?"

Josh ducked his head, like Austin did when he wanted to avoid a question, and resumed his task. "What other reason would there be?" He snatched a few bottles of glitter and sequins from the basket and pretended to be hard at work.

"Opal, why didn't you leave your bear in the cabin? You know it's gonna get dirty out here." Sarah, a little girl with pale hair, glanced at the Paddington Bear seated between her and her friend. She reached across the table for the tube of pink paint. Her arm grazed the brown fur, and it toppled toward the ground.

Before Tess could step in, Josh scooped up the bear and brushed away the dirt. The girl's eyes lit up as he handed it over, and she hugged it tightly to her chest.

"Hey, kids." Genevieve raised her voice to be heard over the excited chatter. "What do you say we get these birdhouses started? I'll bet if you ask her nicely, Tess will show us how it's done."

Soon the entire table was cheering for Tess to join them. Teddy bear still clutched in one hand, the little girl next to Josh reached over and gave a slight tug on Tess's arm.

One look at the stuffed animal, adorned in its blue duffle coat and red hat, and her heart melted.

"Do you want a paintbrush?" The girl grabbed hers and offered it to Tess, dimples sinking further into her round cheeks as she smiled.

"I'd love one. Thank you." Tess sank into the empty chair beside her.

She smiled down at Opal and played with one of the toggle buttons on the stuffed bear's jacket. "And who is this handsome fella?"

"His name's Paddington. But you can call him Paddy." Opal reached for the tube of pink paint and squirted some onto her paper plate.

Tess couldn't help but smile. Happy to spend her morning with the kids, she reached for one of the unclaimed birdhouses and got to work.

An hour passed, the kids fully engaged with the activity. Tess set down her paintbrush and, out of habit, glanced at her wrist to check the time. The sight of her bare skin reminded her once more that her watch was upstairs on her dresser. It had been over a week since she'd removed it for the wedding, and she'd been reluctant to lose the sense of freedom that had come with the unburdening of that silicone band.

She wiped the pastel stains from her hands and turned toward Josh. "I'm going to go check on Trudy and see how the snacks are coming. Do you think you can manage the group 'til I get back?"

"Sure thing. I think we can handle a little paint, right, Gen?"

"Absolutely." Her copper ringlets bounced with her nod.

With one final glance around the table, Tess rose and retraced her steps toward The Lodge, where she found Trudy busy in the kitchen.

"Anything I can help with?" Tess propped her forearms against the counter and eyed the freshly cut watermelon by her elbow.

"Can't say as there is. I'm about finished with the snacks, and the lemonade's all done." She swiped a towel over the condensation gathering on the side of the pitcher and poured a tall glass. "However, could you be a dear and take this to Austin?

I think I saw him head out back not too long ago, slaving away over some bushes."

So that's where he'd gone off to. Maybe she'd finally get a chance to talk with him, after all. Eager to find him, Tess reached for the glass and was halfway out the door when Trudy stopped her.

"Oh, and Tess," the woman's voice grew soft. "I don't pretend to know what's going on, but be patient with him. He'll open up when he's ready. Always does." She gave Tess a reassuring pat on the arm and ushered her out the door.

Austin's chest ached every time he saw the two of them together. The way the sun glinted golden brown against their identically wavy hair. How Josh looked out for the little girl whenever the other kids teased her about the stuffed bear.

Just like an older brother would.

That Josh did it all without that knowledge made Austin's pride in him swell all the more. It also tightened the knot around his middle the longer the week progressed. Sooner or later, Josh would learn the truth, but God help him, Austin prayed that day would not come within the next week.

He'd already left two voicemails for Meghan using the satellite phone, but she'd yet to return his calls. She'd mentioned something in her last email about some upcoming work in a remote village, and he really hoped that wasn't this week. If his car wasn't in the shop for some unexplained oil leak, he'd have spent the better part of the day in town trying to track her down.

He hated having to manage this situation without her. If she were here, she'd no doubt know how to handle the situation. But without a single word so far, he was on his own.

With decisive movements, Austin worked to shape the bush in front of him. Arms outstretched, he tackled the tallest bough and severed it with one clean snip. He wedged his shears against a particularly thick branch and hacked it free from the tangle of evergreen. His eyes slid shut, and he inhaled a deep breath of the sweet, woodsy scent. Another bead of sweat trickled down his temple, and he blinked away the salty sting.

Nothing like manual labor to take one's mind off things. Or at least that's what he'd hoped for when he'd ransacked the shed an hour ago for a pair of gloves and pruning shears. Anything to keep his hands, if not his mind, occupied.

A rustling noise drew his attention, and he snapped his head up to see Tess round the far corner of the building. A few strands of mahogany hair fell loose around her face as she pushed back the shrubbery, twigs snapping underfoot from the exposed ground cover.

"If it's at all possible, could you not kill all the camp's official plant?" He smiled to let her know he was teasing and resumed his task.

"What are you talking about?" Tess propped a hand against her hip and inspected one of the bright red stems. Her scrunched-up brow reminded Austin of a kid in a dusty museum. Mildly confused.

He released a dry laugh and tossed a few more branches onto the growing pile. "Where did you think the name for this place came from?"

Austin had trimmed most of them back already, but a few branches still stuck out in odd directions across the ground. The same plant flanked the entire rest of the property beneath the evergreen bushes, providing a sprawling decoration of pink-studded greenery wherever one looked.

Tess shrugged. "Figured it was historic or something. Maybe Native American?" She pointed her foot at the trailing evergreen shrub and its pink and white bell-shaped flowers. "So, what are they, then?"

Austin twirled one of the flowers between his fingers and offered it to her before returning to the bush in front of him. "*Arctostaphylos uva-ursi.*"

She frowned in confusion. "English, please?"

He had asked that same question the first day he'd stepped foot on this land, and his grandfather's voice came back to him. He pruned another branch and spoke. "In Latin, *uva* means grapes, and *ursus* is bear. Put them together, and you get bearberry, or as some people call it, kinnikinnick. Grows all over this mountain."

"And I assume bears love to eat it?" she teased.

"Exactly." He bent to pick another flower, and silence wrapped around them in an uncomfortable embrace.

Next to him, Tess shifted until her shadow fell across him.

"You've been avoiding me," she said, her tone direct and to the point. She handed him the glass, and he frowned into the lemonade.

"No, I haven't."

"Then what do you call this?" She extended her arm to motion toward the sprawling hedge wrapping the house.

"I'm working."

"I can see that." Tess grew quiet once again before her tone softened. "I know something's up. Whatever it is, you can tell me. I might not be the best at giving advice, but I've been told I'm a good listener."

Austin raised the glass to his lips, savoring the cool liquid and the few seconds it afforded him to gather his thoughts. Should he tell Tess what was going on?

One look at her friendly smile, and he knew the answer.

He blew out a heavy breath and leveled his gaze with hers. "Josh's dad was here."

Tess's eyes grew wide before her forehead dipped in confusion. "Here? You mean at the camp? I thought he walked out before Josh was born. How would he even know to come here?"

"As far as I can tell, he doesn't know."

"Then what brought him all the way out here? Are you sure it was the same guy? A person can change a lot in fifteen years."

His head felt like a two-ton boulder when he nodded. "It was Brian, alright. But he wasn't here for Josh. Get this. He's Opal's dad."

"No." Tess's mouth sagged. "So that's why you asked me to do the check-ins."

His shoulders slumped as he recalled the way he'd tucked tail and run. "I saw him standing there, after all this time, and I couldn't face him. Not yet, anyway."

He'd had fifteen years to think about what he'd say to the man, and now that he had his chance, he couldn't muster a single word. Who was he kidding? If one and a half decades wasn't enough time, five days wouldn't make much of a difference.

Tess's cool fingers brushed his calloused skin and released the pruning shears from his grasp. With a gentle tug, she pulled him toward one of the benches dotting the backyard 'til they were seated side by side. Her hand, small yet strong, found his.

"How can I help? If anything, it's clear you need someone to talk to. A friend."

Austin smiled at her kind offer and wished they could somehow escape for a while, away from all the troubles plaguing him, however much a fantasy that wish might be. "I'm fine. All that matters is that Josh doesn't find out. I won't stand seeing him get hurt in all this."

He stole a glance at Tess. The crease between her brows deepened. She seemed to study the tufted grass at their feet. He tried not to fidget in his seat while he waited for her reply, but the silence ticked by before she finally spoke.

"I understand wanting to protect him. And I know there's a lot going on here I don't fully understand. But is this really the best way?" Her hazel eyes bore into his. "His own dad will be back in a matter of days, and you're not going to tell him?"

"No."

"Why not?"

This was a mistake. He never should have said a thing. Family issues deserved to remain in the family, no matter how well-meaning the person might be. Austin released Tess's hand to work the tension from his neck. "You don't understand."

"Then help me to. I know this must be difficult, especially with Meghan out of the country as well. But you can't shut people out. Life doesn't work that way."

"It's worked fine for fifteen years. Meghan and Josh have gotten along for this long, and I'm sure she'd agree. Believe me, if she were here, I'd ask her. But in case you've forgotten, she isn't. And I doubt the cell reception is any better in Cambodia than it is here."

Tess tilted her head in question. "And what about the little girl? Opal."

"What about her?" Why couldn't Tess leave it alone?

"Doesn't Josh deserve to know he has a sister?"

"Half-sister," he ground out, the words leaving a bitter taste in his mouth.

"Sister," she shot back. The look she gave him said she wasn't about to back down.

Not wanting to fight with Tess, Austin rose from the bench and took a step toward the main building. He needed space. Time. Distance. Knowing Tess, she wouldn't let any of this go without a fight, and a fight was the last thing he was looking for.

"Where are you going?" Tess was right beside him, near to fuming, if her tone was any indication.

"To my office. This camp isn't going to run itself." He swiped the gloves and shears from the grass and stalked off toward the shed, leaving her questions and accusations behind him. He had enough to deal with right now without anyone questioning his choices, and he didn't need Tess's pity or her anger, at the moment.

CHAPTER

Twenty-Seven

AUSTIN LOOKED UP at the ceiling in the dark room and counted the swirls of knotted pine etched into the wooden beams. An hour had passed since Tess and the others went to bed, but he remained seated on one of the wooden chairs at the dining table with his guitar.

Tonight, he'd craved the feel of the nylon strings under his fingers as his soul sought for wisdom. He plucked the strings one by one as if their music were a prayer. Songs of praise, questions, aching longings he couldn't put into words. God heard them all.

The weight of so many responsibilities weighed on him. Everywhere he turned, there was something to lose. So many things riding on his shoulders. If he messed up again, what would the consequences be this time?

Pine boughs creaked in the wind, and Austin listened to their quiet sounds as they floated through the open window. He propped his guitar against the table and leaned his forearms against his thighs, giving in to the stillness.

Tess's words played on repeat in the forefront of his mind. As much as he hated to admit it, she was right. He'd been kidding himself to think he could keep something like this from Josh, but it wasn't his place to share such a secret.

"Lord," he whispered into the empty room. "What am I supposed to do?"

He closed his eyes and listened for something. Anything. But only silence answered.

Austin tested the strings once more, as if their music held the answer. A floorboard squeaked at the top of the stairs. He placed a hand over the strings to silence them. Padded footsteps sounded before another door clicked shut. When no further sound came, he set aside the guitar and paced across the room to the old fireplace.

The birthday cards from last month still sat in a neat row across the mantel. He smiled at the memory of the not-so-surprising *surprise* party. Had that been four weeks ago? He smiled at the card from his parents out in California and moved down the row, rereading the notes of well-wishes and clever jokes. Meghan's card stood out from the rest, the colorful handmade paper rough between his fingertips. He still couldn't believe how many stamps it had taken to send a simple piece of paper halfway around the world. No doubt they doubled the weight of the entire envelope.

Austin's chest swelled at the outpouring of love represented in the handful of cards in front of him. Family. Friends, both old and new.

He returned Meghan's card to its proper place, and his sleeve caught on one of the cards at the end. One by one, they toppled over like a row of dominoes. In the dark, he scrambled to snatch them up before they could fall into the sooty fireplace. He was rearranging them once more on the mantel when another, smaller square of paper fluttered to the floor.

He bent to retrieve it and recognized Tess's flowing script centered on the page. He squinted in the dim light to read the few lines: *A sweet friendship refreshes the soul—Happy Birthday to a new and faithful friend.*

Austin's shoulders sagged. He hadn't been much of a friend today—that was for sure. And Tess had only been trying to help. He could see that now, and he wanted to punch himself for reacting how he did.

"Lord, help me walk in a way pleasing to you. I'm trying everything I can here, but I know it will never be enough. Teach me to be content with your will and not mine, and give me grace enough to surrender the things I can't control over to you. Even if your answer isn't my own."

Tess stared at the glassy water from the edge of the bank. Gentle waves lapped against the shore, kissing her bare toes. Towel draped across her shoulder, she closed her eyes and willed her heart to match the steady rhythm drumming against the warm sand. The pounding in her chest slowed with each exhale.

Breathe in. And out.

All night, she'd tossed and turned, replaying her and Austin's argument until the walls of her bedroom grew rosy with morning's alpenglow. She shouldn't have pushed so hard, should have sensed it in the tension of his voice that he needed someone to listen rather than to question his judgment. Heaven knew she could be stubborn—a trait that had worked to her advantage in her racing career but failed her when it came to more important things, such as relationships.

That morning, she'd slipped out of the house unnoticed. Not that it had been particularly difficult, what with the kids racing off to their prospective activities with the same enthusiasm as a runner at the crack of the starting gun. What had she expected, anyway? For Austin to be waiting for her with a smile on his face as if nothing had happened yesterday?

Of course, the low rumble of his SUV had disappeared down the hill a good ten minutes before she'd descended the stairs. And as far as she knew, he'd yet to return.

She opened her eyes and squinted at the bright sunlight. What she wouldn't have done to have her polarized goggles with her this morning. With a quick tug, she tightened the elastic of her ponytail until her scalp prickled. The sensation brought her back to the here-and-now.

For a few blessed hours, she could lay aside thoughts of a certain camp owner and his family problems and return her focus to why she was here, in her swimsuit and goggles, on the edge of the mountain lake. She was supposed to be training, getting back to her old times so she could have a shot at making the qualifiers next year. Since arriving at the camp, she'd been more than lax in her training. Now, with her ankle nearly healed, it was time to stop daydreaming and get back to reality.

"It's been long enough."

With a determined step, Tess waded up to her ankles and sucked in a breath at the frigid temperature. Still, the shock of cold water was nothing compared to Austin's icy retreat yesterday. Her skin quickly numbed to the effects, and with a few more steps, she was waist-deep. Without another moment's hesitation, she dove headfirst into the water, arms slicing across the surface like a knife through butter on a warm summer's day.

The clear turquoise water glittered around her, inviting her back like an old friend. No pretense. No empty promises. No expectations for her to be anyone other than her true self. She knew what to expect from this sort of relationship. The waves didn't care if she came to them broken or whole, didn't notice if a few salty tears slipped into their swirling eddies.

Taking a breath, she carved her arm into the smooth surface and propelled herself forward. Water foamed at her ankles with each flutter kick as it all came back to her. The rush. The pull. The freedom. She reached the center of the lake, where the water's temperature dropped, and she relished the way the cool water soothed her tired ankle. Turquoise gave way to a palette of deep indigo to rival the monsoon storm clouds that had been rolling through the valley all month.

A familiar melody, one from Sunday's worship circle, flooded her mind, giving her an oddly uplifting sense of peace. If she weren't in the middle of a lake, she'd have hummed along. Her head plunged beneath the surface, and the music swelled as she came up for another breath.

The song echoed once more, the lyrics washing over her with refreshing clarity. *How great thou art. How great thou art.* With each stroke, the words of the song shifted to the scripture Trudy had quoted later that day. *"I press on toward the goal to win the prize for which God has called me heavenward in Christ Jesus."*

Tess slowed her movements. What goal was she pressing toward now? Her racing career? The camp? Austin? Somehow, the old dreams of reaching the Olympics didn't seem as bright as they once were. Was that God shifting her focus toward His true calling, or was it distance that had given her time to reflect? She had a sense it was the former, and, surprisingly, the thought didn't terrify her as much as it had a few weeks after her first surgery.

She'd spent her entire adult life chasing after one goal. To prove she was worthy. Perhaps this summer was the wake-up call she needed to refocus her attention on what truly mattered. Not earning a trophy, or validation of her own accomplishments, but building relationships with people. People like Caden, Trudy, Josh and the other staff members, the hundreds of campers who walked through their doors... and Austin. He may choose to shut her out again, and she could very well get hurt, but one thing she was certain of: she would learn to be a better friend.

She cupped her hand and pushed against the water, propelling herself forward at a more leisurely pace.

So maybe she wasn't in control of her own life. And maybe that was okay. It didn't make the daily struggles any less difficult, but there was comfort in knowing she didn't have to have all the answers. God was bigger than her circumstances, and if He called her to this mountaintop, she'd trust He had a plan.

At the other side of the lake, she turned and retraced her path, floating on more than water as she cut through the rippling waves. The nearby aspens quivered overhead, their leaves emitting a soft round of applause when Tess's feet sank into the muddy sand yards away from the small beach.

Droplets of water clung to the lenses of her goggles. The film obscured her view of the nearby shore, but she tore them off the second she heard someone clear his throat.

Tess looked up. Austin stood a few yards away, her towel in his left hand and a large metal thermos clasped in his right. His heather gray T-shirt clung to his arms as if he'd just finished one of his morning runs. His guarded expression gave her pause but only long enough for her to ascend the beach before accepting the offered towel. Once dried, Tess slipped a pair of running shorts over her swimsuit and wrung the moisture from her damp ponytail.

"Coffee?" His fingers brushed hers in the exchange, the sensation warming her more than a sip of sweetened coffee any day. If he noticed, he didn't indicate as much. Dark circles ringed the bottoms of his eyes, telling her he hadn't slept much, either, in the last twenty-four hours. "How's the training going?"

He seemed in no hurry to get back to the camp, so Tess took that as a good sign. "I'm nowhere near my old time, but that will come with practice."

"That's great. And the ankle?"

"Better. With a little more therapy and a lot of work, it might even be good as new."

"I always think it's a miracle how the body can heal itself the way it does. Believe me, I've seen it all." He shook his head slightly. "If only some things could mend as easily as broken bones."

His voice trailed off, and Tess had to lean closer to hear the last sentence. Would he elaborate? She filled in the silence. "Well, you can't say something like that and expect to leave me hanging."

"No, I suppose I can't." A ghost of a smile played across his lips.

Tess relaxed. This was good. Maybe it was small talk, but at least they could still communicate with one another.

Austin must have sensed as much. He lowered himself to the sand and invited her to join him on the warm, dry slope. Together, they sat in relative silence, watching the bugs flit across the water without a care in the world.

"All my life, I've always felt this need to take care of those around me, as if their happiness was somehow my responsibility. I know Meghan never needed my help, but I was that annoying younger brother who'd decided it was my job to look out for her, you know?"

"No, I don't. Caden wasn't what you would have considered a *responsible* kid growing up."

"Versus now that he's all grown up?"

"Precisely." She did nothing to hide her laughter, and Austin returned the gesture. He might think it odd if she were to tell him, but she could envision him trying to keep her brother in line and failing miserably like she always had. It was no wonder he'd turned out to be such a kind-hearted person. "I think it's great you looked out for your older sister. Really. I'm sure she appreciated it, no matter what she might have said."

Austin released a slow breath and smiled absent-mindedly into the sand at his feet. "I was reminded of something last night."

"And what's that?" She could feel her own smile growing in response to his relaxed tone.

"I'm lucky to count you as a friend. That is, if you still want to be friends after how I acted yesterday."

Tess's heart ached for the man next to her. Of all the things battling within him, there was one worry she could remove from his ever-open hands. She scooted closer in the sand. Set the thermos down. And wove her fingers around his. "Don't worry. I'm not going anywhere."

Austin looked down at their intertwined hands, a look of surprise mingled with relief etched into his upturned brow.

She nudged her elbow against his. "And you? How are you doing?"

His throat bobbed, like a fish testing a lure. "Honestly? I still don't know."

A bubble gurgled to the water's surface before a small fish darted back beneath the surface. "Hmm." *So much for the lure.*

"What?" There was a note of humor in Austin's voice as he turned to face Tess.

"I didn't say anything."

"You were thinking something, though. Weren't you?" His eyebrow lowered in challenge, his features softening.

Tess worried her bottom lip. Last time, she'd made things worse by speaking her opinions out loud. She couldn't take a repeat of yesterday, but what if he was finally open to letting someone else help him? *God, is this one of those times I'm supposed to trust You?*

His shoulder grazed hers as he leaned over to whisper. "It's okay. I can take it." The warmth in his voice nearly undid her, and she found herself giving in to his plea.

"It's just," she paused long enough to strengthen her resolve. "I know you don't agree with me, but no matter what's happened, no matter how much water is under the bridge, I still think Josh should know where he comes from. It doesn't have to be now," she quickly added. "However, one day, he's going to want to know more, and someone will have to give him an answer."

Austin lifted his head and gave a decisive nod. "You're right. Josh deserves to know who his dad is. I've been praying a lot about it, and I've decided I'll wait until the parents pick up their kids on Friday. Then I'll find the right time to talk with

Meghan. If Josh wants to meet the man after that, then I guess I'll know what phone number to call."

"And you'd be okay with that?" It was such a stark contrast to yesterday's reaction that Tess had a hard time believing he'd capitulate so easily.

"If it's what Josh wants, and Meghan gives the go-ahead, I guess I'll have to be. Even if . . ."

"Even if, what?" She was pushing her luck by asking, but something told her he needed to give voice to his fears. Right here. Now. Before they ate away at him any further. Tess tightened her hold around his hand, infusing as much strength into him as possible.

With a sidelong glance that said he saw what she was doing, Austin relaxed his shoulders and peered out over the water. "I'm not sure I can forgive him."

There was such depth to his statement, it echoed inside her as if she were the one who'd spoken the words.

"I think this is where Trudy would quote some sage advice. But since you're stuck with me for now"—she paused when his lips curved upward—"all I can say is this. I've been in your shoes, and I know how much bitterness can rule your life if you let it. My old pastor used to say holding a grudge was like jumping into a ditch of poison ivy and expecting the other person to break out in a rash. I'm not saying it's the same, but if I can forgive Ryan, in time, and with God's help, you'll be able to forgive Josh's dad as well."

Austin grew quiet for so long, she feared she'd overstepped again. But when he turned to face her, the look in his eyes was anything but defensive.

He studied her, his gaze so unwavering, Tess had the feeling he could see straight into her soul. "You know, I think I underestimated you that first day you showed up on my doorstep."

"Oh, yeah? What makes you say that?" She teased, sensing the new spring of hope budding between them.

"Because," he brushed his thumb in a slow arc across the back of her hand, "I should have known right then and there that God had sent someone into my life who would change everything."

CHAPTER

Twenty-Eight

FRIDAY MORNING RUSHED in. A cool wind rustled through the trees with the promise of rain, and the humidity released the forest's earthy fragrance of pine and sage. Eyes closed, Tess took in another cleansing breath before she made her way toward the house. The ground was still wet from last night's gentle showers, and her hiking boots sank into the spongy earth with each purposeful step. The sensation brought back memories of home, of backcountry trails littered with leaves and houses filled with smiling faces. A place not so different from here.

A single drop of rain splashed against her cheek, and she picked up her pace. No need to get caught in another storm. Judging by the dark clouds hanging low over the camp, more rain was on its way. As she sidestepped a puddle in the road, she balanced the stack of boxes between her arm and her hip. The contents jangled with the movement.

Who'd have thought she'd find the stash of old board games hidden away in the shed, of all places? But she should have thought twice before questioning Trudy. When it came to this camp, there didn't seem to be any secret the woman didn't already know. Including the one about her and Austin.

She smiled, recalling how Trudy had pulled her aside the previous evening, eyes twinkling. How she even knew about her and Austin's conversation on the beach was beyond her, but the note of approval in Trudy's smile was enough to assuage any doubt Tess might have had.

This was one secret she didn't mind sharing.

If only she could stop telling herself it was too good to be true. With Josh's dad returning today and the remaining questions of what would happen at the end of the summer, the future was still a mystery.

I press on toward the goal to win the prize for which God has called me heavenward in Christ Jesus. All week, she'd clung to those words, turning them inside and out as she learned what it meant to hand over her past, her present, and her future. She still didn't know what she was pressing on toward, but she had a feeling—no, a hope—it would somehow involve Austin and this mountaintop camp.

A gust of wind chased her inside, and she set the box on the coffee table. Harper, who'd been busy doing her best to keep the kids entertained, jumped up from the braided rug and joined her.

"Hey, Tess. Do you have a minute?"

"Sure. As long as we can talk and unpack at the same time." She could sense the restless energy of the children. "Better not test their patience any longer than necessary."

"I can do that. I don't know how many more jokes I can come up with." She grabbed the first box and set it to the side. "Actually, I was sort of hoping I could pick your brain for a minute about being a professional athlete."

Tess reached for the Monopoly box on top and slid Harper a look. "Shoot."

Harper's eyes lit with excitement, and she barreled ahead. "What's it like being a professional athlete? I mean, when you're not here, of course. I know there's a lot involved, and racing is a different world than soccer, but I'm sure there've got to be a few similarities."

Tess laughed. The girl's enthusiasm reminded her of herself at that age. Ready to conquer the world one race at a time. "There's never a dull moment. That's for sure."

"I'll bet it's amazing. I'd do anything to play professional soccer." She sighed, the Game of Life clutched to her chest as if it were the signing contract she was surely dreaming of.

Tess would be lying if she said she didn't miss it, but life on the track was not the fairy tale she'd dreamed it would be when she was Harper's age.

"Like any job, it had its ups and downs. There's the travel, training, and adrenaline highs of competition. I loved racing, but that life means you miss other things." She slid the box of Pictionary next to the Scrabble board and looked up. "I wouldn't give up the experiences I've had, but I'm learning there's more to life than living from one win to the next."

"I get that. So, will you go back now that your ankle is healed? Or do you have other plans?"

If only she knew.

"I'll let you know when I figure that out." Tess gave Harper a smile and withdrew a container of dominoes from the bottom of the box.

"Who's ready for a game of Monopoly?" Kyle scooped up the game and carried it to the dining table.

A posse of children gathered around him, arguing over who got to be the Scottie dog and who got to be the battleship. He set up the game board amidst the excitement and was about to distribute the cards when he looked up.

"Harper, Tess. Care to join? We've still got the thimble and the wheelbarrow left." He waggled his eyebrows and held up the pewter game pieces.

Up for a challenge, Tess turned to Harper, who met her with a matching grin. "What do you say?"

The girl bounced on her toes with one foot already angled toward the table. "Let's show them how it's done."

The wind picked up, spraying the cabin windows like a drive-through car wash. So much for the storm holding off until the afternoon.

Austin peeled his gaze from the soggy drive and looked back to the room packed full of kids and staff members. This morning had gone as smoothly as a canoe ride in a rainstorm without paddles . . . headed upriver. The bad weather made for a restless group of second-graders. And it did nothing to fix his anxious mood. In another hour, parents would start to arrive, Brian included. And no matter how much he wanted to avoid it, he couldn't put off talking with the man forever.

"*Evasion*, for seventy points." The Scrabble tiles clicked against the board where Josh laid down his next word.

Opal huddled close to him with her teddy bear forgotten at her side and handed the wooden tiles to him one-by-one.

Despite his earlier misgivings, Austin couldn't help but be proud of the way his nephew had taken the little girl under his wing all week. No one had asked him to befriend the shy seven-year-old and her stuffed bear. Least of all, him. He'd been too afraid the truth would come out if they spent any time together, but seeing them like this, he knew he'd been wrong to think he could keep Josh away from his half-sister. Even if they didn't know it yet.

"How is that seventy points?" Austin peered across the board, counting the little numbers in the corners of the tiles. "Even with the double word score, I only count twenty."

Josh flicked the rule book against the table and gave him a smug grin. "You forgot the bingo score. I used all seven of my letters, so that's an extra fifty points."

Opal scribbled the number on the scoresheet, the *seven* looking more like a misshapen *one* in her wobbly script.

Austin sat back on his haunches, impressed and a little dismayed his fourteen-year-old nephew had beaten him yet again. He and his grandpa had played this game too many times to count, and he'd never pulled something like that off. Maybe the kid could teach him more than a thing or two, after all.

Seated around the dining table, Harper, Kyle, and Tess passed the time hovering over the Monopoly board with a handful of campers. Sean and Skye were busy teaching the others how to play Clue. And Genevieve and Trudy had disappeared into the kitchen half an hour ago and hadn't been seen since, yet the smell of watermelon and grilled cheese told him they were hard at work.

Another half-hour passed, and the sounds of game pieces and chatter filled the room until Trudy announced it was time for lunch. Reluctantly, the kids packed away the board games, and they ate in contented silence until the first of the cars pulled up the gravel drive. As the parents filtered in, each kid retrieved his or her bundled belongings from the pile by the door and gave a round of hugs to the staff members. Despite the rain, the teenagers followed them out one-by-one to the lawn, to see the kids off.

By eleven-thirty, the last of the parents were trickling in. Most of the staff was already out front by the cars, saying their goodbyes to the campers. Josh had gone out back to retrieve the kids' finished birdhouses and was busy handing them out as each person left. A handful of kids remained in the front room while their parents chatted away.

Usually, Austin enjoyed this chance to talk with the families. Oftentimes, he found that, like himself, they'd visited the camp when they were children and couldn't be happier to share their wonderful experiences with their own kids. There had even been a few occasions this summer where he'd run into old acquaintances. They'd chatted about their shared memories and gushed over how little the place had changed.

Unfortunately, today was not one of those days.

"I can't tell you how much my Sarah enjoyed this weekend," one of the mothers said to Austin. "I've been wanting to get her into one of these programs for years, but you know how busy kids are these days. All those sports camps and activities. But I'm so glad my friend Trish told me about this place when she did. When I heard she was sending Opal here for the week, I just knew I had to sign Sarah up, too, seeing as they're best friends and all.

"Anyway, long story short," she paused for a breath and continued, "I managed to move around a few things on the calendar, and I couldn't be more pleased. Sarah adores it up here, and I can't blame her. It's so beautiful, and not to mention peaceful. Isn't that right, honey?" The woman turned to her daughter, who was busy playing Chutes and Ladders with Opal at the coffee table.

The woman had cornered him by the fireplace and had been talking nonstop the past five minutes. He was only half-listening as she carried on with her one-sided conversation. Even if he hadn't been so distracted, he probably wouldn't have been able to get a word in anyway with the way she was rattling on. However, the mention of Opal caught his attention.

"You know Opal's parents?"

"Of course." She waved her hand as if it were a silly question. "Our kids are in the same class, but Trish and I go way back. However, we haven't seen much of Brian since their divorce finalized last year. It's a shame, really. He and my husband used to have so much fun watching football games together, but I guess things weren't working for them."

Divorced. It seemed Brian had managed to mess up yet another relationship. Austin felt a twinge of satisfaction, but it was soon eclipsed by sympathy for Opal. No matter his feelings toward the man, no child deserved to grow up in a broken home. He dropped his gaze to the little girl, the one who looked so much like his own nephew, and wished that somehow things could be different for the both of them.

At that moment, a dark green SUV rolled up the drive and disappeared from sight as it pulled into the small parking area out front. Austin tensed. In less than a minute, Brian would step through that door and back into their lives. He scanned the room and released a breath when he didn't see Josh. It was bad enough they'd have a small audience, what with the remaining campers and their families slowly filtering out of the room. All he wanted was to keep things polite and civil, and to see Brian on his way as quickly as possible.

Outside, a car door shut. A pair of footsteps echoed up the porch steps and across the wooden deck toward the front door. Austin tried to focus on the woman talking beside him, the other parents nearby, the kids talking with their new friends ... anything to distract his overactive mind and keep him grounded in the present instead of the past.

He slid a reluctant glance toward the door as a large man in slacks and a rain-splattered polo entered.

"Brian. What a surprise seeing you here." The woman beside Austin clapped her hands, a harsh sound that clanged in Austin's ears. She stepped forward and welcomed the newcomer with a smile. "I was just talking about how much David and I miss seeing you, and then here you are."

She moved her arms in front of her as if he were a magician appearing out of thin air. "I figured I'd see Trish, but it's a treat running into you. I'll have to tell David when we get home. I'm sure he'd love to catch up as well."

Brian dipped his head in a polite greeting. His strong aftershave filled the normally spacious entry room, the familiar scent bringing with it a wave of fifteen-year-old memories.

"In fact," the woman continued before he could speak, "why don't you and Opal come over for dinner sometime this week? I know David's been itching for an excuse to fire up his new smoker."

Sarah's mother seemed in no hurry to leave. In fact, since Brian's arrival, Austin could easily step back and let her carry on her monologue before Brian ever realized who he was. After all, he'd been a kid the last time they'd seen each other. While Brian had merely aged, still sporting the same slicked-back hairstyle as before, Austin had grown into an adult.

He'd been the one to help keep his family together. He'd learned to step up and face life's challenges instead of running from them. All those past experiences had turned him into the person he was today, and while he didn't always get it right, he'd been trying his best to live a life in accordance with his faith—the same faith his grandpa instilled in him all those years ago in the heart of the Colorado Rocky Mountains.

Brian said something in response to the woman's ramblings that made her laugh. The sound fell flat against Austin's ears. Before he registered what she said next, she turned her full attention toward him and paused, as if waiting for his response. Brian also turned, and for the first time, familiarity seemed to ruffle his brow.

"Wright? What are you doing here?" His surprise seemed genuine, but everything about his presence had Austin on edge.

Austin knew better than to stoke the flames. Oh, but how he wanted to tell the man just how badly he'd messed things up. How he'd broken everything and left them all to pick up the pieces. But he wasn't a child anymore. Sure, his skin grew clammy the longer he stood there, but he cleared his throat and spoke up, all the same.

"Brian. Long time no see." Austin shoved his hands into his pockets. He could be civil without having to welcome the man with open arms. "Here to pick up your daughter?"

Brian nodded. "Her mom had something come up last minute and asked if I could come get Opal instead. You have a kid here too?" His tone was friendly, if not a tad guarded.

"Oh, don't be silly, Brian," the woman interrupted, having yet to pick up on the subtle tension in the room. "Austin owns the place. And, might I add," she said, eyes aglow with praise, "he's done a wonderful job."

"That true?" Brian asked, seeming mildly impressed as he looked around the room. His gaze landed on Opal and Sarah seated next to each other on the couch. Neither of the girls looked up from their game.

Austin waved to another mother and daughter as they made for the door and returned his attention to Brian and Mrs. Chatty. "My grandpa left it to me after he passed. I thought about selling it at first, but the idea of someone else running this place didn't sit right with me. Meghan said I was crazy to bring the camp back, but I couldn't let it go to ruin either."

The mention of his sister's name seemed to grab Brian's full attention. "How is Meghan? I haven't thought about her in ages. I'll bet she's been busy saving the world one rainforest at a time." He chuckled, as if becoming a single mother at twenty-three hadn't changed all her plans. "I wish I could say I remained as altruistic as her, but environmental law doesn't pay half as well as contracts and litigation."

Keep it polite. The sooner he takes Opal and leaves, the sooner things can go back to normal.

"Meghan's doing fine." It had taken years to get there, but she'd made a good life for herself and her son. Austin stared at the man, waiting for him to ask after Josh as well. When he didn't, he added, "And, by the way, so is Josh."

Brian's forehead dipped. "Who?"

The muscles in Austin's neck grew tense, but he forced his posture to appear relaxed for the sake of the other families still present. If Brian wanted to play it that way, he'd let him. He slid his hand from his pocket to massage his neck but waved instead as two more families walked out into the rain. A gust of cold air blew through the house and slammed the door shut behind them.

Unfazed, Brian reached for Opal's pink and purple backpack and threaded an arm through the tiny shoulder straps until it hung loose at his elbow. "That's okay, man. I never expected her to stay single forever or anything. Meghan is a great girl. I know things didn't work out between the two of us, but I hope she's happy. Tell her hi for me next time you see her."

Tell her hi? Austin tensed, the muscles in his neck going rigid. Did the man really think he could get off that easily?

In the distance, low thunder rumbled over the mountains. The temperature in the house dropped another degree.

Mrs. Chatty wrapped her arms around her torso. "That storm's coming in faster than I expected." She looked between the two of them, a slight frown on her face, as if sensing more than a shift in the weather. "Well, I'd better get Sarah's things together and be off before the roads turn to mud. It was nice running into you, Brian. I'll have David text you the details about dinner."

With a few more parting comments, she left them to go in search of her daughter's bag and coat.

"Don't mind her," Brian reassured, backpack still dangling from his crooked elbow. His Rolex glinted under the fluorescent lights. "She's always like that. To be honest, I don't know how David keeps up with her half the time, but they seem happy. Unlike Trish and me." He looked at Austin. "Go ahead and say it. I know what you're thinking."

"You do?" Austin doubted Brian even had a clue.

"Yeah, that I ruined another good relationship. Gave up when things got hard." He shrugged. "I'll admit, I've made my fair share of mistakes. Trish and I both. We tried the whole couples counseling thing, but there are some things you can't fix."

"Like with Meghan?"

"Yeah. Like me and Meghan. But kids, you know . . . they make everything so much more complicated than two people drifting apart. At least I can know Meghan and I made the right decision. I might not have Trish anymore either, but at least I have Opal." He smiled across the room at his daughter.

Austin couldn't stand to listen to Brian's justifications any longer. Whatever empathy he'd begun to feel for the guy disappeared the moment he wrote off Josh's very existence. He lowered his voice so as not to draw attention to their conversation, but he couldn't pretend any longer.

If Brian wouldn't step up and take responsibility, then that was his problem. "So that's it, then? Your second family justifies you running out on your first?"

Brian's forehead dipped, his face growing stern. "Listen, I liked Meghan. A lot. But we were kids. She wasn't my family."

"And what about Josh?" Austin challenged. He'd keep pushing back until Brian at least accepted responsibility for his actions.

"Josh," the man frowned, "isn't the guy she's with now?" The man looked genuinely confused, but Austin didn't care.

This was Austin's chance. He took the opening and charged ahead. "Drop the act, Brian. Meghan told me how you left without a backward glance as soon as she told you she was pregnant."

Brian took a step back and bumped against the thick pine wall. "What are you talking about? Meghan would have told me something like that. She . . . we . . . had a kid? If I had known—"

"Oh, come on, man. Megan told me everything. You knew, but you chose to leave her and your son anyway."

The door on the other side of the kitchen slammed shut. Pounding footsteps echoed across the patio, and a head of short brown hair disappeared behind the trees.

Josh.

Austin bit back a groan. He hadn't even heard him come back inside.

Torn between wanting to lay into Brian and chase after his nephew, Austin rounded on the hulk of a man standing unwanted in the middle of his living room. "Don't for a minute think we're done here." He took a few steps toward the door, intending to track down Josh and explain.

Brian's face reddened. "I don't know what you're playing at, but I'm taking my daughter and leaving."

Austin's patience was running thin. He didn't have time to play referee to whatever the man had to say. "Do whatever you want, Brian. You always have. But right now, I need to go find my nephew."

He yanked a rain jacket from the closet, and the empty hanger clattered to the ground. He had one arm through the sleeve when the front door swung open. He had to jump back to avoid getting hit.

Skye bolted through the opening, heaving in a lungful of breath as she sloshed her water-logged boots over the threshold. Her face was flushed, and her wide eyes made Austin's stomach sink.

CHAPTER

Twenty-Nine

THE SOUND OF raised voices spilled through the open windows with an edge of desperation that made the hair rise on the back of Tess's neck.

Genevieve's voice rose up from the front lawn. The sounds of crunching gravel punctuated her words. "Josh, what are you doing?"

"When I get to town, I'm calling my mom for the truth. No more lies." Tess could barely make out Josh's words as he raced away from the house.

"What are you even talking . . .?" The rest of Genevieve's question died in the wind.

Hurried footsteps followed Josh's, and a second later, a car door opened and slammed shut. A compact engine revved out front, an echo of the building storm.

"What does he think he's doing?" Austin stammered. "He doesn't even have a learner's permit yet." His eyes grew wide. In a panic, he dropped the rain jacket and reached for the emergency kit, complete with survival gear, flares, and a hand radio, before charging into the rain.

Tess followed Austin, watching as Josh reversed her Prius from beneath the large spruce and directed it toward the main road.

Alarm bells blared in every corner of her mind. How could she have been so careless, leaving her keys in her car like that? Josh was an unlicensed driver. He had no business driving off in near flash-flood conditions, let alone in a car without all-wheel-drive.

Austin stopped a few feet in front of her, patting his pockets in a frenzied panic.

Brian pulled up the rear of the group, dragging a very upset Opal behind him. He had his keys clutched in his fist, ready to storm off, when Austin rounded on him.

"Give me your keys." A note of desperation edged Austin's voice, and Brian's defenses seemed to cool.

"What?" The man's bushy eyebrows shot up.

"Now."

Brian nearly dropped his key ring before handing them over to Austin, who launched toward the dark SUV the moment they were in his hand. One look at Trudy's panicked expression, and Tess raced after him, dropping into the vacant seat beside him.

"What are you doing?" he asked, bewildered.

She fumbled with her seat belt and clicked it into place. "I'm not letting two people I care about get themselves hurt, so I'm coming with you."

He looked from her to the road and blew out a heavy breath. "Fine. Just hold on."

Without losing another second, he threw the car into drive, and they careened down the gravel drive. Streams of water rushed down the rutted gullies of the dirt road. In his haste, Austin overshot the first curve. Tess clutched at her door handle as the front tires caught the edge of the shoulder. Austin tightened his grip on the steering wheel and fought to regain control.

Thank goodness Brian was smart enough to have four-wheel drive. But Tess's car was a whole other story. The sedan would be lucky to make it down this mountain on a good day. But on a washed-out road like this? If Josh hit one of those ruts at any speed, there was no telling what could happen.

She remained silent and maintained a white-knuckle grip on the passenger door armrest, her thoughts, no doubt, on the same thing.

They skirted the next curve, and the forest thickened around them as they descended the mountain. A smattering of moisture clung to the windshield, but too little for Austin to bother with the wipers.

Please, God, keep him safe. She whispered the prayer over and over as the two of them skirted the heavily rutted curves down the mountain.

The wall of trees cleared ahead just enough for Tess to see down to the next switchback. She sucked in a breath and pointed toward the road below. "There."

Austin slowed the car, and Tess flung open the door to jump out. She barely registered the slick mud seeping over the tops of her shoes. Icy rain pelted against her exposed skin, and wet tendrils of hair clung to her face. In a second, Austin was right beside her, mouth set in a grim line as a sickening thunderclap reverberated over the exposed slope.

The ground shook as if a thousand runners were charging down the mountain, and all Tess could do was stand frozen in the mud. Without warning, another flash of light, so blinding she was forced to close her eyes, bolted across the sky. The air fizzled and cracked like a shotgun, and every instinct told her to run.

A pair of tire marks were gouged into the mud, and Tess's car was nowhere in sight.

All of a sudden, everything looked all too familiar. The tire marks, the broken glass, the steep mountain cliff and hairpin curve. Maybe if Austin hadn't spent nearly a decade of his life responding to accidents one after the other, he'd have been able to breathe.

What greeted him at the edge of the road made his stomach churn. Shattered glass glittered along the side of the road and down the slope. Austin steeled himself for the worst and peered over the edge. Tess's car lay ten yards below them, the hood smashed against a single tree that held it suspended, feet away from the nearby cliff.

A shadow moved in the driver's seat, and Austin froze. Dozens of images flashed through his brain. Cuts, contusions, broken bones. . . . It was one thing to go in after a stranger. He could push aside the emotion and do whatever needed to be done to stabilize the patient. The sounds of the forest and highway below dimmed, and he sank further into the what-ifs. What if he couldn't do it? What if he couldn't save Josh, after everything that had already happened?

"Austin? Are you alright?" Tess's voice cut through the haze.

He looked down to see his hands shaking before looking back up into her concerned gaze. His backpack was propped against her foot, and she had the radio clutched to her chest as if waiting for his instructions.

"He'll be okay, Austin. I promise." She reached for his hand and gave it a tight squeeze. "I'll contact Trudy and the fire department. Now, you go down and check on him."

Her reassuring smile was enough to quell the knot in his stomach. He squeezed her hand in a silent *thank you* and set off down the steep slope. He wove between the boulders and tree shoots, all the while praying for a miracle, until his hand found the nearest door handle.

"Josh. Josh, are you there? Are you hurt?" The window was cracked, and dirt obscured his nephew's face. Austin yanked open the door and pushed back the deflated airbags. Without pausing, he brushed his hands over the boy's head and arms for signs of breaks or contusions. A few cuts would likely require stitches, and he suspected a sprained wrist and some hefty bruising. But he was in one piece.

Josh groaned when Austin probed his wrist, and he swatted his hands away. "Don't need you . . . fussing over me like a kid."

A flood of relief cascaded over Austin. At least Josh still had the wherewithal to talk back. That had to be a good sign.

"Is there anywhere that hurts? Do you feel dizzy or lightheaded? Do you remember what happened?" He rattled off the questions with rapid fire succession. He didn't expect Josh to answer them all, but his responses would go a long way to ruling out any major injuries.

Josh shook his head, the movement appearing stiff and a little painful. "Yes. No. And I'm pretty sure I was attacked by a tree."

Austin's shoulders relaxed, and he breathed out a prayer of thanks as big as the mountain beneath them. "Got to watch out for those trees that show up in the middle of the road, right?"

Josh laughed, a raspy sound that gave way to a fit of coughs. "Don't make me laugh, or I'll have to punch you."

Austin grinned. "Wouldn't dream of it."

Sand and gravel shifted above him, and he looked up to see Tess standing on the edge of the road, radio in one hand and his backpack in the other. "How is he? I've got the fire department on the line, and they say they can be here in about ten minutes."

"What did you do, bring the entire town with you?" Josh scrunched his face, evidently not keen on having an audience.

"Nope, only me and Tess. But it sounds like the cavalry will be here in a few minutes."

There was another grunt of disapproval, and Austin couldn't help but feel sorry for his nephew.

"What do you say? Do you think you can make it back up to the road? Or do you want to stay here for a bit?" He waved at Tess to let her know all was well and turned back to Josh.

The boy fidgeted with the steering wheel. "You said it's only Tess right now?" His question wasn't much more than a whisper.

Austin understood the concern behind his question. What he was really asking was if Brian was with her.

"Yep. Just us three, and I know for a fact she'll be delighted to see you safe and sound."

Josh seemed to consider his options. For a long moment, Austin thought he'd opt to stay put and catch his breath, but the boy surprised him yet again. "Okay. Let's go."

CHAPTER

Thirty

TESS SAT IN the cool waiting room of the Estes Park Medical Center and hummed to the buzz of the nearby coffee maker. Genevieve's head lolled against her shoulder as the teenage girl slept. The pages of Trudy's book crinkled next to her as if they hadn't already been there for over three hours.

Skye and the others had insisted on waiting with them as well, but after the second hour of no news, Trudy persuaded them to head on back to camp with her husband. As soon as there was something to share, they'd let them know.

"What do you think is taking so long?" Tess whispered to Trudy.

The indistinct murmurs of nearby voices mingled with the rattling of the air conditioning unit above them. Memories of another hospital assailed her like the unwanted stench of bleach and antiseptic, and she tried to push them from her mind.

Lowering her book, Trudy reached over the plastic armrest and gave Tess's hand a squeeze. "I'm sure everything is fine. Austin said they needed to run a few standard tests before they could release Josh. You know how hospitals are."

Unfortunately, she did. She also knew all too well the way a life could change once a person passed through those sliding glass doors.

Tess stared at her hand in Trudy's, grateful for the woman's support. Not long after the paramedics had brought Josh in, Trudy arrived at the hospital and wrapped Tess in a comforting embrace. Austin was the one who really deserved her hugs. But he'd disappeared down the hall the moment the doctors wheeled Josh away.

What if Josh had worse injuries than they'd first thought? The adrenaline from the accident would have dulled the pain, but that didn't mean those things couldn't present themselves later. For all she knew, he could have internal bleeding, and all because he'd taken her car. A two-wheel-drive sedan that had no right being in the mountains, in the first place.

Hadn't Austin warned her about her choice in vehicles that first day? Not that she'd taken much stock in his advice then, but now . . .

She brushed an unruly lock of hair from her face, and her fingers came back damp.

Trudy shifted beside her, her bracelets clanking against the armrest as she extracted a tissue from her large purse. "Don't you be worryin' about them." She handed it to Tess with a reassuring smile and waited for her to dab at her eyes before continuing. "One thing you should know about the Wright men is they're tougher than they look. I remember when Austin was not much younger than Josh. He got it in his head one morning to scavenge for raspberries down by the lake. He managed to fill the entire bucket, but little did he know he'd been traipsing through poison ivy all afternoon."

"Oh, no." Tess could imagine the discomfort and embarrassment he must have felt.

"Oh, yes," Trudy laughed. "He was as red as my berry cobbler. It took an entire bottle of calamine lotion to stop the itching. Typical Austin. He didn't complain once, but he steered clear of those raspberry bushes the rest of that summer."

Tess joined with Trudy's laughter as footsteps approached from the hallway.

"Sounds like you two are having fun."

Austin's deep timbre cut through the delirious fog, snapping Tess back to the hospital waiting room. She was on her feet in a second. Arms open, he pulled her into a hug, where she rested her head against the steady rise and fall of his chest.

A chair creaked behind them as Genevieve woke, the same look of concern on her face as earlier.

"How's the patient doing?" Tess infused as much positivity into her voice as she could, if not for Genevieve's sake, then for Austin.

"He's doing fine. Resting a bit." His hand brushed over the top of her head and down her shoulders. "Nothing broken, but he has a concussion. They are still waiting to do some more imaging to rule out any other injuries, and since it's already so late, they plan to keep him overnight for observation."

"When can we go see him?" Genevieve spoke up. Hair mussed and makeup smudged, she looked small and vulnerable, her concern for Josh evident.

Austin's face softened, and he gave them all a reassuring smile. "Maybe later. If Josh had his way, I'm sure he'd be out of here in a heartbeat. But the doctors said it would be better if he could rest for a bit." A phone buzzed in his pocket, interrupting the momentary sliver of peace. Freeing his arms from around Tess, he drew it out and looked at the screen. He frowned. "Sorry, I have to take this."

Austin stepped back and walked to the other side of the room. He returned a few minutes later and slumped into the chair across from Tess and the others. "That was Meghan. She's booked the first flight out from Phnom Penh tonight. She'll lay over in Tokyo and be in Denver by tomorrow evening."

"Bless her heart. She must be worried sick." Trudy stepped toward the hospitality counter and poured him a cup of black coffee. "Did you tell her Josh is all right?"

"Yes. But she wouldn't hear it. When I asked about her work, she said four months in Cambodia was enough. The team could handle the last one without her."

Trudy stirred a packet of creamer and sugar into another coffee and offered it to Tess. "Sounds like Meghan. I'll make up one of the spare rooms for her."

Austin took a sip, visibly relaxing under Trudy's ministrations. "I didn't even think that far ahead. Thank you. I don't want to leave Josh here alone."

"Not a problem. Genevieve and I can take care of things back at the camp if you think you'll be alright here."

"Of course." The girl nodded. "I'll do whatever I can to help."

Tess's heart swelled with gratitude for Genevieve and the rest of the camp staff. She only wished she'd had this kind of community after her accident. She knew Josh was in good hands.

When Trudy seemed satisfied that Austin and Tess had everything they needed, she and Genevieve said their goodbyes and disappeared down the corridor toward the parking lot.

When the two of them were out of sight, Tess followed Austin to the row of chairs in the small waiting room and slid into the seat beside him. She curled her feet beneath her and, despite the armrest between them, rested her head against his shoulder. "What happened to Brian and Opal? I saw them come in not long after Trudy and the others, but I never saw them leave."

Austin took another sip and took his time answering. "He took Opal home, but he promised to come back once Meghan gets here. I talked with him a little bit while the doctors were examining Josh. The guy seemed pretty quiet and shaken up, but I can't blame him. All this time, I thought he'd known about Josh. It must be quite the shock to gain a fourteen-year-old son and almost lose him all in one day."

Tess peered down the hallway and frowned. She'd never thought about it that way.

Austin angled his head to peer down at her, his chin grazing the top of her head. "But I don't really want to talk about Brian right now." His voice dipped low, as if speaking about the man took a great deal of effort.

She breathed in the caramel aroma of his coffee and relaxed. They'd had enough to worry about today. His heart was in the right place, and that was all Tess had ever wanted. "That's alright by me. I quite like the sound of having you all to myself for a little bit."

He shifted beneath her, and his arm settled around her shoulders. "I couldn't agree more."

"I'm fine. Really. Why won't anybody believe me?" Josh looked up from his twin bed and scowled at Trudy, who flitted above him like a protective mother hen, readjusting the wall of pillows behind his back for the seventh time that morning.

Austin bit back a laugh. He'd had a hard enough time bandaging up those raspberry scratches a few months back. By some miracle, Josh had managed to walk away from his accident with little more than a concussion and a few sprains, but with the way he was reacting, one would think the doctor had prescribed something more objectionable than bed rest.

"Young man, you heard what the doctors said. You have a concussion, which means you need to get your rest. No excuses." Trudy fluffed one more pillow before seeming satisfied with her work.

Josh went silent. He crossed his arms across his chest, the bulky ace bandage on his wrist making the movement appear slow and cumbersome. Despite his efforts to be a difficult patient, he wasn't fooling anyone with his tough guy act. The accident had scared everyone, no doubt Josh included. He'd open back up, eventually, but until then, the best they could do was be there for him when he needed them.

"Are you sure you don't need anything?" Meghan asked, fussing with the bedsheets until they lay flat and pristine at the corners.

After what sounded like a harrowing few days of travel, she'd arrived at The Lodge in her rental car to find Austin and Josh arguing over her son's care. According to Josh, he was as fit as a horse, but she wouldn't hear any of it.

"Actually, there is one thing." Josh's face brightened with an idea. "I think my phone and earbuds are downstairs by the coffee table. Nothing about listening to music should violate my house arrest, right?"

Austin sighed. "Sorry, no stimuli for at least a few days, I'm afraid. Doctor's orders. But if you'd like to talk at all, we'd be more than happy to answer any questions you might have." Austin hated to take that away from him, too, especially after all he'd been through the last forty-eight hours. But if it would aid his nephew's recovery, he'd endure a few more days of complaints.

Josh's face fell, and he looked accusingly between the three of them. "What, so I'm supposed to lie here all day? I think I'm at a greater risk of dying from boredom than hurting myself listening to music." He flopped against the pile of pillows and glared at the knotted pine ceiling.

Ignoring her son's dramatic sigh, Meghan turned to Austin and changed the subject. "I'm sorry it took so long for me to get here. I got on the first plane flight I could find, but I wish I'd been here sooner." Since last night, she'd showered and donned a fresh pair of clothes, but Austin knew for a fact she'd slept hardly a wink.

"Stop apologizing, dear." Trudy gave Meghan a reassuring smile. "Austin and Tess have been taking shifts, and the others have been more than happy to help out as needed."

At Trudy's comment, Meghan tilted her head and turned to Austin. "So, the brunette I saw out front this morning with the other staff members. Something there I should know about?" She raised an eyebrow, intent on wheedling out the information as if they were still children.

"You mean Tess?" Josh cut in, smiling now that the attention was off him.

Meghan's grin illuminated her otherwise tired complexion. "Ah, so the girl from the emails is real, after all. I was beginning to think she sounded too good to be true."

Austin shot her a look meant to chastise her teasing but missed his mark. "Don't believe a word he tells you. He suffered a head injury, remember?"

Josh feigned complete innocence and resumed his perusal of the ceiling.

"Mm," Meghan hummed. "I don't know. Trudy had some pretty interesting things to say about the two of you as well." Her mood seemed to revive on their new topic of conversation.

Austin groaned. "Not you, too."

The woman raised her hands in surrender, and Meghan actually laughed.

"Don't worry. It was all good. I'm glad to hear my baby brother has finally found someone. Athlete, philanthropist ... and she's pretty too." Meghan taunted him with another smile.

"As much as I'd like to sit here and listen to you two discuss my life..." He inched toward the door, suddenly more empathetic to his nephew's plight. "I think the doctor's orders were to let this one rest." He pointed toward Josh.

"Not fair. It's boring up here, and I feel fine." Josh scooted to the edge of the bed and swung his legs over the edge.

"Oh, no, you don't." Meghan crossed the room and shoved Josh's legs back onto the thin mattress one by one. "Your uncle is right. You need to rest, and you won't be able to do that with the three of us standing over you."

"But Mom."

"No buts, mister. Now, lie back down." Her commanding tone eased, and she laid a kiss on the top of his head.

Leaving Josh to rest, the three of them stepped outside into the hallway. The door clicked shut, and Trudy was the first to speak up.

"I think I'll go whip up some of my chicken noodle soup. Maybe that will help soothe his stomach, if not his soul." She gave each of them a quick hug before turning toward the stairs. Austin watched as her silver hair bounced with each step until she'd disappeared from sight.

"Not quite the same as installing wells in Cambodia, huh?" Austin bumped his sister's shoulder with his as they stood in the dark hallway. As glad as he was to have her safely back home, he hated knowing she'd had to cut her trip short.

"No, it isn't. But I don't mind the running water and electricity." She smiled, but dark circles ringed the bottoms of her eyes.

"Speaking of people resting . . . when was the last time you got some sleep?"

"Not counting the twenty minutes I managed to get on the plane?" she asked.

"Definitely not."

She shrugged. "You know, I can't even remember. Probably two days ago?"

"All the more reason to catch up on some sleep while you're here. I hear the bunk beds in the cabins are incredibly comfortable." He smiled, and she gave him a playful shove.

They walked to the end of the hall, and he stilled when they reached the top of the steps. A weight seemed to press on him the longer they walked together in silence. He'd avoided mentioning Brian when they'd been on the phone earlier, but his sister deserved to know what she was walking into.

"Listen, Meghan." He stopped her with a hand on her upper arm and encouraged her to sit with him on the top step. "I don't want to cause you any more worry. But I thought you should know. Brian Hughes was here. His daughter was one of the campers."

Meghan grew unusually quiet, but nothing could have prepared Austin for her simple answer. "Okay."

"Okay?" It came out harsh, and he worked to reel back his surprise. "That's all you have to say?"

"What else would you have me do? Get upset?"

"Well, yeah," he stammered. "After everything he put you through, and now this. It would be well deserved."

"Austin."

The soft reprimand stopped him in his tracks.

Meghan shook her head like Mom used to do when they were kids. "There's a lot more to the story I never told you. I forgave Brian a long time ago, and although the timing is less than stellar, I've been praying about when would be the right time to tell Josh about his father. Maybe this is God's answer."

"After all he did? Leaving you and Josh like that?"

"About that." Meghan lowered her gaze to her feet. She grew unnaturally quiet, and Austin feared he'd ripped open the old wound. Sliding her purse up her shoulder, she crossed her arms and finally looked up. "Brian never knew about Josh."

Austin's forehead dipped. "That's not what you told Mom and Dad fifteen years ago."

"I know. It's just ..." Her eyes seemed to grow even heavier than before. "Brian was already gone, and I didn't find out until a couple weeks later. By then, he was with another team in some remote area, and I'd already told Mom and Dad I was coming home. You know how many cell phone numbers I went through during my brief stint with the Peace Corps. By the time I'd had Josh and was finally settled, I couldn't reach Brian if I wanted to or not."

Austin's accusations toward Brian yesterday floated back up to the surface. Had he really misjudged the man all those years? Brian may have been a jerk for dumping her while working overseas, but his sister hadn't handled things perfectly, either. In fact, by comparison, her transgressions far outweighed Brian's. She'd kept secret the fact that the man had a son, not to mention she'd lied to everyone about the details the past fifteen years. Austin knew he should be angry at her for lying to him too, but he couldn't muster the emotions. All he wanted was to somehow erase the years' worth of pain she'd endured.

To tell the truth, he'd always admired the way she'd taken care of herself and Josh all these years. Even now, he could respect the way she was handling everything that had transpired in the last forty-eight hours. Even if it meant baring her soul to her son and his father.

Meghan toyed with the buckle of her purse until the clasp released, and she pulled out a worn photo. Carefully, she unfolded it and handed it to Austin.

His fingers brushed the ragged edges, and he smiled at the memory. Almost ten years had passed since that Christmas party at their parents' house. He'd come back home from college for the holidays, and Meghan had recently moved into her new apartment with Josh in San Jose. It had been a small affair, only the three of them and their mom and dad. Josh was four at the time, and he'd melted into a tantrum minutes after the picture was taken, but even then, it had been a trip worth remembering.

"You kept it."

"Of course I did. As a reminder that God works out all things for His good." She plucked the family picture from his hands and tucked it back in the folds of her bag. "So, in answer to your earlier question. No, I'm not upset that Brian is here. In fact, I'm relieved the truth is finally out in the open. You don't know how tiring it is to keep something like that a secret."

"What will you tell Josh?"

"The truth. All of it. And then I'll introduce him to his father."

"Just like that?"

"Just like that." She gave him a weak smile. "They *both* deserve the truth."

Meghan rose, as if the conversation required action rather than reminiscing. Still processing things, Austin followed behind her. He matched her long strides, his hiking boots a contrast to her slim Converse sneakers tapping away against the hardwood floor.

At the bottom of the stairs, she stopped and turned once more toward Austin. "I appreciate all you've done for us. You're a great uncle to Josh." She nodded toward the front door and outside, where the rest of the staff had been all morning. "But I think it's time you live your life rather than protecting everyone else's. And who knows? Maybe God has already brought you someone who can share that life with you."

Austin followed her gaze. Was he really that transparent?

His gaze bore into the log wall as if he could imagine her seated in one of those uncomfortable chairs, humming to herself as she patiently waited for them. The thought of her waiting for him on the other side made this ordeal bearable. They'd only known each other a handful of months, but already she seemed as much a part of his life as the camp he called home.

"You may be right."

"Aren't I always?" Meghan tossed him a shameless grin and turned toward the stairs. Her footsteps echoed down the hall and disappeared around the corner, leaving him to ponder his future.

CHAPTER

Thirty-One

LAUGHTER FLOATED UP the hill from the lake and spilled through the cabin's open window. Tess scrubbed at a stubborn stain on the wood floor, the sting of vinegar causing her eyes to water.

Skye's screeches carried over Kyle's and Sean's booming voices, no doubt the beginnings of another water war. Tess could only imagine what was going on down there. Having declined their invitation to join, she'd resumed her task of cleaning the cabins, glad to be of use now that the latest round of campers had left. After a long week, the teenagers deserved some serious downtime. A chance to unwind and be kids. If that meant her working a little extra to make that happen, she wasn't complaining.

The stain began to lift beneath her ministrations. With a fresh rag, she went after the fading mark until the floor gleamed almost like new.

Ever since Josh returned from the hospital, things had been different. According to the doctor's orders, he'd taken things easy the past few days, so the other staff had to juggle their schedules to cover his shifts. None of them had complained about the extra work. When Austin wasn't busy keeping the place running, he spent most of his free time catching up with his sister or fussing over his convalescing nephew.

Even Brian had come by a couple of times—despite Austin's conflicted silence—once with Opal, and once on his own. Despite his attempts to make up for lost time, and the news of his recent divorce, it had been uncomfortable for everyone at first. But the more time he spent with Meghan and Josh, the more she could see the family they could have been. Or could still be.

Despite the pungent smell of vinegar and Castile soap, Tess smiled.

Austin must have sensed it as well, the way Meghan's face brightened a few degrees when Brian told a joke, or how quickly he had accepted the fact that he had a son. Josh had taken a bit longer to warm up to the idea, but by Brian's second visit, he was back to his normal, relaxed self.

Austin, on the other hand . . .

She sighed. She didn't know what was going on in that head of his. One minute, he was wrapping his arm around her in the hospital waiting room as if it were the most natural thing in the world. And now . . . she'd hardly seen him outside regular working hours all week.

She should appreciate his devotion to his family. Ultimately, that was all she'd ever really wanted. But for once, she had hoped to be on the receiving end—not the one looking in from the outside. Tess understood what he'd meant when he said family was everything to him. And as much as she hated to admit it, she wasn't family. For a moment, a new future had begun to unfold in front of her in precious glimpses, but they disappeared as fast as a reflection on the water.

She tossed her rag in the bucket with a little too much force, and soapy water splashed against her bare legs and onto the floor. "Nice going, Tess."

With a clean towel, she soaked up the excess water and gathered the rest of the cleaning supplies before she could create any more work for herself.

The water sloshed over the sides as she walked, and she thought about the photos Abigail had sent her last weekend while in town—sandy beaches, lazy vacation days with her, Ben, and a few thousand colorful fish. No dirty cabins or sticky family situations to maneuver around.

Ben and Abigail should have gotten back from Cancún late last night. With the red-eye flight and the time difference, Tess had suggested they stay at her place before heading back to Buena Vista. Even though she and Abigail hadn't lived together for over a year, she'd insisted Abigail keep her spare key in case she ever needed it.

It seemed silly to keep the place all to herself, especially when she wasn't there half the year. Sooner or later, she'd have to decide—go back to her old life or start something new.

A series of loud splashes caught her attention as the teenagers jumped one-by-one into the lake. She longed to join them, to feel the cool alpine water rush over her skin and wash away her heavy thoughts.

From the edge of the drive, she spotted Trudy on the patio struggling with an armload of last night's latest adventure. Tess waved to get the woman's attention.

"Oh, Tess. Good. Would you mind giving me a hand?" A coil of blankets and cords fell in a heap on the wooden planks at Trudy's feet. She looked ready to toss the entire bundle over the railing and into the mud.

"Of course." Tess unloaded her bucket of soapy water and dingy rags onto the grass and took the patio steps two at a time. Once she reached the platform, she tiptoed around the scattered chairs and grabbed an end of a crocheted afghan draped over the nearest table. "Looks like someone had fun here."

For the kids' last night, they'd built a fort on the patio out of furniture and old blankets. Trudy in her quick thinking had dug out some old string lights for them to wrap their creation in. Only now, after last night's wind, it had turned into more of an obstacle course in cables and upturned chairs.

Trudy propped her fists against her hips and grimaced at the mess. "Yes, they did. And by the looks of it, I'd say they used every spare sheet and blanket they could find." She wrangled free the end of another cable that appeared hopelessly knotted around a damp sheet. "Had I known it was going to be so windy last night, I'd have suggested they apply their design skills someplace inside."

"Here, let me help with that." Tess grabbed the end closest to her and began to separate the stringed lights from the frayed cotton.

Trudy's stern expression softened. "Thank you, dear. Now enough about my complaints. How've you been? I feel as if I haven't seen you in a month of Sundays, what with all that's been going on around here."

A light breeze exhaled over them while they worked, the remnants of last night's surprise storm retreating down the valley. Tess didn't want to burden the woman with her worries, but Trudy's soft smile was so inviting. Warm. Safe.

Tess sighed. "I guess I'm trying to work out what happens next. In another week, the rest of the campers will be gone. Genevieve, Harper, and the others will go off to college, and Josh will go back home with his mom. What use will Austin have with a *Special Activities Coordinator*," she put special emphasis on the last bit, "when there's no one left to coordinate?"

Tess worked at a particularly difficult knot. The twisted length of fabric mocked her attempts, as if it could sense her mounting frustration. When it didn't loosen, she gave it another tug before finally giving up.

She dropped the coil of sheets and cables in a huff. "I don't know where I fit anymore."

"Now, what's with the long face?" Trudy's bangles clinked while she worked. "I thought you'd be glad to get back to normal, seein' as you're healed up and all. Don't tell me you've gone and changed your mind about racing."

Tess's limbs grew heavy, the pull of two different worlds weighing on her every thought. "And if I have? Would that be such a bad thing?"

Trudy shook her head. "Not at all. It takes a lot of courage to question where your life is headed. So long as you entrust your future into God's hands, you'll do fine."

Tess had come to care for and respect Trudy dearly, and her approval meant the world to her. "And if that future involved staying here?"

Trudy blew out an exaggerated breath. "Backcountry living ... It isn't everyone's cup of tea. Including yours when you first arrived, if I'm not mistaken." She peered over the edge of her stretched-out blanket like a kid playing hide and seek.

Tess laughed and started back in on the knotted fabric. "You're not wrong. But this place feels more like home now than the city."

"Well, ain't that somethin'. Never thought I'd see the day you'd prefer dirt to concrete. But this place has a way of getting under one's skin."

That it did.

"So," she continued. "What are you planning to do?"

With the final corner free, Tess folded the sheet and stacked it on top of the others on a nearby table. "I have some ideas, but... I don't know. Maybe they're just that. Ideas." In her experience, her plans always fell apart. But now there was so much more at stake than a mere trophy.

"Tess, look at me."

At the shift in Trudy's tone, Tess lifted her head.

"The world is an ever-changing place, full of endless possibilities. Don't let fear stop you from taking those leaps of faith. Life is full of what-ifs, could-haves, and shouldn't-haves. When the timing's right, you'll know it. And you might even be surprised what, or who, God has waiting for you on the other side."

It was as if Trudy could read her innermost thoughts, the ones she didn't even want to admit to herself. "But what if I make the wrong decision?"

"Do you believe the good Lord makes mistakes?"

She had lost more than a few nights of sleep wrestling with that question after the accident. But perhaps the thing she thought would shatter her world had, in fact, been the beginning of a journey to rebuild her life. "No."

"Then don't give up. He isn't finished with you yet. If we stopped dreaming every time things grew difficult, the world would be a much darker place for it."

"Even if those dreams could end in heartache?"

Trudy hummed to herself before answering. "I think it's the ones where we have something to lose that are worth fighting for. Don't you?" Not waiting for an answer, she scooped up the final blankets and gently folded them into a neat pile, giving Tess time for her words to sink in.

Above the lawn, Tess looked out across the patio, down the tree-studded slope, and beyond the A-frame cabins below. A line of cars dotted the end of the driveway, their paint faded beneath a fine layer of dirt. Meghan's rental shimmered in the sun, but Tess could already see a few splashes of mud creeping up from the undercarriage. In another week, it would blend in with all the others.

A woodpecker hammered in the distance, no doubt Morty in his stubborn attempts to reclaim his home. Tess smiled. For the first time, she could appreciate the bird's tireless persistence. There was something special about these woods—intangible, yet welcoming.

Tess let her eyes rove over the rest of the camp. Every inch brought with it fond memories, whispered promises, and blossoming hopes for a future she never dreamed of.

What had once appeared a tired and forgotten camp now seemed full of life. Could she leave it all behind? Or, like the woodpecker, had she found the place her soul longed to stay?

"Trudy," Tess asked, "would you mind if I borrowed your car for a while? I have something I need to take care of back home."

Trudy didn't bat an eyelash. Eyes twinkling, she waved toward her car parked beside Austin's. "Keys are on the dashboard."

"Thank you, Trudy." Tess gave the woman's hand a squeeze and made a beeline for the car.

"Oh, and Tess?" Trudy called out behind her.

Tess paused halfway toward the steps and turned.

"If you check the glove compartment, you might find a box of lemon melt aways for the drive." The skin creased around her eyes, smiling as if she'd shared her biggest secret of all.

Austin went over the plans once more and smiled. This could work. In fact, it could more than work. He'd been so focused on re-creating his grandpa's dreams all summer that he hadn't fully realized the camp's potential until now.

He could imagine a big family Thanksgiving in The Lodge and Christmas in the cabins, ice skating on the lake, exploring new trails on snowshoes, and teaching kids how to build snow forts. There would be movie nights inside by the fire and an endless supply of hot chocolate. They could offer a special package during spring break. He could approach some of the local schools about using the place for science camps or field trips when the weather warmed back up, and he could even rent out the main house and the meadow for weddings or retreats.

His mind involuntarily flicked to thoughts of another potential wedding down the road, but he pushed it from his mind. There would be plenty of time for that later. Best to take things slow and trust God's timing.

Austin downed a swig of coffee and coughed on the dregs lining the bottom. After a sip of water, he looked at the mantle clock, surprised to see it was well past noon. As soon as he started to plan things out, the ideas had come flooding in. There were still a lot of logistics to work out, numbers to crunch, and all that.

But it wasn't impossible.

Families and tourists flocked to the town of Estes Park all throughout the year, and if he played his cards right, he very well might be able to turn this summer camp into a year-round retreat. Of course, he'd have to hire a more permanent staff. He already knew Meghan and Josh would be here to help, and Trudy had hinted at her availability weeks ago, should the need arise.

He smiled at the papers strewn across his desk. This definitely had potential.

Austin rolled up the sheet of paper and tucked it under his arm. Aside from the sounds of distant voices, the house was quiet. Trudy's old Bronco had rumbled down the drive hours ago, Meghan was still in town making phone calls, and Josh was busy with the others at the lake. He hadn't seen Tess most of the day, but from the sounds coming from the kitchen, he had an idea where he might find her.

He couldn't wait to share his ideas with her. He'd spent the better part of the week working out the details, and he wanted her to be the first to see them. He'd never talked with her about his ideas, but the thought of her leaving when the camp closed next week was enough to spur him ahead.

Coffee cup in hand, he pushed away from his desk and strode toward the living room. There was a faint humming, something he didn't recognize, but the soothing melody beckoned him onward. He smiled and tried to pick out which '80s tune Tess was singing to herself now.

"Hey, Tess. Do you have a minute? I'd like to show you something—" He turned the corner and stopped.

Trudy stood at the prep table, her nose deep in one of her many cookbooks. Her foot bounced along to the melody as she hummed. Austin paused in the doorway, and her pink lips parted in a smile.

"Austin, perfect timing. I was about to go looking for you to discuss a new recipe I'd like to try out. What do you think of a mango salad? I thought Meghan would appreciate it—a little taste of the tropics."

"I'm sure she'll love whatever you make." He'd been all fired up to share his plans for the camp with Tess, so the abrupt shift to talk about food caught him off guard. Shaking it off, he reached into the cabinet for a new mug and topped it off with the last of the morning's coffee. He took a sip and looked over the rim at Trudy. "I thought I saw your car head out a few hours ago."

The woman waved a hand toward the window. "Oh, that was Tess. I lent her my keys for the afternoon."

Austin nearly choked on the hot liquid. Tess had left? He steadied himself and willed his mind to slow down. Tess had Trudy's car. She'd return, eventually. "Did she say where she was going?"

"Oh, something about heading home, I think." She turned the page, seemingly engrossed in the recipe.

Austin didn't know whether to go after Tess or wait to talk with her when she returned. Whenever that would be. Not that she had any reason to share in his excitement, but he'd hoped, still hoped, they could somehow have a future. And if opening up the camp year-round could help that along . . .

"Go. I'll watch the camp until you get back." Trudy didn't even look up from her book.

"Trudy, I can't ask you to do that." For one thing, today was her day off. And secondly, he'd already imposed enough on her hospitality during Abigail's wedding and Josh's accident. "It can wait until tomorrow."

Trudy peered up from her book and frowned. With a blank recipe card, she marked her page and laid the book on the table. "You know, sometimes you can be as stubborn as your granddaddy. He loved this place, but even he knew it's only land and a few buildings."

"I never said—"

Her no-nonsense stare halted his rebuttal. "What makes a home is the people we fill it with and the relationships we're willing to fight for."

From behind the stack of cookbooks, she withdrew his Explorer keys and slid them across the table. "You'd better get a move on, or you'll be driving back in the dark." Her tone brooked no argument, and Austin needed no further prompting.

"Thank you, Trudy." He reached for his keys and brushed a kiss against the woman's wrinkled cheek. "What would I ever do without you?"

She gave him a soft pat on the arm and smiled. "You'd be fine. Sometimes we just need an outside voice to tell us what we already know. Now, don't let that girl go. She's the best thing that ever happened to this place."

And to him.

"I think you're right."

CHAPTER

Thirty-Two

ARE YOU SURE about this?" Abigail waited by the sidewalk while Tess lifted the hammer.

"I've never been more sure about anything."

The metal reverberated off the For Sale sign, each decisive blow driving the aluminum frame further into the lawn. She'd worry about the HOA guidelines, online listings, and finding a real estate agent later. For now, nothing felt more satisfying than hammering an old-school sign into the freshly cut lawn.

"I never realized how much I'd been missing until this summer. Even if Austin doesn't need me after next week, I can't go back to the way my life was before. I want what you and Ben have, and I'm not going to find that traveling from one city to the next six months out of the year."

"So, your plan is to sell your place and . . . what, exactly?" Beside her, Abigail twirled a lock of hair between her fingertips and peered up into the window of her old bedroom, where Ben was busy packing up their things.

Tess shrugged. "Who knows? Maybe I'll move in with Aunt Josie like you did last summer. She mentioned something at the wedding about the house feeling empty now that you've moved out. Or I could find a place in Estes Park. I could teach classes at the rec center, maybe even pick up a little coaching on the side. It could be fun."

And if Austin happened to need another set of hands around the camp next summer, she wouldn't say no. He may not have asked her yet, but she planned on broaching the topic the moment she got back.

She stole a peek over the sign at Abigail, who didn't seem to share her enthusiasm.

"Hmm. And you'd be fine giving up your career? All those races, the years of training, gone?"

With a final blow, Tess took a step back and surveyed the sign with approval. "It's not like I'd be giving up racing completely. Lots of other athletes find ways to balance work and life. With some planning and effort, it would be more than doable. It might look a little different, is all."

Okay, so maybe a *lot* different. Six months ago, the very thought would have sent her running toward the hills, but a lot had changed since then.

The long grass dampened Ben's footfalls. When his shadow fell over the sign, Tess turned to see his arm wrap around

Abigail's torso. Her heart warmed at the sight of the two of them together.

Ben laid a soft kiss on the top of Abigail's head. "Almost ready to go?"

Abigail's stubborn frown relaxed as she looked up at her husband. "Once Tess gives up this ridiculous idea of hers. I tried talking some sense into her. These types of decisions should take time, not be a spur-of-the-moment thing."

Leave it to Abigail to be the pragmatic one.

"It might sound like I'm rushing into this, but I've had months to think it through. I know what I'm doing." At least, she kept telling herself that.

Ben traced Abigail's earlier gaze across the clapboard facade, eyes squinting in that way of his whenever he was sizing up a new project. "You know, I could do a few minor repairs around here if you'd like. Do an inspection, touch up some paint. It wouldn't take much to sell this place in today's market."

"Not helping, honey." Abigail gave him a playful swat.

"Just saying." He gave her another kiss to silence her protests and hooked a thumb toward the door. "I'll be inside if you need me."

Abigail rolled her eyes as he slipped from her grasp and ascended the steps two at a time. "You've gone and done it now. If you so much as mention a renovation project around Ben, you'll never get rid of him."

A family passed beside them on the sidewalk, kids slurping down ice cream while their parents pushed a double stroller.

Abigail watched them walk by before settling her gaze once again on Tess.

"You're really doing this." It was a statement rather than a question.

"I guess I am." Ever since her earlier conversation with Trudy, she'd felt a sense of overwhelming peace. For once in her life, she didn't have everything mapped out. And the sensation was surprisingly freeing.

"Well, I'm not saying I fully understand it, but if you're happy, so am I."

Tess nearly dropped the hammer on her foot. "You mean it?"

She'd expected a little more pushback. Less understanding and more caution. This was Abigail, her cousin, and first and foremost, her best friend.

Abigail's rosy smile eased away the last of Tess's concerns. "Of course. And if you need anything, and I mean anything, don't hesitate to give me a call. You already know Ben's all for it. He's probably measuring the kitchen cabinets as we speak."

Tess blinked at the sting in her eyes and looked at her cousin with new appreciation. How had she ever questioned her place in this family?

Abigail pulled her into a hug, and Tess welcomed the familiar embrace.

When she pulled away a few seconds later, her eyes settled on something over Tess's right shoulder. "Um, Tess? I think you have a visitor." She inclined her head toward the street.

Curious, Tess pivoted on the grass to look behind her and froze.

There, standing beside a black and white Explorer, was Austin. His dirt-stained hiking shoes and faded jeans were a sharp contrast to the metropolitan cityscape behind him. Like the rest of him, the rips and tears were hard-earned. He was more real to her than any man she'd ever met, no matter how different their lives may seem. And he was standing mere feet from her front lawn.

Abigail chuckled at her stunned expression before she slipped toward the front door, leaving the two of them alone.

Tess's bravado vanished. Every intention of bringing up her plans fell to the wayside, and in their place, uncertainty crept in. "Austin. What are you doing here?"

"Nice to see you too." He smiled, but his feet remained rooted to the concrete. The breeze toyed with the ends of his short, dark hair, asking for someone to run her fingers through it.

Tess willed her hands to remain at her sides. "Sorry. I guess you caught me by surprise. How'd you know I was here?"

"Trudy."

Of course.

"She was the one who offered to watch the camp for a few hours."

"Oh? And why is that?" Tess didn't dare let her imagination run wild with the possibilities. She'd led herself to believe in fanciful dreams far too many times. But the fact Austin was here had to mean something.

Aware she still held the hammer in her hand, she bent and propped it against the side of the sign, all the while waiting for Austin's response.

He shifted his weight from one foot to the other and frowned at the dandelions sprouting from the cracks in the city concrete. "I had a lot of time to think on the drive down here." He rubbed a hand across the back of his neck and let it fall. "Actually, that's not true. I've had more than enough time to think, and I made up my mind a long time ago."

Tess's pulse gained momentum as he took a step toward her.

His gaze traveled from the condo behind her and caught on the family at the other end of the sidewalk. The busy street was far from their secluded sanctuary in the mountains, where there was nothing but forests to overhear your most private thoughts, and she had a sense this was a conversation best kept between the two of them.

Austin cleared his throat and turned his attention toward the opposite end of the street. "You know, I drove past this little park a few blocks back. Would you mind if we took a walk?"

"A walk sounds perfect."

She fell into step beside him. Their shoulders bumped slightly every time they passed someone on the sidewalk, and Tess was all too aware of the silent questions radiating between them.

At the end of the street, they turned south and continued beneath the bridge toward the river that skirted the fringe of Denver's high-rise center. Beachgoers gathered at the water's edge with their kayaks and inner tubes while curious onlookers watched from the grassy knoll.

"I'm sorry about your car. I'll sort everything out with the insurance, so you won't have to worry about that." Austin stepped closer to Tess as a woman on roller skates zipped by. He kept their close proximity long after the woman had passed, his hand mere inches from hers.

Tess couldn't have been happier for the busy Saturday afternoon. "It's only a car. And besides, someone once told me if you're going to live in the mountains, you'd better have something with four-wheel drive."

"Is that so?" He slid her a look, a smile tugging at the corners of his perfectly shaped mouth. "You wouldn't perhaps be open to a few suggestions, would you? I happen to know of this great little town up the road."

"Depends. Do you know of anyone looking to hire an ex-professional triathlete?"

Austin chuckled. "I don't know about the 'ex' part, but I was thinking..." His voice trailed off, and Tess had to lean in to hear him over the kids screaming in the shallows. "I know I have no right to ask this of you, but would you ever consider staying on a little longer?"

Her lips curved. "How much longer are we talking?"

"Would indefinitely be a possibility?" He stilled beneath a canopy of trees on the edge of the park and turned to face her. "I don't need an answer right away. Whatever time you need, it's yours. I just wanted you to know you have a place at the camp if you want it. With Trudy, Meghan, Josh . . . and me."

Tess didn't need another second to think it over. She knew her answer, but her traitorous tongue couldn't seem to form the words to say as much. Instead, she inquired about Austin's other news. "So, Meghan and Josh are staying? I thought he would only be there for the summer."

"He was, but Meghan's decided to move back for the time being. Let Josh get to know his dad for a little while before they make any permanent decisions."

"That's great. I'm happy for them." Truly, she was. But that wasn't what she wanted to convey to Austin at this moment.

"I wasn't sure how it would go over with Josh, but he seemed open to the idea. All that's left is to tell Opal."

Tess's hand found his, and she wrapped her fingers over the rough skin. "She already adores him, and I know Josh feels the same way." She looked up at him, a weightlessness lifting her up from her toes. "And in answer to your question, indefinitely sounds perfect."

Despite the crowds, Austin pulled her behind the shelter of a large cottonwood tree and dipped his face toward hers.

Her heart was safe in Austin's care. And even though the future looked uncertain, she could rely on the unfailing nature of a God so loving, He'd brought a man like Austin into her life to show her how sweet it could be when she chose to live by faith. Those insecurities may never completely go away, and she was okay with that, so long as she didn't allow her fears to prevent her from running the race God had set before her.

And from where she stood, it would be the most exciting race she'd ever run.

When Austin finally pulled back, she felt as if she were flying, but his furrowed expression gave her pause.

"Are you sure about this? I know you had dreams before meeting me, and I wouldn't ever want to stand in the way of you achieving them. If anyone deserves to be happy, it's you." He said it with such seriousness, she couldn't help but laugh.

Little did he know that his willingness to let her go only made her love him all the more. "You make me happy, you Bigfoot-loving idiot. I can't imagine leaving. Not the camp, not Josh or Trudy. And especially not you."

"Is that so?" His eyes practically glowed as the sun dipped behind the nearby foothills. "Does that mean you'll think about staying?"

If only he knew how he'd already turned her world upside down in the best possible way.

"Lucky for you, I'm all in."

EPILOGUE

ONE WEEK LATER

TESS WATCHED A family of mallards draw near the crowded beach. The trio of ducklings chased after their parents as they disappeared beneath the shadow of the boathouse. Their trailing wake cast a series of ripples across the placid surface all the way to where she stood along the shore.

She curled her toes into the warm sand. The familiar sensation grounded her amongst the waves of excitement spilling over the beach. Sunlight glinted off the water into her eyes, and she squinted against the morning sun. If she closed her eyes, she could feel the same excitement she'd come to love at the start of every new race.

It amazed her still how quickly things were falling into place. After two days on the market, she'd found a tenant to lease her condo to, and she and Austin had prepared Camp Kinnikinnick for its last week of summer campers. With a light heart, she'd said goodbye to her old life. And in the days since, she and Austin kept busy making plans for the future.

Trudy's voice carried over the others', her southern drawl distinct from where she, Meghan, and Skye sat in their folding chairs near the dock. Having declined the offer to participate, they seemed content to cheer on the rest of the camp staff in their end-of-the-season triathlon.

Well, triathlon might be pushing it. At least in the traditional sense. Once the final campers of the season were gone, Tess and Austin had spent the past few days charting out the course and its details. This would not be your typical swim, bike, and run. Contestants would still be required to travel by water, wheel, and foot, but with a twist.

The sand shifted beside her, and Austin's familiar scent mingled with the spruce-tinged mountain air. His shoulder brushed against hers, his skin warm from the sun, and he spoke loud enough to be heard over the nearby excitement. "It might not be the National Championships you were hoping for, but I hope you like it."

It could have been an egg race, and she wouldn't have objected. So long as she could share this moment with Austin.

"It's perfect."

The sun glowed through the aspens overhead, their shadows dancing across the sand like a crowd of cheering spectators.

Austin's bare arm grazed hers once more. "Just so you know, I don't think the rest of us stand a chance with you in this race. At least when you were wearing your ankle brace, us mere mortals would have had a fighting chance."

How she loved it when his mouth tipped up like that. It made her want to reach up on tip-toes and kiss him, even with the nearby onlookers. Instead, she settled for a smile. "I believe in you. And Bigfoot... But mostly you."

His eyes crinkled at the edges. "Hm, you're going to make me regret teasing you, aren't you?"

"Wouldn't dream of it."

Somewhere behind them, a sudden splash of music spilled over the beach. Tess turned to see Skye bent over an old cassette player, fiddling with the ancient dials as the song *Walking on Sunshine* blared from the stereo speakers.

"Josh found it in the closet upstairs, along with a bunch of tapes. And guess which decade made up the overwhelming majority?" The warmth of his smile was nearly enough to make her forget the entire race. Nearly.

"I'd say your grandpa had great taste in music." There was no way Austin could have known about her favorite song. But the gesture made her break into a sappy grin.

"T-Minus sixty seconds," Trudy called out. "Everybody to the starting line." The woman reclined against her colorfully woven lawn chair, eyes fixed on the watch Tess had lent her for the race.

It had taken a few tries to show her how to maneuver to the correct app on the touchscreen, but now that she'd found it, she was all set to announce the start of the countdown. With a flourish, Trudy gave two sharp blows to the silver whistle hanging from her neck to call people toward the water's edge.

Everyone made their way to the row of four canoes lined up on the beach. Their bows dipped with the gentle sway of the water. Josh hopped into their canoe before Tess was halfway across the beach, evidently ready for the race to begin. The boat sank a few inches under his weight, bobbing like a one-sided see-saw.

Austin reached into the canoe beside them, where Genevieve was already waiting and clipped into his life jacket.

"Forty seconds." Trudy blew on the whistle three more times, as if the first two piercing sounds had gone unnoticed.

Austin grimaced. "Whoever gave her that whistle ought to be tarred and feathered."

"It's not that bad." At least no one had given her a starting pistol.

He tossed her a wry grin as he shouldered into his life jacket. "Try saying that with a straight face."

As if to drive home his point, Trudy let out another series of rapid-fire whistles. Poor Meghan had her fingers in her ears, and Tess fought hard not to laugh.

"Come on, Tess," Josh shouted from the canoe, his frown aimed at Austin. "Stop fraternizing with the competition and get in the boat. We're about to start."

Austin's eyes lit with amusement. "Looks like you've been summoned."

"I think you're right." She reached into the hull for the second oar and smiled. "Wouldn't want to let my teammate down after all." Rocking the boat as little as possible, she climbed in behind Josh and plopped onto the raised seat.

Austin followed behind her and joined Genevieve in the boat beside them, the grin never leaving his face as he readied himself for Trudy's countdown.

"Ten seconds," Trudy announced over the music. Gaze fixed on the digital watch, she waited as everyone grew quiet. "On your marks. Get set. Go."

Shouts and splashes drowned out the shriek of the whistle as each team pushed off from the shore.

Harper and Kyle shot out in front of the group. Leaning into their strokes, they led the queue into the middle of the lake where they were soon overtaken by Josh and Tess. With Josh in front, he set a grueling pace, one Tess was happy to oblige. She dug her oar into the clear water and heaved her body weight at a sharp enough angle to keep them headed in a straight line.

They reached the opposite end of the lake in record speed. A backward glance told her they were still in the lead but only by a single boat-length. In the straightaway, Austin and Genevieve had shot ahead with the other two teams close on their tail. Josh and Tess dropped their oars to the port side and leaned into the turn. Icy water splashed over their knees and ankles, and they resumed their paddling toward the starting beach.

The front of the canoe plowed into the silty sand, jolting Tess and Josh forward with the sudden stop. Barely in the lead, they jumped out and hauled their boat up the sand to Trudy and Meghan's excited cheers.

"Go, Josh!" Meghan shouted as Tess and Josh yanked off their life jackets.

"What about your own brother?" Austin piped up as he dropped his canoe beside her.

"Sorry, Austin." Meghan shrugged, not looking the least bit sorry.

The final two teams pulled up behind them. Without missing a beat, they took off up the hill toward the row of wheelbarrows at the top, shedding their life jackets as they ran.

"Looks like you'd better get a move on." Meghan grabbed the cassette player and took off after the others. "Last one to the top is a slowpoke."

Tess smiled at the sibling rivalry. With the final buckle undone, she ripped off her vest and sprinted ahead of Austin.

Josh reached their wheelbarrow first and leapt in. When Tess caught up, she grabbed hold of the wooden handles and tilted the legs up off the grass.

In the lead again, Harper and Kyle took off down the field. At Josh's urging, she raced after them and was soon halfway across the field. Steering a wheelbarrow was nothing like riding a bike. Every dip and rise threatened to upturn their cart with Josh in it. Tightening her grip, Tess slowed enough to maintain their balance and reached the other side without incident. In one leap, Josh was back on solid ground. Tess dropped the wheelbarrow where she stood, and the group charged toward the trail that led to the low ropes course.

At the ropes course, everyone had to work together to cross the four cables strung between the trees. So, when they reached the final platform, it was a mad dash to the finish line.

Tess pumped her arms, drawing neck-and-neck with Austin's long strides. "Ready to admit defeat?" she teased over the sound of her own heavy breathing.

"As soon as you are." He sent her a devilish grin and increased his speed.

The half-mile back to The Lodge was a full-on sprint. Her lungs burned from months of inactivity, but she pushed herself as hard as her legs could carry her through the trees. Footsteps sounded behind her as the rest of the group charged down the trail.

After a few more yards, the forest opened up, and the log building came into view. Trudy and Meghan were already waiting for them, a red ribbon strung between them on the top porch step.

In a few more strides, Tess was at the bottom step. The wood groaned beside her as Austin matched her pace. Another leap, and they climbed the stairs shoulder-to-shoulder until Trudy's and Meghan's cheers met them on the top step. Together, they broke through the ribbon moments before Josh and Genevieve charged up the stairs behind them.

In a blur, Austin drew Tess into his arms, and his mouth crushed against hers. She leaned into his kiss, and all thoughts of the race fled from her mind. No doubt Austin could feel the thump of her heart against his chest. Not from the canoe ride, or the wheelbarrow sprints, or that final charge up the steps. No.

Whenever she was around him, she felt as if she were caught up in the race of her life, and no number of trophies or ribbons could compare to the rush of Austin Wright.

He pulled back too soon and allowed her to catch her breath, his own chest rising and falling in rapid succession.

Footsteps pounded up the steps behind them as the rest of the group spilled onto the patio. No longer alone, they turned to take in the satisfied smiles of everyone around them. Meghan was busy snapping pictures as everyone circled around the food table for cookies and lemonade. Even Morty hammered his applause in the distance. Only Trudy was looking in their direction, a sparkle in her pale blue eyes, before she also moved to join in the excitement.

Tess relaxed against Austin's side, his arm around her shoulders, basking in the sense of community around them. Her heart felt full. And she knew—even if she never competed in another race, never made it to the Olympics—this would be enough.

"We should do this every year. Make it a new tradition." She could already envision the different events they could throw in, how it could evolve with time. They were bound to make changes the longer they managed the camp, and she, for one, couldn't wait to see how things would unfold.

Austin nuzzled his face into her hair and drew in a deep breath. "I like the sound of that."

She tilted her head back, and he smiled down at her. "What do you think about paddle board races next year? Or a timed scavenger hunt?"

His chest reverberated with a low chuckle. "I think we can work something out."

Tess lifted a simple prayer of thanks, grateful to have been welcomed into this rag-tag family and how they'd helped her realize her true worth. A promising future was unfolding before her, and she had to pinch herself to believe it was real.

His fingers traced down her arm and intertwined with hers, as if to convince her this was anything but a dream. His lips brushed her hair with a feather-soft touch.

"Hey, you two." Meghan hollered from one of the picnic tables where the kids were busy chowing down on pulled pork sandwiches and coleslaw. "Quit daydreaming and grab some food before it's all gone."

Biting back a grin, Austin led the way, and the two of them joined in the celebration. Trudy handed out glasses of lemonade, and Meghan offered them each a plate mounded high with food. She'd even saved them a couple of chocolate chip cookies, which would have disappeared in a blink had she not hidden them from the hungry teenagers for safekeeping.

With Austin at her side, Tess looked around the table of smiling faces and couldn't help but return the gesture.

She'd learned when she held life with an open hand, God could do amazing things. He'd taken one shattered dream and molded it into a more beautiful story than she ever could have imagined. All it took was one race to change her trajectory in life, and looking back, Tess couldn't be more grateful.

"...I press on toward the goal to win the prize for which God has called me heavenward in Christ Jesus."

—Philippians 3:12-14

Trudy's Lemon Meltaways

What better way to enjoy a taste of the Colorado sunshine than with these citrusy confections? Reminiscent of long summer days and lazy afternoons, the combination of lemon and vanilla is sure to bring a smile to your face. And who knows? Maybe they'll inspire you to have a few adventures of your own.

Ingredients

1 ¾ cup flour
2 Tbsp cornstarch
¼ tsp salt
1 cup powdered sugar
¾ cup butter, room temp
zest of ½ lemon
1 Tbsp lemon juice
1 tsp vanilla extract

For the icing

1 cup powdered sugar
1 Tbsp lemon juice
zest of ½ lemon
pinch of salt

In a medium sized bowl, whisk together the flour, cornstarch, and salt, and set aside. In a stand mixer, combine powdered sugar, butter, and lemon zest and whip until pale and fluffy, 1-2 minutes. Mix in lemon juice and vanilla. Add in the flour mixture and combine. Once cookie dough is completely mixed, turn out onto a piece of plastic wrap and shape into a log, 1 ½ - 2 inches in width. Wrap dough tightly in the plastic wrap and chill in the fridge for at least one hour.

When ready to bake, preheat the oven to 350 degrees F and line a baking sheet with parchment paper. Unwrap the dough and slice into round disks. Bake cookies 11-15 minutes, or until the edges appear slightly golden along the edges.

In a small bowl, combine powdered sugar, lemon zest, and lemon juice. Add more lemon juice or water if the icing seems too thick. Set aside and allow cookies to cool before icing. Once the cookies are cool to the touch, spoon the glaze into the center of each cookie and spread in a circle toward the edges.

ACKNOWLEDGEMENTS

This book wouldn't have been possible without the help of so many people, from the encouragement of friends and family to the critique partners and editors who helped me stay sane while writing this story.

To the critique groups through ACFW, I can't even begin to thank you all for your help, the weekly chapter exchanges, for answering my endless list of questions. I'd like to especially thank my amazing editors, Erynn Newman and Suzie Oakley. Thank you for all the time you spent pouring over these pages to make this the best it could be.

To the amazing authors who encouraged me on this journey including Susan May Warren, Tari Faris, Alicia Whittle, and all the other members of the My Book Therapy and ACFW communities.

Readers, reviewers, and other bookworm friends. Thank you for journeying with me through these stories and allowing me to share a bit of my heart with you all.

To my parents, who have always believed in and supported me. You have been my biggest cheerleaders, and I am so incredibly grateful. You've taught me to never give up on my dreams.

And to God, who leads us up mountains and walks with us through the valleys. "I can do all this through him who gives me strength."

DID YOU LIKE THIS BOOK?

If so, please leave a quick **review** or **rate it** on:

AMAZON, GOODREADS, or wherever you leave reviews :)

You can also...

Host a **book club**, Give a copy as a **gift, Tell your friends and family,** Post a picture of you reading on **Instagram** and tag me at @AlyssaSchwarzAuthor, or Request this or any of my other books at your **local library**

Check out the entire Prescott Family Romance series!

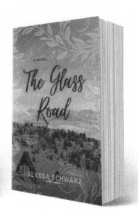

UP NEXT IN THE PRESCOTT FAMILY ROMANCE SERIES

Fields of Glass

Micah Prescott will do anything to save his family's sheep ranch, even if it kills him. With a city-based firm pressuring him to sell and the bank threatening to call in his loan, he has less than a month to figure out a solution to keep the property his father strove so hard to protect. But when a storm rolls in, washing out the only bridge to town and bringing with it an unwanted visitor, he finds his options quickly dwindling.

Sales associate Francis Grace Riley knows what it means to be underestimated—first by her family, and again in the male-dominated world of business. Convinced she can secure a deal where others had only failed, she takes off to the mountains in search of one stubborn rancher, only to realize there is much more riding on the outcome of this trip than her job.

From the moment Micah rescues Grace on the side of the road, sparks fly—that is until he learns who she really is. Stuck there until the bridge is repaired, the two of them must learn to work together if they have any hopes of achieving their goals. But when things start to go wrong on the ranch, and sheep begin to disappear, they're left questioning who they can trust ... and what they're willing to sacrifice for those they care for.

To learn more and stay up to date with the cover reveal and all upcoming book releases, subscribe to Alyssa's e-mail newsletter, **Book Nook With A View, at** **www.authoralyssaschwarz.com**

LET'S CONNECT!

www.authoralyssaschwarz.com
Facebook — Alyssa Schwarz, Author
Instagram — @AlyssaSchwarzAuthor
Pinterest — Alyssa Schwarz Author

Subscribe to Alyssa's email newsletter, Book Nook With A View

ABOUT THE AUTHOR

I love a good story, especially if it has a happy ending! From mountain adventures to Downton Abbey-esque romances, I firmly believe we could all use a little more inspirational and heart-warming tales to keep us up at night—tales that take us on far away (or not so distant) adventures and speak words of life and truth into our lives. Though I write mainly contemporary fiction, I try to find fun ways to incorporate the past. Whether it's a family secret, or a century-old journal, history has a way of shaping the lives of my characters for better or for worse. If any of these story ideas sound like your cup of tea, then pull up a chair, take a sip of your favorite drink, and find your next happily-ever-after.

Made in the USA
Middletown, DE
23 December 2022

16789535R00210